# Chaos Theory
## *The Exceptionals Book 2*

## Sarah Cass
## Mary Terrani

**Urban Fantasy**

**Sarah Cass**
www.authorsarahcass.com

**Divine Roses Ink Publishing**
www.divinerosesink.com

**A Divine Roses Ink Book**
Urban Fantasy
Paranormal Romance



**PUBLISHER**
**Divine Roses Ink**
http://www.divinerosesink.com

# Other Books by Mary Terrani

Decking the Halls

**The Exceptionals**
Escaping Humanity

# Books by Sarah Cass

**The Tribe Series**
The Tribe
The Wolf
The Chief
The Raven
**The Dominion Falls Series**
Changing Tracks
Derailed
Dark Territory
Runaway Train
Home Signal
**The Lake Point Series**
Santa, Maybe
Deep-Fried Sweethearts
Stalled Independence
Witch Way
A Thorough Thanksgiving
Eve's New Year
Heartstrings & Hockey Pucks
Luck of the Cowgirl
Stars, Stripes & Motorbikes
Free Falling
Love for Hire
Haunted Hearts
**Stand Alone Novels**
Masked Hearts
Leap
**The Exceptionals**
Escaping Humanity

# Dedication
## For Mary Terrani

Sarah,
We did it again. Continuing the journey with these amazing characters. I am so excited about the road we are on. You know me better than I know myself and how to keep me going. I love you.

To Tommy,
No matter what point we are in our lives you are always there, encouraging and pushing me to be better and continue towards my dreams. Thank you for everything you do and most of all just being you. Love you

To Jenny,
Thank you for sticking with Sarah and I though the ups and downs of this journey. All the research, promotion and helping me to find my voice at conventions, or in most cases being my voice. Your perspective has been invaluable. Even though our plans have been put on hold we will get there. Love you.

# Dedication
## For Sarah Cass

To Mary,
Sometimes it seemed like this wasn't going to happen, but here we are at release time again. Our journey with these characters has been a roller coaster for sure, but I'm so glad we took the ride. Love you.

To Erik,
Thank you for always supporting me. I've had some crazy dreams and plans, including moving our whole family 1,000 miles from where we were. It hasn't always been easy, but your support means everything.

To my kids,
I hope you never stop chasing your dreams. It can feel crazy at times, but it's always worth it. You all have made me a proud mom with all you've done, and I cannot wait to see where your dreams lead you.

8

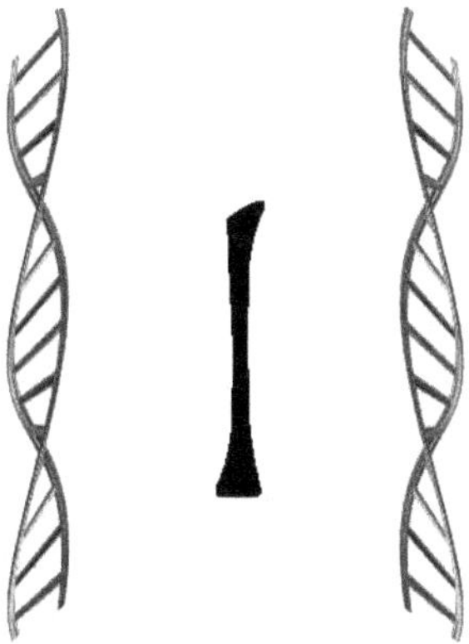

Dawn approached too fast. Soon she would have to find shelter. Inessa had been traveling for the better part of six months now. Only at night. During that time, she'd kept moving to avoid the risk of being caught by anyone remotely anti-mutant.

Beyond the cities that now lay in rubble people gathered. No. Humans gathered. Trying to rebuild. To grow some food on the land left behind that had not been scorched and destroyed. Some were successful and she'd seen the joy of people coming together and forming families out of the darkness.

For the most part she'd avoided settlements, although sometimes the appeal of a hot cooked meal outweighed the danger. She only caved in mutant sympathetic settlements.

Seeing a person's aura gave you an inordinate amount of information once you learned the proper way to read them. Auras were a tricky thing. One color could have a myriad of meanings. Since the ability to see them was the primary mutation she developed, she had made sure to learn fast how to understand them.

10

Some days it was all that kept her alive.

The horse danced beneath her, pulling her back to the present situation. Few options remained for shelter in the middle of nowhere like she was. While Indiana had mostly come out unscathed, it only survived due to the amount of open land. Filled with cornfields instead of possible hidden groups of mutants.

The ground remained battle scarred, mostly from the after-war skirmishes that still raged between the military and the mutants or their sympathizers. Still, it was wide open with only a few barns to shelter her. The closest had animals inside, so it was still in use.

Somewhere there had to be an abandoned barn. With a kick to the ribs she got her horse moving again, galloping through the faint pre-dawn light in search of a rundown barn, a cluster of trees, anywhere to take shelter for the day. A place to sleep and recover.

A few more miles through the fields she spotted the perfect barn. Not so rundown that it could cave in on her, but obviously falling from disuse.

Unfortunately, it was occupied. By one person.

Inessa frowned, studying the aura in the barn with care. It was an Exceptional. For the most part she left Exceptionals alone as well. Too many were far too paranoid and her general friendliness and understanding tended to freak them out more. It was far too lonely an existence for the people person she'd once been.

Just as she thought she'd have to move on, to leave this mutant alone, her memory caught up to her. There was something familiar about this person.

She knew him.

A grin crossed her features and she led the horse to the barn, slipping down just outside. It was easy to tell he was sleeping, and she hated to startle an Exceptional that was alone. The sun coming up over the horizon left her little choice. She pulled the door open and led her horse inside, pulling the door closed.

As she'd hoped the loud creak of the door had managed to wake the sleeping mutant, but now he hid. His indecision clear in his aura, she moved forward, "Dr. Carter?"

A tiny squeak of surprise escaped, but he didn't move. As expected, suspicion tempered his moves. There was something else too. He was different, something major had happened. An injury, although his pain had been minimal. A side effect of his mutation probably helped.

"Dr. Carter, maybe you remember me? I'm Inessa Jelen. Last year you set my leg after the destruction of the city. You saved my leg, you saved me. Do you remember?" Inessa took a cautious step forward, tossing the reigns around a post. "Of course, my leg isn't important now that New York City is nothing but rubble."

"Inessa," he whispered. "I remember."

"Good. Then you remember that I'm a mutant too, right?"

"You joked about your name." His voice remained a whisper, hard to hear. "Said it was hilarious. Inessa means pure, and you were anything but."

"That's right."

"Complex displaced fracture of the fibula, complete fracture of the tibia. Result of crushing with loose fragments. You needed surgery. I couldn't move you once I was done, left you in the care of a friend of yours. We were supposed to return. Take you back when you were able to travel. I never made it back."

"No, you didn't. I feared the worst for you." She moved around the corner of the stall he hid in. "Don't feel bad though. Dixon took great care of me. Once I was well enough to fend for myself, he left New York to find his family."

"You healed well, then?"

"I sure did. I'm surprised to find you out here in the middle of nowhere. You told me about the compound, I've been trying to get there. It's slow going, just me and the horse. What about you? Where's your wife?"

"Charlotte." A wave of grief crashed over him. Grey with blasts of deep purple consumed his aura. "I don't know. We got separated. Indianapolis and St. Louis were among the last cities hit. We were trying to help some orphaned mutant children. She went to St. Louis. I came to Indiana. I just remember the explosion. The screams. Screams of the children. My own screams."

Inessa knelt in front of Dr. Carter, setting her hand on his arm. "Dr. Carter?" There was no way to stop her gasp when he lifted his head. The right side of his face mutilated with scars. The eye she remembered as a stunning blue now white and dead.

His left eye moved in her direction, but it was slow and couldn't seem to look right at her. "I was found by a sympathizer. Thankfully I was able to keep myself out of pain by numbing my own nerves, but I had no medical care."

"Where is the sympathizer?"

"She's gone. I guess she was already sick when the war came. Weak heart. She died a few weeks ago during a skirmish." Dr. Carter's hand shook as he ran it through his hair, "She helped me keep the wounds clean, and even stitched up some for me, but there was no way for me to get real medical care. My face and blood are among those tagged."

"How have you survived?" Inessa took a shaky breath and sat next to him. The wounds were bad, but she was relieved his suffering had been kept to a minimum. For her surgery, she'd been appreciative of his unique mutation. Without any access to anesthetic he'd been able to operate while she was fully awake, and she hadn't felt a thing. His ability to dull nerves or make them fully alive in an attack had been one she had declared the 'coolest' she'd ever seen. "What about food? How can you go anywhere?"

Tracy had laid me in with some supplies every couple of weeks. I've been stretching them out. Right now, I've been trying to figure out how to get back to the compound when I can only see shadows and light in one eye. I must find out if Charlotte is alive. If she survived the attack on St. Louis." His breath came out in a long-exhaled attempt to keep calm. "She's all I've got now."

Inessa smiled, "Well then Dr. Carter, I think I can help. I really do hate being by myself and I was heading to that compound too. If you aren't afraid of horses, my buddy Shiksa and I can help you travel."

"Afraid of horses? I was raised on a farm and bred horses." For the first time since she had shown up a bit of hope brightened the layers of his aura. Even still the sadness and longing for the love he remembered kept it dull.

"Good. Then at dusk we'll set out again." She squeezed his arm. "Don't you worry, Dr. Carter. I'm the best at keeping away from troops and snitches. The best liars can't hide the nastiness of their auras. I'll get you home and back to your wife."

"Thank you, Inessa. And please, call me Neil. I'm hardly a doctor anymore."

"Okay, I'll call you Neil. I have one stipulation to that though."

"What?"

"Don't give up hope. Don't ever give that up. It's all we've got."

Dusk faded to twilight around the small group gathered at the edge of the abandoned neighborhood. Chance stood to the side of the grave, absorbing the scene before him. Small self-sustaining globes of fire provided by Talisa and Charlotte lent a soft glow to the scene.

Warren had Abby wrapped tight in his arms, possibly the only thing that kept the grieving mother on her feet. She clutched a box to her chest while she sobbed hysterically. The amount of pain they must be in was unfathomable. He knew the shock of finding out an adult was your child, that was almost normal in their upturned lives. To imagine losing Charlotte only a few short weeks after finding her, though?

The panicked rush of pain formed a lump in his throat before he could stop it. Charlotte's hand settled on his arm at his rush of emotion, but it faded enough that he didn't get the matching concerned glance.

He did get one from Talisa, though equally as brief as Charlotte's touch. She remained where she stood, steadfast between Abby and Roark. This week should have been one of celebration with their return. Unfortunately, the fates landed them immediately in crisis and then attending a funeral.

James had disappeared back into the compound not long before everyone arrived for the ceremony. He avoided anything that had to do with Annie's cremation or funeral. Then again, all of that involved Warren, and Chance was pretty sure James was avoiding him too. Any time Warren saw Chance's second in command, he went on a rampage of vitriol.

Chance shook off the thoughts at a small mental nudge from Talisa that they needed to begin. "Thank you all for gathering tonight. We are here to celebrate the life of Anna Maria Johnson, Annie. Though she was only with us for a short time, we were able to see what an amazing spirit she had. She was a beautiful young woman, with an even more stunning beauty deep in her soul."

A high-pitched wail from Abby interrupted Chance. "My little girl."

"Yes. Yes, she was," Chance agreed quietly. "Even though we did not have a lifetime of memories with her, she had them with you both, and all of us. When Annie found out she was dying, the only thing she wanted was to be reunited with her family. We thank the spirits that she was able to find that here with us all. Now we commit her to the care of the spirits, and with those that have gone before us."

Chance stepped forward to lay his hand on the wooden box that contained Annie's ashes. The moment he began to recite a Lenape mourning prayer, a white-hot pain surged up his spine. He recognized the sensation as a precursor to what would be an intense vision. Though he sank to his knees, he managed to keep his hand on the box.

*"Hey Chief, Lucas said you have everything ready for my vision quest." Annie stood in the doorway, a bright smile on her face. In one hand she held a mug of steaming tea, the other rested on her growing belly.*

*"I do. I was able to find the final ingredient this morning. Are you sure you want to do this pregnant? Vision quests can be awfully intense."*

16

*"I'm sure, I'll be all right. I know once she is here, I won't want to be away from her for it. The Spirits, and Talisa, will watch over us and protect us both."*

*Chance chuckled, Talisa was almost more protective over her grandchild than she was with her children. "As long as you and James are sure about it, we can begin at sundown."*

*"Thank you, Ravenhawk. I'll go see about reining in James before his nerves rattle him apart. The last thing you need is a useless head warrior." Annie kissed Chance on the cheek. "I really appreciate all you have done for me."*

*"I'm just glad you're with us, Annie. You'll have to tell me what your secret to keeping James in check is."*

*"I don't think you can do what I do, Chief." Annie winked before she headed for the door.*

*Chance laughed. "You know what? Never mind. I don't want to know."*

*"Just make sure my husband stays in one piece while I do this. Thanks again." With one last wave, she slipped out of the door.*

A deep gasping breath found him back in reality, the box of Annie's ashes now in his arms. Talisa knelt beside him while the rest of the party stared at him.

"Sani?" Talisa's gentle touch to his temple almost burned like fire in the aftermath. It had always been that way.

"W-we need to get inside shortly. Steele will have people in the area." He lied to cover the truth of the vision, not even the slightest bit sure how to process it.

Talisa's voice entered his mind smooth as glass, like it belonged there. *You look as though you've seen a ghost.*

*Because I did.* Chance met her confused gaze. *Let's finish this and then we need to talk in private with James.*

"Chance?" Abby squeaked his name, her fingers reaching for the box.

"My apologies, Abby." He rose to his feet, letting her take the box back. Once again, he set his hand on it and continued the prayer the vision had interrupted. After, he gestured for Abby and Warren to place the ashes in the grave.

Abby's sobs grew impossibly louder as the family moved forward to the grave.

"We'll be in shortly." Warren's voice was brusque, and he didn't turn toward them to speak. "Would you let us grieve in peace?"

Chance squeezed Warren's shoulder, then turned to depart with the rest of the group. When they made it back to the compound, he didn't stop to explain anything. Tal and Roark didn't ask but followed him straight toward James' room.

The Spirits wouldn't have shown him a vision of Annie very much alive and pregnant if it wasn't possible. How could it be possible when they'd just buried the woman he'd had a conversation with in his vision?

Roark pushed the intercom button next to the door. "James."

James' voice crackled through the speaker. "Leave me alone."

Chance wasn't going to argue with him over it. Answers were needed. He punched the override code into the panel. "James, we need to talk."

"Look, you can't force me to go. I have my reasons." His lead warrior growled at him from his table. A laptop sat in front of him closed, a light blinking furiously on its side.

"The funeral is over, son. No one is forcing you to go out there." Talisa laid her hand on Chance's arm. "What happened out there, C?"

18

"That was a doozy of a vision, Chief." Roark's eyes knitted in concern. "And for some reason it brought you here. What is it?"

James' brow furrowed; his dark gaze stuck on Chance. "Vision?"

"Annie. I saw Annie."

"Like, her spirit spoke to you?" Talisa glanced toward James, then back to Chance.

"No. Not even close. It wasn't her spirit, it was her. I was helping her prepare for a vision quest." Chance didn't look away from James, gauging him carefully for any reaction.

"How could that be possible? Warren and Abby are putting her ashes in the ground as we speak." Roark's voice strained in confusion. "It makes no sense."

"I don't know, I only know what I saw. Somehow the spirits think it's possible for her to have a life with us. A full life." Chance blinked a few times as the headache grew worse. He'd need to treat it soon, but first he still needed answers.

James' anger had faded, and now he kept his eyes downcast, avoiding everyone in the room. "Anne saw a vision about her vision quest when Lucas helped her."

"So, let me see if I understand this." Talisa rubbed her temples as though she shared Chance's headache. "The young woman that was cremated, and we just had a funeral for, the one that is James' mate—*she* came to you to discuss her vision quest?"

"And she was pregnant." Over the shocked exclamations of Roark and Talisa, he nodded to her. "You're welcome to see it for yourself if it helps."

She nodded, her arm settling on his shoulder before he closed his eyes to avoid double vision from seeing the scene replayed. Talisa in his mind was a new, odd sensation, yet familiar all the same. With Lucas and Ilana he'd had to become accustomed to it; somehow it almost felt as though Tal had been there all along.

When he opened his eyes again after the vision had replayed, he noted the sad smile that lingered on Tal's face. "Now you see why I was confused?"

"Pregnant and married to James? Warren is going to have kittens." Talisa sighed. "How exactly do we bring a woman back from the dead that's been burned and interred? Even if I could recreate her body exactly as it was without the self-destructing DNA, I can't recreate a soul or personality."

"Well…" James' fingers grazed along the edge of the laptop. "I might be able to help you with that, Mom."

"James Logan Nashuk." Annie's voice echoed from the laptop loud and clear when he opened it. "You cut me off mid-sentence."

"Fuck me," Talisa muttered, her hand pressed to her head.

Chance stared at the laptop in disbelief. "Welcome home, Talisa."

Charlotte stormed through the hallways of the compound. Out of the goodness of her heart she'd remained behind at the funeral on the off chance she might be needed. While she'd maintained a respectful distance, any hope of keeping her cool had disappeared.

The dizzying auras alone was enough to unbalance her. However, hearing Warren rail against James once Annie had been buried sent her over the edge. While she might be among the calmest of her family, there was only so much even she could tolerate.

Politeness out the window, she punched the button to enter James' room without knocking. "You know, I love Uncle Warren, but if he doesn't knock this shit off, I'm going to ask Elan to poison him with her claws." Her continued tirade faded on her lips when she realized James wasn't alone. All three of her parents stared at her along with her brother.

Chance laid a hand on her shoulder. "Everything okay?"

"Yeah. I mean, yeah. I'm just frustrated. I wanted to make sure James was okay." She let out the last of her heated breath. "You know, see if anything changed."

"We came down for similar reasons." Talisa eyed James intently, and in a fashion similar to Lucas, a gentle nudge hit Charlotte's brain. No words, just an urging of sorts. Talisa continued as if the mental nudge hadn't happened. "Warren will come around. He's grieving, things will run their course."

Charlotte took her mother's cue without argument. She worried her bottom lip between her teeth in her focus. James' aura shimmered in front of her, and rather unexpectedly it bordered on calm. Several strands shot out from him and connected to Roark and Talisa and then veered off somewhere else in the compound to Lucas and Elan. One connected to her and Chance. One however went past Chance and stopped on the laptop on his desk.

James' brow furrowed. "Shorty?"

Charlotte held up a finger in a silent request for another moment. She returned her focus to her brother, willing all the other threads away but the one that had caught her off-guard. It definitely led to the laptop. That's when she saw it. Initially she'd dismissed the oddness as a reflection from the monitor, but that wasn't what was happening.

James moved when she did toward the laptop. Impatience edged into his tone. "Seriously, Shorty. What is your deal?"

"Why the hell does James' laptop have an aura?" Charlotte asked by way of an answer. "There should only be an aura if there is a soul, a life."

"Hey, Charlotte." Annie's voice echoed from the laptop. The blurry image of the neighborhood on the screen cleared. A figure walked down the road until she was right in front of the screen, and it was undeniably Annie.

"Fuck me." Charlotte jumped back into Talisa.

22

Talisa gently gripped her shoulders. "Well, that answers that question. We are going to have to tell Warren and Abby about this."

"Please don't," Annie protested. "We don't even know if anything can be done yet, and if you tell my dad he will take the laptop away. I won't be able to see anyone but him or Mom. I can't stay like this forever, and I'd rather stay with James."

Roark stepped forward. "What exactly do you mean, Annie?"

"Computers hold information. Data. Binary code. A brainwave, or in this case from what Charlotte is seeing, a soul." Annie's brow wrinkled in concern. "If you were to connect this laptop to the network, I would be seen as a virus. Dad's antivirus will try to get rid of me."

"*No.*" James gripped the edge of the laptop.

"Relax, James." Chance set his hand on her brother's shoulder. "We're going to talk this through and figure out what our options are. Abby and Warren are going to have to be brought into the loop at some point."

"She's right." Talisa interjected. "With the way Warren is processing right now, he'd take the laptop and never let us near it again."

"So, what do we do?" Chance folded his arms across his chest. "The Spirits have shown me it's possible. Just not how."

"How do we create a clone body without a soul? And once we do, how do we get Annie back into that body?" Charlotte turned around to face Talisa. "Not to mention, how much time do we have for Annie to stay in the computer like that? And how do we work on any of this without Warren finding out and flipping out?"

"Easy Char." Roark held his hand up. "We're not going to figure it all out right this second. There are a lot of variables we need to look at."

"I understand it isn't going to be easy. I just appreciate any help you can give me." Annie's voice came from the computer again. "The Spirits think it's possible. They have shown me a lot since I transferred into the computer."

"But not how to do it?" Talisa said with a wry smile.

"No, they said you would be able to figure it out." The image of Annie shrugged.

"Once we figure that out, we may need supplies. I don't know what you use to make a new body." Chance frowned, "Or where we would need to go for those supplies."

"One step at a time Chief." Roark sat down in the chair behind him and pulled Talisa onto his lap. "Is the lab even big enough for this?"

"RB and Kenzie were finishing up the temporary lab that we moved the Exceptionals that you brought home with you to." Charlotte moved to the couch.

"You're awfully quiet James." Chance glanced over at his second in command. "You're almost…well I'd say you're calm."

"I'm fine Chief." Red surged through James' aura but retreated as quick as it had come forth.

"Do you need some time for all of this? RB can keep helping me as he has been. No one is going to hold it against you." Chance offered.

"I said I'm fine." James snapped back.

"Amendchewagan" Annie's voice interjected.

"You have no idea, Annie." Talisa laughed.

"Mom? What will this do to James? What about their connection?" Charlotte could only wonder at the oddity of it all.

It had never happened before, that much was for sure. Would this hurt them both, and alter their connection? Even worse, would it sever the connection when they tried to fix it?

"I don't think it will hurt them, Charlotte." Talisa's brow furrowed in all-too-familiar fashion. Such an expression meant she was pondering some things likely more complicated than they could expect to guess on the first try.

"I won't do anything that is going to hurt James." Annie's panic made the speaker crackle with her urgency. "I've hurt him enough already."

James huffed. "Anne, stop."

"I'm not going to stop. I know how much pain you were in when I refused the bond. I'm not going to do that again," Annie argued back.

James snorted. "Now who's stubborn?"

"She's already learning Lenape. I think I like her already." Talisa smiled, though her eyes still had the distant look of being deep in thought. "We aren't going to figure this all out right this minute. Why don't we leave James and Annie alone for right now? Your father and I will see what we can come up with to bring her back. Char, do you want to help?"

"Sure, Mom. James may be getting his mate back, but I want my friend back too." Charlotte shrugged absently, a lingering hint of jealousy tugging her heart. Rather than dwell on it, the idea of keeping busy seemed a good distraction. "It's not like I have anything else going on."

Inessa held onto the reins as the horse slowed. Off in the distance sat what appeared to be a small farming community, a handful of houses, a small plane, and some planted fields.

Without her ability, from any angle but the one where they currently stood, she wouldn't have been able to see anything but trees. From their exact vantage point she could see a small break in the trees where vehicles could enter.

All else was silent.

"We're here," she said quietly to Neil.

"You sure?"

She laughed. "I'm quite sure. I've been able to see this place for miles. It's lit up like a Christmas tree. I hope the military never obtains an Exceptional like myself."

"God help us, if they ever do," Neil whispered. The tension in his voice mingled with excitement and nervousness. "We're already being watched. We'll have to take care. If we do anything wrong, we'll be attacked first, questioned later."

While she appreciated the warning, she didn't need to be told they were being watched. Despite the extreme care and quiet they'd maintained; she could see the auras of the men in the trees. "I'll be careful. I can see them. Hopefully they'll recognize you before they attack."

"I don't exactly look like I once did. I wouldn't hang my hopes on that." Weeks ago it would have worried her, his comment would have been so laced with self-loathing and fear. After a few weeks in her presence, the comment now had a bit of humor mixed in with it. She wasn't sure if it was her influence, or just being close to home that did it.

She urged the horse forward, taking a deep breath as the figures in the trees moved in response. "You said I'm to ask for Night Hawk, right? James."

"Yes."

26

"And he's Charlotte's brother. He'll recognize you if the others don't."

"Exactly."

If it weren't for the very real danger in the situation, Inessa would have found it amusing to watch the figures in the trees come closer, in synch, with every step the horse moved nearer. Then, without explanation, they all stopped.

She gasped in surprise, keeping them still as the auras began to move further away. "They're retreating. Why are they retreating?"

"I'm not sure. This is not standard procedure. I heard no signal."

"No. You wouldn't have. It was telepathic," she whispered. "At least I'm assuming so as there's a telepath heading our way."

"Lucas."

Another brother of Charlotte's, the indirect twin of James. At least, that's how she'd come to refer to the two men's association. The knowledge relaxed her along with the fact that she detected no threat in his aura.

*You have nothing to fear from me.*

The brush of Lucas' mind to hers drew her closer still. "I know. You mean me absolutely no harm, I can see that. Thank you for calling off the SWAT team. I really didn't want them to shoot first and ask questions later."

"At least you're more likely to live with a well-placed arrow as opposed to a bullet wound." Lucas chuckled as they drew closer. His gaze drifted to the man behind her, eyes softening at the sight of him. "Neil. Thank the Spirits. We thought for sure you were dead. Only Charlotte was convinced that you were not."

"I thought I might be for a while there," Neil acknowledged. His voice caught mid-sentence. He cleared his throat. "Charlotte? She didn't think I was dead. Really?"

"Really. Everyone will be thrilled to find you are, in fact, alive." Lucas held up a hand, clasping it with Neil's to assist him off the horse. "On top of the return of Mother and Father, this has been a good day."

"Returned? But how?" Neil grasped Lucas' shoulder. "James saw them die. How can they be here now?"

"That's a long story. Come, we will go into the tunnels so you can see Charlotte. The rest of the news can wait." Lucas smiled at Inessa. "One of the men will take your horse to the stables. The Chief will want to meet you in person. I've alerted him to your arrival."

Inessa nodded her appreciation. "I look forward to meeting him. Neil has told me so much about all of you. Should I wait up here so you can bring Neil to his wife? I don't mind."

"No. You are welcome down in the tunnels. Ravenhawk will be waiting for you down there." Lucas set Neil's hand on his arm, guiding them to the nearest house.

For a while they remained quiet. The only sound came from Lucas' occasional warning of how many steps they were taking. By the time they got down into the tunnel, Chance stood waiting on them.

Chance stepped forward to embrace Neil. "Neil. Thank the Spirits. We haven't yet told Charlotte. Lucas said you were coming, but we didn't want to get her hopes up. Do you require medical care first?"

"No. These wounds are old, and fully healed physically." Neil smiled, "Inessa has made sure our trip went smoother than I would have thought. We ran into no one. The few times there were any troops within a few miles, she found us some place safe to hide."

"Inessa." Chance turned his attention toward her. For a moment, she had to force her way through the shield of defensiveness in his aura. Underneath she could see his genuine gratitude but getting there was tough. "Thank you for bringing him back to us safe. I'm Chance."

His defensive aura was almost enough to put her on guard, but she wasn't that sort of person. She was a people person who had cracked through tougher walls than his just by being herself. Inessa shook his hand, offering a bright smile. With a bit of effort, she focused on the warmth she found lingering under the grays and blacks of his mistrust and pain. "Nice to meet you, Chance. Lucas, why don't you go ahead and take Neil to his wife? I think I'll be all right in your Chief's capable hands."

Lucas bowed slightly. "I will. Thank you, Inessa."

Chance waited until they'd made their way down the tunnels before gesturing toward the path they'd taken. "Right this way. I don't know how much Neil has told you about us."

"We've had a few months together, so I know quite a bit." Inessa shrugged at his surprise. "Hey, I'm a people person. I struggle to be quiet in any capacity. Plus, he was so depressed and scared, I had to keep him moving forward. Thank you for allowing me to enter without any trouble. I know how tight your security is."

"Lucas says you're very open for him, and that we have no reason to mistrust you. I have learned to take his word on things. So, thank you for bringing Neil back to us." After that, his walls softened slightly, but he still tried to keep guarded. He probably didn't realize nothing was protected from her mutation.

"He saved my life once. It only seemed right that I help him get home to his wife. His love for her is the clearest thing he had and kept him balanced when he could have given up." Inessa kept her focus on the tunnel walls for a moment.

The cool metal was a welcome distraction from the dichotomy of the man beside her. Not to mention the fact that she found him exceptionally attractive. It was an honest enough thought. That didn't bother her. However, it had been so long since she'd been with anyone that she had to put those thoughts away before she attacked the poor man without warning.

She cleared her throat, focusing on their conversation again. "Dr. Carter was amazingly talented. I hate to see him lose his ability to perform surgery. So much tragedy came out of this stupid war."

"Too much. Here, let's get you something to eat." Chance led her into a small kitchen. Several crock pots lined the counter, delicious smells of fresh food like she hadn't eaten in months made her stomach rumble. "We try to keep a steady stream of hot food ready. Many people come in and out throughout the day. Not everyone bothers to put a kitchen in their own unit here. It's easier to have some community food at the ready."

"With a community food mentality, you'd think you'd have a much bigger kitchen than this." The words were out of her mouth before she'd thought about it. Her cheeks grew warm when Chance turned an amused gaze her way. "Sorry. That slipped out. It's just—it seems a bit cramped in here."

"It is. We plan a larger cafeteria sort of room in our new wing. That's not slated for completion for another month, though. We take our lessons as they come." Chance smiled as he led her to the crock pots. After he'd handed her a bowl, he helped himself to some chili. Once she'd gotten some for herself, he held out a chair for her. He took the seat beside her, his gaze focused on her. "Lucas says you are from New York City."

"Indirectly, yes. I was born in Poland, but we moved to the states when I was five." She spun her spoon in her chili. If he asked her about her family, she just might fall into a place she didn't like going. A place she hadn't been since she'd stumbled on Neil and got a traveling companion to distract her from her own worries.

"You were on Broadway when the attacks started?"

"Literally." Inessa rubbed her arms as the memory shivered through her. "I had that night off from the ballet, so I had gone to a friend's performance on Broadway. I was sitting front row when the stage manager halted the performance because we didn't hear the sirens. He said the military was attacking those with mutations, and those with powers were fighting back. It was an all-out war across the island. By the time the first concussion of a blast shook the theater, the screams were deafening."

Chance set his hand on her arm, pulling her from the depths of her own intense study of her chili. For the first time since she'd met him, his guard was down. Concern and warmth poured toward her in soothing, peaceful waves of green and indigo. "I remember the battle well. That was the first, and the worst."

Somehow the colors of his aura melted into a watercolor of confusion. It was then that she realized she was crying. "It's horrible to watch people die," she whispered.

"I know."

"No. You don't." She wiped at her tears, forcing her focus back to the safe haven of her bowl of chili. To distract herself, she counted the beans. "You see them die, but you see their shells, their surface. I see it all. Their pain, their fear, their entire life dim and fade to black."

Beyond the screams that day, she had to watch so many deaths, so many painful wounds and emotional losses. Good friends trapped under the rubble, those she could see, but not reach. Sudden deaths, long and lingering deaths. It was now at a point where she knew she'd be able to see the grim reaper coming long before it happened.

She cleared her throat against the renewed burgeoning well of tears. "Sorry. Can we talk about something else? I haven't been around people in so long, the last thing I want to do is blubber like a baby in front of the first ones I see."

"Of course." His hand squeezed her arm gently. "How about we find you a unit for you to stay in? You can have a hot shower, even listen to some music or watch some TV?"

"Music?" The mere word brought some life back to her, so she straightened. "What sort of music are we talking about?"

Chance chuckled at her response. "I'm sure if what you're looking for isn't in our database, it won't take any time to find what you want. We have the world's best computer geek here."

"A hot shower and music? Goddess, I think if you proposed right now I'd say yes just for offering me those two things. Throw in some dance shoes and there'd be no doubt."

He quirked a brow. "I'm afraid we don't have any of those, but I'll keep that in mind."

Talisa studied the screen on the side of the young girls cryounit. The readings hadn't changed one iota since they'd arrived back at the compound. Still, she'd come down to the cavernous room they sat in for the pure isolation of it.

Plus, the work soothed her. For the past year of imprisonment and separation from Roark, the work had kept both herself and her husband sane. She could almost call it a form of Stockholm Syndrome considering how willing she'd been to give up on her work once upon a lifetime ago.

"I thought I'd find you here." Roark's voice remained low and quiet but echoed around the room nonetheless. "Trying to get your bearings?"

"It is a lot of chaos right now. After a year of nothing but science, it's a little much. Even though I missed it terribly." She sighed into the embrace he wrapped her in. "You came down here, as well. Not just to look for me, either."

"Busted," he muttered in her ear. A low chuckle followed his words. "Telepathy?"

"No. Not this time. I merely know my husband well."

"That you do."

"What are we going to do about—"

"Nope."

Talisa craned her neck around to meet his gaze. "Excuse me?"

"We are taking five minutes away from it. So shut your trap, woman."

She turned in his arms, a brow raised to stare him down. "I know you didn't tell me to shut up. Because if you had, that would be asking for a neutering."

The tiniest of whimpers hit her ears at the suggestion. "Not funny."

"A little funny."

He pulled her closer, his arms tight around her waist. His nose nuzzled against her neck. The welcome warmth of his hold seeped into her tense bones until she could almost say she was relaxed. Almost, but not quite. A soft sigh stirred against her neck. "Maybe ten minutes."

A hint of laughter rumbled about in her belly, jockeying for release. "When, in our entire relationship, have we been allowed ten minutes without interruption?"

"Never."

"Not even when we first met and you screwed me silly in the first ten minutes."

"That damn Warren interrupted, what could have been an awesome day."

"Even before you became an Exceptional you always were insatiable."

"You were too."

"Never said I wasn't." She grinned up at him when he finally lifted his head. "Why don't we focus on this group for a few minutes. Down here in this quiet room. We might not be able to do much, but maybe we can get some info out of these units to figure out where these people came from, and what we unwittingly did to them."

"That sounds like a plan I can get behind. Let me guess, you want to start on the little one."

"You read my mind," she said in a droll tone.

Roark laughed heartily and smacked her lightly on the ass. "Smartass."

"Couldn't resist." She turned her attention back to the stasis unit beside them. "She is so young. Must be, what, six? Based on appearance, of course."

"Of course." He handed her one of the tablets laid out on the table near the units, then took one for himself. "But as anyone who's paid any attention to this mess of a war knows, anyone born an Exceptional ages differently."

"Which means she could be anywhere between one and three human years, at best." Tal activated her tablet, pleased to find it already hooked into the units. One good thing about the computer mutation of Warren was that even in the depths of his despair, his mind couldn't stop moving at super-speed.

The man always had to be programming or de-programming. Tal couldn't imagine what the results would be if Warren ever stopped thinking. The world itself might stop turning.

She scrolled through the existing readouts on the unit again. "This really doesn't tell us much."

"Well, I'll be damned."

"What?"

"I'm surprised we didn't notice this sooner. Then again, maybe I'm not."

"Roark."

He held up his tablet to her. Somewhere along the way, he'd gone to another screen, where the evidence of a sample collection device could be seen within the unit. "Looks like when we, or Steele, or Warren, or who-the-fuck-ever designed this thing, we planned for contingencies."

"Hot damn. You're sexy when you're being smarter than me."

"Bullshit."

"Okay, not smarter than me, but smart." She leaned up to give him a quick kiss. "Now let's get our samples. As long as we're at it, we might as well get them all."

"I'll start on Mr. and Mrs. Meowza over there. You get her, and the others."

"Deal." Tal flicked through the screens until she found the link to the device within the program. "Looks easy enough to manipulate. Is it just me, or does it look like this damn thing even labels them for us?"

"I'll be interested to see just what the hell they're labeled as." Roark glanced her way. "Maybe we left ourselves messages, if we did this, of course."

"You say that like it's something we always do." She studied the available options. "Skin samples, blood, even hair. Thorough."

"I've got Felinity started."

"Would you stop it, you big dork?"

"Nope."

She rolled her eyes but didn't argue further. It didn't take telepathy to see he was happy to be feeling useful, every bit as much as she did—well, feeling useful and away from the chaos for at least a few minutes.

Then, midway through extraction, her device froze.

"Damn it," she muttered.

"What the fuck?" Roark smacked the top of the unit he was hovering over. "Get moving, you hunk of junk."

36

"You're frozen, too?"

"Yeah. What happened?"

"Odd. Maybe a failsafe of some kind?" She set aside her tablet to study the machine before her. The panel on the board appeared frozen as well, but when she tilted her head she noticed an almost graph-like screen flickering beneath it. "Handprint?"

"You think?"

"Maybe. You try the panel; I'll try the tablet." She wondered if the same restriction would work from the devices.

"No dice. You?"

"Nope. Wait." She tilted the panel, then noticed a seam at the top. Once she'd popped it open with her nail, a red light flickered along her face. "Got it. It was a trick. It's a retinal scan. There's a seam at the top of this panel. It's almost hidden. Good, clean work."

"Nice."

"Sometimes we're smarter than we look."

"You always are, and that's saying a lot. You're fucking hot, and brilliant to boot."

"Stop talking dirty to me, I'm working." She chuckled low.

"Damn, woman. Can't help it. Makes it worse knowing there's no wall between us now."

"Don't remind me, or I might stop working."

"No. Wall."

"Fuck."

"Please?"

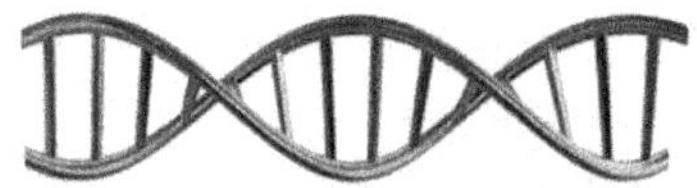

Charlotte moved along the corridors through the living area of the compound towards what was considered the more practical areas, wringing her hands. Despite his attempt to keep his tone neutral she could tell that whatever news Lucas had for her was important.

The lab, Warren's office, and a few storage rooms lined this section. The area still held no decoration other than the occasional posting on the wall to show directions. Most people avoided this area unless they needed to be seen in the lab.

Behind the door off the corridor a large common room spread out. The walls held various decorations on it, mostly artifact that they had been able to save or recover before the remainder of the tribe had been driven from their lands. Charlotte, Abigail, and the other women had done it in an effort to remind them of what they had lost and what they still fought for.

The door to the conference room off the main area came into view. It was the only thing that stood between her and whatever revelation Lucas had for her. Her hand froze over the keypad as the deep breath she took left her body with a shudder. A familiar aura wavered on the other side of the door, but she dared not hope.

She tapped the keypad and all breath left her body. All she managed was a small, squeaked, "Oh God."

Lucas stood off to one side fixing a few cups of tea. In the chair closest to the door sat Neil, her long lost husband. To confirm the calm, soothing colors of his aura were real, and the thread that connected them shining so bright brought tears to her eyes.

"Charlotte?" Pinks and blues streaked through a murky gray to his aura, all of it matching the anxious tone in his voice.

38

The moment Neil leaned on the table to stand, Charlotte shot across the room. She threw her arms around his neck tight to hold on to his realness. Her lips captured his before he could make any word of greeting or protest. Tears slipped down her cheeks unbidden, to lend their salt to the sweetness of the long-awaited kiss.

The sound of Lucas clearing his throat was the only thing that made her pull back.

"How? When?" Charlotte brought her hand up to cup his cheek. She had to feel him to know he was real. It was the only thing that mattered. He was home. He came back to her just as he promised. "I have missed you so much."

"Not a day passed that I didn't think about you." Neil brushed his lips across her forehead. "I wish I had been able to contact you."

"Shh, it's going to be okay. You're home. That's all that matters." She brought her other hand up to cup his other cheek. That's when she felt it. Puckering and ridges of skin under her fingertips. "Neil?"

The pink and blue in his aura were shoved to the background and replaced with dark and muddy gray when Charlotte pulled back. "It looks worse than it is."

Charlotte smirked at him until she realized he couldn't see her. Her hand came up to her lips and pressed against them in order to stop their trembling. "What happened?"

A hand on her shoulder startled her. Lucas had approached without her realizing it, or even remembering he'd been in the room. *I have made you both some tea. I will give you the privacy you need. Reach out if you require anything.* He bowed his head to her, then to Neil as if the man could see him. Then, he slipped from the room without another word.

Neil cleared his throat. "I know I must look a fright. I wouldn't blame you if—"

"Neil David Carter, don't you dare finish that sentence!"

"But Charlotte, I'm not the man I was."

Her lips pressed to his again in a soft kiss meant to silence his protest. When she pulled back, she took the time to rein in her mutation. While she could never truly turn it off for long, this would give her the opportunity to survey the damage. She studied the scars that lined his face, cut across his eye and the corner of his mouth. With the tips of her fingers, she brushed along the puckered ridge of the worst scar until she reached the side of the cloudy eye that stared lifelessly through her. "None of this matters to my feelings. I love you just as much as the day I went to St. Louis."

The gray spiraled out of his aura as if it were going down the drain. A soft blue replaced it. "I love you too. So much. I am so sorry I didn't listen to you that day. You told me you had a bad feeling about it."

"Neil, don't." Another kiss before she continued. "You are home and safe and that is all that matters right now. Everything else we will figure out. Now sit. You look exhausted. How did you get home?"

"Inessa. You remember the woman with the broken leg in New York?"

Charlotte nodded and waited for him to continue when it dawned on her that he couldn't see her. She swiped a tear from her cheek. "I remember her. Did she stay?"

"She did. I believe Chance was getting her settled. Lucas brought me down here so I could see you."

"I'll have to thank her when I see her for bringing you back to me." She slid one of the mugs of tea closer to Neil. "Here you should drink this. Lucas made it."

40

Neil's chuckle made her smile, "Which means we should drink it without question right?

"Precisely." With a shaky breath she guided his hand to the mug. "H-how much can you see? We'll rearrange our unit if you want. Whatever you need." The more she spoke the more the silent tears fell.

"Shadows and light mostly with the left. Nothing with the right." The fear spiked back through his aura.

"Hey." Charlotte ran her fingers through his hair. "None of that. The only thing that changes is I can't hog all the covers tonight. You don't know how happy that makes me."

"I don't want to be a burden to you, Charlotte."

"You will never be a burden to me. For better or worse, remember?" She slid onto his lap and wrapped her arms around him.

"I've been gone for almost a year. You could have moved on; found someone else." He wrapped his arms around her waist.

"Right, because dating opportunities are vast in the middle of a war."

"Has anyone ever told you that your family is particularly sarcastic?" His lips pressed to her temple.

"Well, not that I can think of. No one has ever mentioned it before. Nope." Charlotte couldn't help the laughter that bubbled up.

"Well let me be the first."

"I knew you weren't dead and you promised you would come back to me. Granted we did miss our reservation in the hot spring." She shifted on his lap to rest her forehead against his. A long sigh of release drained from her lips.

"How did you know?" Confusion mixed with a hint of hope.

"The threads. Ours never dimmed. Never faltered. It's always been there just like my parents."

"Lucas mentioned something about your parents when we got here." His brow furrowed in confusion.

"They are alive…and home. We just got them back too. What do you say we go back to our unit? Maybe a nice hot shower?"

"That sounds wonderful actually." His smile was weak but it was something.

Two vines of ivy snaked out from under her clothes to carry the mugs. Once she stood, she took his hand and waited for him to do the same. "You know I couldn't even bring myself to part with that god-awful couch you loved."

Neil chuckled, "You kept that? I would have figured that would be the first thing you tossed." His arm wrapped around her shoulder as they moved through the common area.

"Oh, it was a thought. A fleeting one, but a thought nonetheless." Her arm wrapped around his waist. She let him set the pace, not wanting to rush him. All she cared about was that he had come back to her.

He ran the tips of his fingers over the numbers on the door when they stopped in front of it. "This is it right?"

"This is it." Charlotte moved in front of him and placed a soft kiss on his lips. "Welcome home, Neil."

Danny paused long enough for Ethan to shut the door to their parents' room. He stuffed his hands in his pockets. The last thing he wanted to do now was go back to his own unit. He'd been sleeping on the couch in his parents' unit under the guise of supporting them. Truth be told, they needed the support. Both of them had been nearly inconsolable since Annie died.

That being said, he wasn't sure he was ready to face Elan. While he knew she did it because she felt like it was the only way to save her parents, the fact that she left without talking to him or even just saying goodbye hurt. Being face-to-face with her soon was inevitable, but what would he say to her?

"You talk to her yet?" Ethan broke through his internal monologue.

"Not yet. I haven't seen her since she stopped by Annie's room. I don't know what to say."

"What the hell were you thinking comes to mind." Ethan sighed. "But we don't know if her parents would be back if she hadn't gone."

"You know the bad part?" Danny glanced at his brother as they walked, "I completely get the why. If it had been Mom and

Dad, I can't say I wouldn't have done something similar if I thought I could save them. But she left without a word. I got a crumpled note with three words on it. And they weren't I love you."

"Harsh."

"Tell me about it. Worst part is I don't know if she even wants to talk to me. I mean I did kinda shut the door in her face when she came by right after Annie died." He pursed his lips at the wave of guilt he felt from his brother at the mention of their sister. "Would you stop beating yourself up?"

"Damn twin connection." Ethan ran a hand through his hair. A deep sigh echoed from Danny's twin. "Ilana says the same thing, but I can't help it. I should have gotten to know her better. It wouldn't have killed me to be nice to her. Instead, I let her die thinking I hated her. I was just so freaked out by the whole thing."

Danny patted his brother's shoulder. "Dude, you don't have to tell me. She knew things about us and yet we didn't have any of the same memories she did. Annie didn't hate you, though. She might have been hurt, but she didn't hate you."

"Not helping, bro."

"I know, I know. Sorry. I'm at such a loss. About everything."

"Me too."

Danny glanced back the way they'd come. "I'm worried about Mom and Dad. They've barely left their unit. I thought maybe Talisa and Roark being home might have helped some."

"Oh, stop with the damn distraction." Ethan stopped in the middle of the hall.

"Huh?" Danny stopped short when his brother did. "What are you talking about?"

"Just go talk to her. You need to."

44

Danny groaned. "We have bigger problems."

"No, not really. She's your damn wife. Mom and dad have each other."

"But—"

"Hear me out." Ethan held up his hands, effectively stopping Danny's continuing argument for the moment. "I'm not saying your first question shouldn't be what the fuck, but we are in the middle of a war—a revolution. I may not have spent much time with Annie but she did teach me one thing. Don't live with regrets. Steele could find this place tomorrow and blow us all to kingdom come. We could end up in the middle of another battle. Shit, look at Ariel."

"Yeah. I get it. Hell, every time we identify a new Exceptional and an extraction team is sent out something could happen." Danny rubbed the back of his neck. "I have no idea where to start, though. I feel so selfish about the whole damn thing. It's amazing that her parents are not only alive, but back—but I needed my wife to deal with our sister dying. God, I am an asshole."

Ethan rolled his eyes. "You are not an asshole, you're human. You both had shit going on you had to deal with. Now you need to talk it out, or in your case yell it at each other and then screw each other silly."

"It's like you know us or something." Danny made the effort to chuckle, though it came out hollow.

"Twin connection goes both ways big brother."

"How in hell do I even start this conversation? Oh, hey Elan I'm so glad you're home. What the hell were you thinking running off like that without telling me? Without backup? How could you leave me like that with nothing but a damn note that said you had to?" Tears welled in his eyes at every word.

Elan's voice came from behind him, quiet and almost unsure which was weird for her. "That's a pretty good start. Doesn't sound as angry as I'd expected, though."

"Jesus, Mary, and Joseph on food stamps, woman!"

Ethan cleared his throat. "And that's my cue to leave. Glad you're home sis. Try not to tear up the corridor, you two. Fighting or otherwise."

"Ethan…" Danny frowned at his brother. He knew they needed to talk but he didn't know if he was ready to do that yet.

"Nope. Not staying around so you two can avoid it. I'm going to go find Ilana. I'll talk to you later." Ethan headed back toward the common area.

Danny focused on his feet until Ethan disappeared. They weren't that far from the common area, but it felt like an eternity. Part of him wanted to grab his wife and yank her to him, kiss her senseless, and forget about the whole thing. But if they didn't talk, it would fester until it exploded and that wouldn't be good for either one of them.

"I'm sorry about your sister." Elan's voice trembled.

"Yeah me too…thanks." Danny stuffed his hands in his pockets to keep him from doing exactly what he just decided not to do. "Got your parents back. That's a good thing. And a few extras I hear."

"Told them to leave those pods behind but they didn't want to listen to me." Elan shrugged.

"Pods filled with Exceptionals, and word is a free-standing Exceptional along with. Chaz is his name, from what I hear." Anger welled again when he noted the miniscule twitch of his wife's lips. He knew her well enough to see the name meant something to her. Of course, knowing what had happened to her in the past under Steele's control. "I'm guessing he's a friend of yours."

"Something like that."

"Look Elan. I don't want to dance around this. Ya left me. No goodbye. No conversation. Just that shitty-ass note."

"Danny…"

He held one hand up, the other clenched at his side. "Let me finish. I need to get this out. You owe me that much. Like I told Ethan. Worst part is I can totally understand why you went after them like you did. I get that. It's how you left. What if something happened to you? What if you hadn't come back? You robbed me of a chance to tell you I love you before you left. Of any sort of contingency…"

"Danny there wasn't…" Elan attempted to interrupt again.

"Woman, I said let me finish." He advanced on her and backed her up against the wall. The logical side of his brain told him this was the stupidest idea he'd had in a long time. He knew she hated to be cornered. The pissed off side said, 'screw it let's see what happens'. "I know it's selfish of me, but I needed you too, damn it!" One hand came to rest on the wall next to her head.

"Danny I'm sorry, but I had to." Elan's skin thickened in response to his proximity.

"You had to." He nodded for a second before he leaned in and pressed his lips to her forehead. "I love you Elan. Now I'm going back to our unit. When my wife is ready to finish talking this out…you know where to find me."

James carried the laptop clutched tight in his hand. He strode down the nearly dark corridor with no problem. His enhanced eyesight made the little snippets of light more than enough to see the path to where the pods were stored.

A quick check of the computers told him where his parents were, and that they were not working on the issue of Anne, so far as he could tell. He had no idea what on earth could be more important than getting her soul *out* of the computer before she died—again.

He stormed into the makeshift lab, only to find them both bent over an odd metal pod. They were discussing something with an intensity that surprised him, but he couldn't understand them. Sure, they spoke English, but it almost seemed like some sort of code.

"I miss the stars," Talisa mumbled.

"I do too. Doesn't mean they aren't still shining." Roark flipped through some screens on the tablet he held. "Look. They're shining bright. Hello, James."

"What the hell are you doing?" James came within inches of slamming down the computer he held but thought better. Even though Anne wasn't a physical creature, he didn't think slamming around her current home would be a good idea.

Tal lifted her gaze to study James. "What does it look like we're doing?"

"Having a really weird conversation, instead of working on Anne's problem." James jabbed his finger toward the pod. "What the hell is that?"

Tal sighed, a deep sigh that seemed to resonate from her soul. "I had to get away from the voices for a while. It relaxes me to be working, it's the only thing that was a comfort for over a year, James."

"As for this," Roark gestured to the pod, "This is what we brought back with us. We aren't ignoring the problem of Annie, James, but look at her. She's just a child. She doesn't deserve to be frozen in time any more than Annie deserves to be trapped in a computer."

"No," Tal cut him off before he could speak. "We aren't saying she's more important than Annie, but she is important, too."

James growled low despite himself. "I don't like having my mind read."

"When you project and scream at me, it's hard to ignore." Tal set down her tablet. "Do as your dad says and go look at her."

James moved closer when Tal stepped aside.

"And I don't have to answer to you, James. Remember that." Though her words were harsh, Tal touched his shoulder gently. "Nothing around here is ever simple. I know having your mate come back to you is very important, I wouldn't ever deny you that, but I am still your mother."

Roark leaned on the pod. "How is Annie doing?"

"Strong for now, but she isn't sure how long she can maintain. Being in a laptop is very restrictive on a lot, including power." James studied the girl inside the pod. Something was oddly familiar about her, though he couldn't place why. "Who is she?"

"We're not sure. We have some tests running now. Once we're sure she's not a danger to us, nor us to her, we might try to wake her." Tal frowned, then glanced over to where four more of the pods lay. "Of the five that we saw any hope of rescuing, she is the one that appears to be the strongest."

"What about Anne?" James met his mother's gaze, unwavering when her eyes flashed with warning. "What are her chances?"

Tal's gaze softened, then darted to the computer on the table. "No soul can live as data for long, you know that in your heart. We need to gather and speak at length about our options. A new body makes the most sense, but it'll be tricky as hell to do, even with the best technology."

"That's not good enough, Mom."

"I know. It's the best I can do for now. I'm not sure we even can, since her original DNA was made with a faulty design." As if she sensed his growing tension, she set her hands on both his cheeks. Automatically, he leaned toward her until their foreheads touched. She smiled at him warm enough to calm his internal struggle almost as well as Anne could. "You know I will do everything I can, don't you?"

"Yes," he admitted somewhat begrudgingly. Despite himself, his anger eased even more.

"I would never do anything that would hurt you. Losing Annie would, so I don't want that to happen." She held his gaze tight, unwavering and strong as she'd always been. "You have to trust that your dad and I are going to do everything in our power to do that."

Instinctively, he did trust his mom, but another instinct to protect Anne battled against it. His jaw clenched against the protest rising in direct opposition to his better judgment.

"That's the mating instinct," Tal soothed. Her features softened into a sad smile. "Probably made worse because you never were able to complete the bond, and the fact that she is a data stream in a computer now."

Through gritted teeth he managed to speak something non-offensive. "She is my focus."

"I understand that. We are also working on the problem. Believe it or not, your dad and I have a bit of intelligence between us and can work on multiple problems simultaneously."

50

Roark's deep voice broke into the conversation with surprising gentleness. "I know you're unable to step back to look at the big picture now, but we can. There are many reasons for us to be looking over this child, James. Trust us."

"I trust you," James said directly to Talisa. For reasons likely attributed to the programming from Steele, he'd always had a shaky bond with Roark. "Don't make me wait long."

"You'll wait as long as necessary." Once again, Tal's voice took on a hard edge, a sort of command his synapses instinctively responded to.

"Mom."

"Either stay and help so you can see what we're doing or go. Blow off steam in the gym. Plug your girlfriend in so her batteries don't die."

Roark snorted. "That sounded all levels of wrong."

James chuckled along with them. The infusion of humor helped break some of the tension he'd been unable to shake since Annie's non-demise. "He's not wrong, Mom."

"Hey, I've got mad skills when it comes to gutter humor." Tal winked before lifting on tiptoe to kiss James' forehead. "Go."

"You'll keep me informed." It wasn't a question, but a statement.

"Of course."

"Thank you."

Elan remained in the now empty corridor for several long seconds. Danny's reaction confused the shit out of her, and she hated when she didn't have a handle on the situation. When she went into their room, would it continue with that last bit of affection, or would his true anger erupt?

She'd earned every bit of anger, and she'd been trained to not balk from her punishments when they came, so that didn't bother her. What did was the unknown of what would happen when she went in there.

After a few long, slow breaths, she pushed off the wall to follow her husband. Unlike the past few days, the moment she got to the door, it slid open for her. The room inside was a wreck, which was sort of her style, but not Danny's. He might not be a neat freak, but the room look like he'd spent some time venting his anger—over her, or his sister, or both.

"Did some redecorating, I see." She immediately regretted the comment, but it managed to draw a snort from Danny.

"Yeah, well, time's been a bit short. My temper has been, too." Danny shoved a few items of clothing into a dresser drawer.

52

She walked up beside him, unable to curb the instinct to thicken her skin against his possible anger, not that he'd ever hurt her. "What now?"

"Wish I fucking knew."

"So, it's not just me."

"Not by a long shot." He shook his head. "Damn it, Elan."

"It's how I operate. It's how I was trained."

"I'm sick of that fucking excuse."

"I'm well aware you're sick of my past, I am too." She'd snapped without meaning to. The flash of fire in his eyes sent her into full defensive mode. "You were there to help break me of his fucking mind control bullshit, you saw how deep it is in me. I'm sorry it hurt you, I'm sorry I caved to it yet again, but sometimes…"

"What?" He grabbed her shoulders, ignorant of her thick skin and now-poisonous nail tips. "Sometimes, what?"

"I…" She couldn't say it, didn't dare say it. If Danny knew that sometimes the old commands beat through her skull like the world's most dangerous ear worm, he'd send her immediately to her mother and Lucas for another de-brainwashing session. She shook her head. "It doesn't matter. I'm just sorry."

"You can't even tell me?" Hurt creased his features again, his hands dropped from her shoulders. After a moment, anger worked its way back through. "Is this even a marriage, then?"

"I did wrong. I know this. I handled it poorly, I hurt you, I'm the world's worst wife. I've said I'm sorry, I don't know what else to do!"

"You can stop!"

"Stop what? Being me? I am who you married."

"Stop hiding shit from me." Danny dropped to sit on the corner of his bed. His elbow propped on his knees; his face buried in his hands. "Stop making me worry that every time I turn around, you'll be gone, and I'll never get to say goodbye, or tell you again that I love you."

"This was an extreme situation." She dropped to her knees before him. After a moment, she pulled his hands away from his features to meet his gaze. "Outside of this, when in the past year have I given you any reason to worry? You know this was different."

"I know." He sighed, his forehead dropping against hers. "Everything is just such shit right now. I don't know which way is up."

"That way," She offered, a tentative smile tugging at her lips as she pointed to the ceiling.

He stared at her hard, his expression unreadable for several long seconds. "Really?"

"Well…it is."

"You are such a smartass."

"I've been told I get that from my mother."

A slow, genuine smile finally crept across his features. He cupped her face in his hands gently. "That's what they say."

Elan's eyes fluttered closed the moment his lips touched hers. A tremor of hope that they might get through this damn mess after all warmed her normally cool heart.

"I love you," he whispered.

"I love you, too. Can I be forgiven?"

"You will be. Might take me a couple days to get all the way there."

"If it takes a month, I get it." Elan met his eyes. "You're the only one here that gets me."

"Some days I wonder if I do."

"Some days I don't get myself, either. So, I guess that makes sense."

54

Whatever reply he was going to make got interrupted by the chime of the door. Danny groaned, glaring at the door. "Not now."

"I apologize," Running Bear's voice echoed into the room through the comm. "I would not intrude, but Caiman's presence is needed."

Elan had never heard RB in any sort of panic, but if there was such a thing for him, he sounded damn close. Her hackles rose, unsure of what danger he'd need her for. "Is there an attack?"

"No. It is…the one you brought with you." RB couldn't know how his words affected her husband beside her.

Danny's grip on her hand tensed, a deep frown lining his features.

"He is in an uncontrollable state. Lucas is unable to reach him." RB hesitated at this unusual statement, because in normal situations Lucas could calm a wild bear. Chaz, however, was anything but normal.

"That's the training." She glanced hesitantly at Danny. "I'm the only one here that can get through to him."

"Of course you are." He scoffed. "Why would anyone think differently?"

"Come with me," she offered. "You'll see what I mean."

"No thanks."

"Caiman?" RB's voice raised minutely in pitch.

"I'll be right there." She rose. "I wish you'd come. I have to help him before he hurts someone or runs out of here and back to Steele."

"Go. I might be there. I don't know."

"I love you."

"Yeah. Love ya too."

Abby rubbed her temples. Her steps led her more on instinct than sight as the migraine caused by the emotional onslaught left her almost stunned by its intensity. She was supposed to be napping, it would probably help if she did, but she was so tired of sleeping.

All she'd done since Annie's passing was sleep. To be honest, sleep was the only thing to stem the tide of emotions. Though she usually could block the intensity to a low hum, lately it was as though her shields didn't exist.

The emotions of everyone around her bombarded her to the point she couldn't control them. The situation had devolved to the point where she didn't know if they were her own emotions, or if she was feeding off the feelings of everyone else around her. The day Annie had passed had been a mixture of both, she was sure. Warren and the boys felt the loss as deeply as she did.

Then there was the matter of James. Despite Warren's insistence that Annie meant nothing to James but a conquest, Abby knew different. Even if James swore up and down that the only emotion he possessed was anger, Abby had seen different. Not just with his mother, but now with her daughter. James felt love for Annie, even if he was unable to truly recognize the emotion.

At an intersection of tunnels, she paused. Her own guilt won over everyone else's feelings beating against her. She should be happy, overjoyed even, that her best friend Talisa had returned along with Roark. For so long they'd waited and hoped, but she couldn't find it in her. Instead of heading toward where she could sense her friends, she made her way topside.

Fresh air burned in her lungs, a stark contrast to the recycled air they had become accustomed to inside the compound. She inhaled deep to let her lungs fill in hopes that a different kind of pain could negate what she'd been living with.

The freshly turned soil of Annie's small grave came into sight within a few minutes. Anguish ripped her up inside, stopping any air from entering or exiting at all. It no longer mattered if the air was fresh or recycled, her lungs wanted some sort of oxygen.

A gasping inhale so loud it startled a sparrow out of a nearby tree filled her lungs back up. She exhaled shakily, kneeling beside the patch of ground. "There's nothing I can say to make this right. Nothing I can do to change anything. In my head as a doctor, a scientist, I know there was nothing we could do. As your mother, I should have moved heaven and earth to find a way to keep you here. You'll never know how sorry I am that I couldn't make you better, baby."

Her breath hiccupped to catch up with the run-on phrases. "We are working on a headstone for you. I hate that we don't have it up yet. Chance promised he will make sure some pretty flowers grow here in the spring. Oh, how horrible am I that I don't know your favorite flower? Or color?"

The cool dirt she scooped into her hands matched the cold she felt seeped throughout her soul these days. "You didn't deserve this. You deserved so much better."

"You all did." Talisa's voice startled her; she'd not heard her walk up.

Abby exhaled slowly, a rush of confusing emotions rattling her further. "How did you find me?"

"Still getting a handle on this telepathy stuff." Talisa knelt beside her. "You were mentally screaming. Not that I blame you, no one would. And, we really haven't had a chance to talk."

"Sorry."

"Please. I am the last person you need to apologize to."

"But I do. I do need to apologize. You're my best friend. I should be overjoyed that you guys are home. I just…"

"After what you've been through, I don't blame you one bit. I can't even imagine what hell I'd be going through if the same happened to me. I'd probably be the worst person on earth. I can't even begin to understand your pain, but that doesn't mean I'm upset about it. You've earned it." Talisa wrapped an arm around Abby to pull her close.

Abby sank into the support willingly. Whatever comfort her friend could offer, she'd gladly accept. "Warren is so angry. I've tried to get through to him, but he's not even listening to me. He doesn't understand. I don't know if it's because it's dealing with a daughter and not a son, or he's just blinded by finding her and losing her so quickly."

"Or both. Roark will be the first to tell you that daughters are different than sons."

"I know but this goes way beyond that. He's furious with James. Thinks he robbed us of Annie's last moments on purpose. I don't believe that. I know James cared for Annie, even if he didn't understand how or why. I know he did. I've never seen him so calm and focused like he was around her."

"Lucas and Char said they were mates. I don't always understand the Spirits reason behind why they do things the way they do but I know there was a connection between them." She leaned her head against Abby's.

"He was getting so bad I asked Lucas for herbs to put in his tea to," Abby cleared her throat, "help him sleep."

58

"Needed a break?" Talisa chuckled.

"My blocks have been off since Annie got here. It was one blow after another. At this point my nerves are shot. I thought if I came out and visited Annie it would give me a reprieve." Abby stared at the slight mound of dirt as if it held all the answers. "Tal, what am I going to do? I feel like I'm losing my husband."

"First of all, we're home, and you don't have to do everything by yourself. We are here to help. If Roark and Chance need to kick Warren in the ass then they will. If you need to bawl your eyes out then you do that. If you want to help Roark and I in the lab with the stasis pods we brought home with us you can do that too."

"In all of this I just wish there was a way to get my daughter back. To really get to know her. For her and James to figure out the connection between them and to have my family whole again. I would do anything to make that happen. Having you guys home helps but I still feel like there is this gaping hole in my heart that will always be there without her."

"Abby…" Waves of guilt pulsed off of Talisa.

"Stop, why are you feeling guilty? It's not your fault. You were kind of imprisoned by the maniac that did this to us." She blew out a breath, "Besides I know you would have helped save her if you could have."

"I wish I could have been here though."

"You're here now. That's what is important." Abby glanced in the direction of the compound. "I should get back. Warren is starting to wake up and he's not happy."

"You have to take care of you too Abby."

"I will. Right now I need to take care of Warren and the boys. I can't lose any of them. It would kill me."

"We won't let that happen."

Chance stood outside the unit he'd given to Inessa earlier that day. Nerves rattled him in a way unfamiliar to him. He ran a hand through his hair to vent some frustration.

Many jobs fell on his shoulders as Chief of the tribe, and in turn a leader of the rebellion. In a typical day one thing that was never his job was hunting down something for a new arrival to the compound.

There was something about this woman, though. She drew him in, put him at ease when he was so used to being on his guard. He hadn't been at ease since before the war. That alone threw him off, let alone the fact that she was beautiful.

The door to her unit loomed in front of him like some great mythical beast he couldn't slay. He raised his hand to knock not once, not twice, but three times. Each time it ended up right back by his side again. One glance at the bag he held in his other hand caused a smile to tug his lips. Music. One of the two things he had mentioned earlier that had made her smile.

"Spirits give me strength." He raised his hand one last time, and this time succeeded in knocking. The door opened so quick after the knock he had to push his nerves aside again at the sight of her. "I hope I'm not disturbing you."

Inessa's bright smile burned away any worries he'd had. "Is everything all right?"

"Fine. It's fine." Chance held up the bag. "Music. I was able to get a few CD's together. I thought you might want to go through them to see if anything caught your eye. I wasn't sure what sort of music you liked, so I grabbed a little of everything."

Humor sparked with a light in her eyes. "That's too kind. You didn't have to bring it by. I know how busy you must be."

He mentally kicked himself for babbling. She was a woman, like any other they brought in to add to the tribe, he didn't need to be an idiot about it. "There's a lot going on right now, but I'm not needed anywhere right this second. Granted now that I've said that it could backfire on me."

"Would you like to come in? That is, if you don't mind telling me a little more about this place. It's amazing, but there is so much to it." Inessa's hand touched his arm, her warm smile continuing to light through him like a ray of sunshine.

Tension drained from his shoulders. "Sure. I'd be more than happy to. If you'd like, we could go for a walk so I can show you around a bit more."

"Oh, that sounds delightful. Let me grab my shoes." Inessa disappeared for a minute. When she returned, her smile remained just as bright as it had been when she'd walked away. "Lead the way."

Chance had no idea what made him do it, but he held out his arm to her. To his pleasure, she linked her arm through his without hesitation. He led her down the hall toward the main common area of the compound. "Down here is the door to another section of units for people to live in. There's a few that people have moved into, but this section is far from filled."

"How many people live down here in these tunnels?"

"We're around a hundred and fifty. Every day more Exceptionals are located, though. We try to get to them as quick as we can, but our resources are limited." He'd forgotten what it was like to walk these halls at a leisure pace. The woman on his arm made him want to take his time. Usually a walk down this hall was rushed and all business with James filling him in on whatever crisis needed attention. There never seemed to be a shortage of crises to be had.

"Where did you just go?" Her curious tone invaded his thoughts without malice.

"Hmm? Oh, sorry. I was just thinking how nice it was to walk like this and not be running to fix something." He gestured to the door on the left, his smile returning without hesitation. "Over there is the area where we will be adding the cafeteria, hopefully in the next month or so."

"There are no machines down here. How are the rooms being built?"

"Everyone that stays here pitches in somehow. We have a few telekinetics to help move the dirt out when we are building a new section and move in the metal as we build. We tend to dig using plants or water." At the next door he pulled a clipboard off a hook. He ran a finger along the top page to check the schedule. "Now this is something special. We typically have to sign up for time in here."

"Sign up for time?" Inessa peeked around him as he opened the door.

"Lucas found a hot spring down here when we were building. If we didn't sign up for time in here it could become very crowded." Chance held the door open for her so she could step inside. He cleared his throat pushing away the image of the two of them in the spring together the moment it popped into his mind. "It tends to stay humid in here."

Inessa wandered the room. A sexy grin crossed her features. "Very relaxing, I imagine. Do you use it often?"

"It stays pretty booked." He rocked back and forth on his feet, his hands stuffed into his pockets. What was it about this woman that broke through his usual control?

"That wasn't what I asked." A hint of mischief glistened in her eyes.

"I haven't in quite some time. I stay pretty busy." The tension crept back up his spine.

"You don't take any time for yourself?"

"I have a lot to do."

"Like what?" She stood in front of him. One hand rested on his chest. Her gaze locked with his, a mix of understanding and challenge lit her eyes in the dim light.

"Well." Chance cleared his throat again. "Have to make sure things stay running smoothly. I am the Chief of the tribe. Construction and expansion need to stay on schedule if we're to keep up with new recruits." His hand came to rest on top of hers.

"You can't do it all alone. Don't you have help?" Her other hand joined the first.

"Of course, I do." What was this woman doing to him? No one had affected him like this in years, not even Karry when they dated before the war. They'd gotten pretty serious at one time, but there was nothing like this untamable fire with her. The only other woman that had ever made him feel like this was Talisa.

"You're flushed. Are you alright?" He eyebrow quirked at the question.

"Fine. It's just humid in here." He gave her hands a gentle squeeze. "We should continue the tour. Someone might have signed up for time in here."

"Did you see anyone on the list when you looked at it?" Inessa took a step closer to him.

"What list?" Chance couldn't take his eyes off her. All sorts of alarm bells went off in the back of his head. This was insane. Crazy. And yet here he was contemplating just how close he could get to her.

"The one on the door where people sign up."

"No didn't see anyone signed up."

"Then we don't have to run out of here." The fingertips of one hand crept up his chest.

"I can't show you the compound from here though." He searched her eyes, one hand coming up to tuck a golden lock of hair behind her ear.

"Maybe all I want to see at the moment is in this room. You need to relax Chief and I have just the thing for that." The grin on her face made his breath catch.

"Inessa…" A groan escaped when she backed up and kicked her shoes off. "I don't know if this is such a good idea."

"This is a perfect idea. No strings. Just two consenting adults that need a break." Her top came up over her head and was tossed on the nearby bench.

In the back of his mind a small voice told him just how bad of an idea this was. They had just met. She had only been there a few hours. They didn't know each other well at all. On the other hand, it had been a long time since he had done anything for himself and an even longer time since he had been this close to a woman. "No strings? I'm not sure I know how to do that."

"Sure you do." She tossed her pants on the bench with her top.

Now he felt like one of those old cartoons with two versions of himself dressed as an angel and a devil trying to talk him into the different options. He pulled his shirt over his head and tossed it aside, "This is insane, you know that right?"

"Sometimes we all need a little insanity." She grinned even brighter than before. "I don't know what you're doing to keep in shape down here but keep it up."

Chance chuckled his arm snaking around her waist and pulling her close, "I stay busy."

"Well I think I know something we can add to your workout routine."

"You do? Why don't you show me?" Vines shot out of the walls and blocked to door so that no one could walk in on them.

"My pleasure."

Warren stood outside Annie's room, unable to enter, but not willing to walk away quite yet. He'd wasted so much time being suspect of her. Unlike his wife, who'd managed to get to know the young woman, he'd missed out on so much.

After a long, deep, bracing breath, he touched the keypad to enter the room. If nothing else, he knew one way he could get to know her well. She had his ability to manipulate computers, which meant that hers had everything.

That computer would be her as much as if she stood there. If he could spend some time with it, he could know what Annie hadn't had time to know because of Steele's manipulations as well as his own mistakes.

The room rang with quiet emptiness in a way that made his ears hurt almost as much as his heart. The last few hours of her life played like a never-ending film reel through his mind.

He scanned the empty quarters once quick with his eyes, confused to not see any sign of the computer anywhere. Another quick scan with his gift revealed the same emptiness. Even if the battery had technically failed, he should be able to detect the device in there somewhere.

Though he knew his senses hadn't failed him, he threw back the covers on the bed, and yanked open drawers in hopes of finding the computer.

"What the fuck?"

He straightened slow as instinct told him what had happened. To confirm his suspicions, he tapped into the hall security camera around the time of Annie's death. The image of James leaving Annie's room with her computer sent another blast of white-hot anger through his gut.

"James."

Warren slammed the drawer he'd been holding shut. He stalked out of the room toward James' quarters. The man had no right to Annie's computer. What good would it do the brute anyhow?

Without precursor, he pounded on James' door. The temptation to force the door open sat close to the surface, his nerve endings burning with the desire to do just that. "James. Give me that computer! It's not yours to have."

For a moment he swore he heard two voices shout in surprise, but then there was only silence.

Warren pressed on the call button beside the doors, his fingers twitching with the barely restrained energy it would take to open the door without permission. "James. I know you are fucking in there. Give it back to me, now. It isn't yours!"

The door slid open. James, who by all accounts should have been in the hospital ward stood calm, if angry as a devil. His brows met in a fierce scowl. "Fuck off, Warren."

"She was *my* daughter!"

"She was my *mate*!"

"Lying son of a bitch. That computer is mine, now give it."

James held him back with one arm, a threatening growl cut through Warren's impatience, barely. "Do not enter this room. I won't be blamed for what happens if you do."

Warren bristled under the threat. The second he spotted Annie's computer on James' nightstand, all reason fled. He leapt into the room, only to rebound into the hall faster than he could blink. The opposite wall met his body with an unforgiving clang of metal.

The echo rang through Warren's mind. He rose, lips curling back. The familiar code of Annie's computer seemed to almost call to him, a call he wouldn't refuse. He launched forward again. "Give it back to me, you insolent, half-wit Neanderthal!"

James blocked Warren's oncoming blow as if it were nothing more than a fly, which made Warren's blood boil more. He came at the brute of a man time and again, only to be rebuffed.

"*Warren.*" Hands grabbed him, dragging him from his intended target. He fought against the hold until a familiar set of brown eyes, and the bronze-skinned woman they were attached to blocked James from his view. Talisa shoved him back toward the wall, a low growl rippling past her lips. "Warren. Stop this."

"He stole her computer." Warren fought to get free, but Tal was stronger than she looked, always had been.

"Warren," the calm voice of Roark came from behind Tal. "Calm down."

"I won't. He stole the only thing of hers we have!" Warren tried to fight off Tal again.

"Daddy, stop." Quiet as quiet could be, Warren could have sworn he heard Annie's voice. A spark of life from her computer faded right after.

Warren stilled, his eyes wide. Now he was hallucinating.

"Warren." Now that he'd stilled, Tal's body relaxed a smidge. Her brows crinkled in concern. "Warren, this isn't like you."

"He lies." Warren glared at Talisa, "And you're helping him. You're keeping me from the last bit of her because you believe his lies about being her mate."

"It wasn't a lie." Tal released her hold on his arms to grasp his face. "I don't lie. You know that. You know me."

"Maybe I don't." Warren brushed her off. "You have been with Steele for over a year, after all. Who knows what he did to you?"

Tal took a step back. "You're not thinking rationally. You're grieving."

"Great job circling your wagons around your ass of a son. Maybe you should have stayed gone." He shoved Tal away hard as he could and stormed off.

"Warren!"

Inessa curled closer to Chance, careful not to wake him. After nearly six months on her own, she was not about to deny herself the warmth and company of a man. From what she'd been able to tell based solely on his aura and what little she'd learned about Chance; he'd been without company even longer than her.

Of course, if the deepness of the sleep after sex were a yardstick to measure with, he'd been celibate a long, long time. She bit her lip against her own giggle at her musings.

If only she could sleep so well herself. Her nerves had been on alert for so long.

As if the Goddess heard her whining and thought she wasn't complacent enough, she went and made things worse.

The lights shut down. For that matter, all power shut down. The quiet hum of the ever-present machines stilled into a silence deeper than any she'd heard in ages.

Fear gripped tight to her heart. Panic sliced through the pleasant calm of post-coital endorphins. It took every bit of effort to hold back the scream building deep inside. She'd been afraid of the dark since the battle in New York City when she'd been trapped in utter darkness under a half-burning building.

Her throat tightened, but she remained still as possible, silently praying that Chance's awareness to their situation would wake him quickly.

As expected, he began to stir after a few minutes of their practical entombment. Once he shifted in his sleep, she tried to pull away.

"Nuh-uh," the mutter was aided by the arm he used to hold her still.

Despite her raw nerves, she giggled. "Nuh-uh?"

"It's an army fly-over," Chance whispered. "Ground troops are checking the neighborhood homes for Exceptionals."

"Really?"

"Yes. Happens often. Lucas just informed me of our status."

"Well, aren't telepaths damn handy?"

"Most especially in war."

With that, the tension that had eased creeped its way back into her muscles. Every moment of pleasure she'd allowed earlier dissipated into the crushing darkness. "Right. War."

He had no way to see her in the pitch black, but she could see him if she lowered her guard enough to take a peek. His aura, initially bright with nearly every color to show his strength, kindness and leadership, began to seal off in greys and black.

Black usually meant imminent death, she knew all too well, but in this case she sensed he was putting up his defenses again.

Damn it. For so long she'd been on her own, and she'd gone and lost control of herself around the first person she got close to. Her own fears could be saved for when she was in her room. Alone. This guy didn't need one more person's fear to hold on to and try to relieve. "Sorry. It's the dark. It freaks me out a little."

"How dark is it for you?"

"It depends on how open I am to the auras. I was focused on you alone in every way." The reminder of the past hour helped a smile tug her lips. Some of the tension melted away. The flash of yellow in his aura hinted at his own amusement. "So, it's damn dark, and if I open too fast I could get overwhelmed.

Somehow his hand found hers. The gentle touch of his thumb brushing along the back of her hand sent soothing waves through her. "And the dark freaks you out?"

"It's a catch-22 from hell." She had no idea why she was telling him any of this. Was it because she'd been so alone, she became a blabbermouth at the first sign of a sympathetic ear? No. She hadn't spilled her personal thoughts and fears to Neil.

"How so?" His voice soothed her with understanding. The sensation wrapped around her with warmth. It held quiet welcome to either answer or change the subject.

"The dark reminds me of New York. The suddenness, the complete end of it. So, it makes sense to be open to the auras during the night hours." Before she could get a grasp on her usual strong control, a shudder ripped through her. Once again, the screams filled her ears, the smoke and dust that had clogged her nose and lungs, phantom pains radiated through her now healed leg.

There wasn't a whisper to interrupt her. Somehow, he even managed to keep his curiosity in check. Sure, it was there, but it lay comfortably settled under layers of blue, pink, and indigo that showed his concern and compassion.

"That night, to avoid the dark, I opened up to the auras only to see them fade into the blackness as death claimed them. They all became part of the night of horror." Her voice caught. She cleared her throat against the rising lump. "Yeah. So. I feel like a toddler, but me and the dark? Not so much friends these days."

"I think that's pretty understandable."

"Understandable or not, I have no idea why I rambled it all off like that. The last thing you need is my problems." Inessa closed her eyes to avoid the sight of whatever he might be feeling. The last thing she wanted was pity. There were so many others much worse off than she was. "My problems are minor in the scheme of things—and you already carry the weight of this war heavy on your shoulders."

"You used that excuse before." There it was again. Seeping in over the relaxed state he'd been in. The weight of his obligations, the tension of responsibility. Even though there was a heaping load of pride in what he did, it weighed on him. The darkness of loss, the pain snaking in and tugging at him like it had tentacles. It was so quick and stubborn that her stomach flipped at the switch.

"What?" His hand still held hers, but the soothing gestures faded. "Is something wrong?"

"Hm? No. Why do you ask?"

"You groaned."

"Oh. Crap. Sorry. I didn't realize that was out loud." She bit her lips, pondering her options. On one hand, he was already closing back off. She knew his mind had likely settled on going to check on everyone. On the other, he couldn't keep living like this. Of all people, she could see it clearly how much the strain was wearing him down.

"Well, it was. What is it?"

"It's you." Once again his tension rose, so she moved fast. In one elegant stretch of a move, she straddled his lap. The moment she did, she almost regretted it. Skin to skin with him again her focus wavered. The way his whole essence relaxed made it all worth it. "Would you like to know what I see when I look at you?"

A lingering moment of hesitation hung between them. Some people liked a reading, others feared what was in it. Although fear probably wasn't the cause, Chance wasn't eager to hear what she saw. Like most people post-war, he probably worried about it being different than he saw himself. He took in a shaky breath. "I don't know."

"You are a rather remarkable human being. When you are just being you, totally relaxed and calm, your aura is the most soothing aura I've ever seen. The only person that comes close is Lucas. Both of you are so very centered, you're connected to the earth, to those around you, and you have a warmth that goes beyond the norm."

"While we trained for different goals in life – I trained to become Chief, his focus was always on being the medicine man – our training was very similar."

"But the war has affected you in a way it hasn't affected him." The minute the words left her mouth his whole being shifted. Defensiveness laced into the tensions from earlier. It wouldn't do, "No, stop. Don't let the tension back in, Chance. Just listen."

"I am the Chief. All those people were my responsibility."

"You didn't kill them. My guess is that every single one of them fought valiantly, and full of pride. They would not have wanted to be hidden away from the fight."

"Women. Children. None of them should have been harmed," Chance's head drooped forward to rest on her chest.

She ran her fingers through his hair, "No they shouldn't have. That doesn't seem to matter to the singular focus of military law. I'm sure you did all that you could to save them. To save whoever it was that you loved so much too."

Not a muscle twitched for a long time. The swirl of emotions went by so fast she didn't bother to interpret them. Of all the things she'd said that one had thrown him. "What do you mean?"

"Of all the losses suffered, of all the grief you carry – and believe me, it's a lot." For the first time in a long time she wanted to help someone. Not just to make her life easier by making his aura calmer, but just to help him. "There is one that you cling to. It is the deepest, darkest grief out of them all. It's what all your darkness is tied to. Like it was your breaking point."

"Talisa." One word brought it right up to the surface. Tangled and gnarled shades of deep purples and grays.

"That's it. You love her, that much is clear."

"I did. She's gone now. Killed in the same battle that changed your life."

More than the flicker of doubt at his own statement, there was something else. A thread of connection tied to the core of the grief. The person he grieved for. "No. She's not. In fact, she's pretty damn close, maybe even in this complex."

"Her son watched her, and her husband get blown up. They're dead."

"In case you didn't know, you can't lie to me. I'll see it every time." Inessa chuckled at the flash of guilt that passed over him. "I get it. You need to test everyone. Apparently even the woman who is eager to screw your brains out again."

Embarrassment, eagerness, pure driven lust. They colored him rather brightly for a moment before fading into amusement, "You're good at changing the subject."

"Yes, but I'm also horny as hell. Did I mention that until the war I was a big ol' slut? I like sex, dude."

"Dude?" Now he was laughing. A good strong belly laugh, "Really?"

"Sorry," her chuckle couldn't be stopped even if it pegged her statement as a lie. "Apparently I've also forgotten how to carry on a conversation without randomly turning it on its head."

"Based on what little I know of you I have to question if you have ever known how to do that."

"You got me. I really haven't. Drove my directors and choreographers nuts with my random bursts of inanity. Probably why my lead roles were few and far between."

"I have to ask." The seriousness was back but was tempered with his humor. "How did you know? We did think she was dead for almost a year. She just got back here a few days ago."

"I didn't know that. I know that she isn't dead. Chance, with my particular mutation I can see your connections to others. To your people, to the land, all of it. When you focused on this Talisa, I could see that your thread to her was not dead. She is alive."

"Oh." For a moment the emotions swirled again while he pondered that so she let him be. Out of nowhere the pure white blast of shock blinded everything else out, "Oh crap!"

"What?"

"Charlotte!"

Inessa quirked a brow, "I'm sorry. What?"

"My daughter. She is – unique. She was kidnapped when she was an infant, experimented on and has four mutations. One is just like yours. She always said Tal and Roark weren't dead, that her husband wasn't. That the threads connecting them weren't gone. We all doubted her. I've already apologized, but we all owe her a huge apology."

"You didn't understand. It's difficult to comprehend when you don't live it." She ran her hands along his shoulders, "I distracted myself from my main point way back when."

Even though Chance was still distracted, he made the effort to focus on her. "What do you mean?"

"I was telling you what I see when I look at you. The main point I was trying to make was that the pain and grief weigh on that calm center. When you are like you are right now you are much more capable of using your brain. Focusing. Being a strong leader."

"And just how am I right now?"

"Relaxed."

"Just relaxed?" The distraction he'd been focused on faded off. Once again his fingers trailed along her skin, "Is that all?"

"Oh it's definitely not all."

"Well you're proving quite a distraction, Miss Jelen. Perhaps I can continue to distract you from the dark. Help you like you've been trying to help me?"

A definite temptation, still she couldn't resist teasing him. "Are you sure you don't have something better to do? There are no crises to deal with. Fires to put out?"

"Benefits of a telepath. I'll know if I'm needed elsewhere."

"Very true. Well then. Let's get back to our exercise program."

"Gladly."

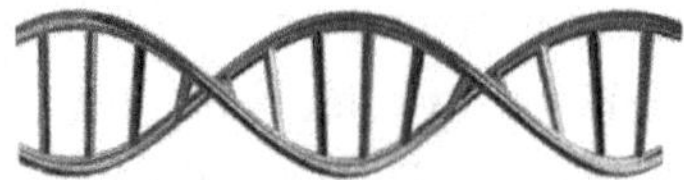

Roark pinched the bridge of his nose as Warren's retreating form stormed down the hallway. He knew their friend was angry and grieving but that didn't make the words hurt any less. "Li, he didn't mean it."

"Yes, he did. In the moment he did." A frown creased the corners of Talisa's mouth.

"Mom, I'm not giving her up." A predatory growl rolled off James.

"Relax son. We're not telling you to give Annie or her computer up. Warren is grieving. He's clinging to the only thing Annie left behind."

"I know we've been gone for a while but something isn't right here." Talisa's gaze shifted down the hallway in the direction Warren had gone.

"You mean other than the fact that I'd like to punch one of our best friends in the throat right now for talking to you like that?" Roark blew out a breath. "We've got to tell them Li. You know he either went to his office to figure out a way to get the computer or he went to tell Abby."

"It's going to take a lot to convince him." Annie's voice drifted into the hallway. "He didn't even acknowledge that I said anything."

"He didn't believe it was real." Talisa rubbed the back of her neck, "We do have to tell them and soon. Warren will be on the warpath until he gets that computer back."

"Question is what are we going to tell them?" Roark attempted to push aside the dread at the thought of that conversation. "By the way, your daughter is only mostly dead."

"And I thought I was the one in the family with no tact." James smirked at his father.

"Don't hurt yourself there son. You almost smiled." Roark blew out a breath in an effort to release some of the tension building behind his eyes. "What do you think, Li?"

Talisa looked down the hallway in the direction that Warren had stormed off. She tilted her head a touch but remained silent. With one hand raised she paused any repeat of the question from Roark. "I think we need to figure things out quickly. Warren just made it back to Abby and he's raging."

"What's there to tell? The computer is staying with me and you and Dad are working on a way to bring her back. End of discussion. I'll kill him before I let him take her from me." James' upper lip twitch as a snarl escaped.

"James, come back in the room where I can see you." Annie's voice drifted out to join them again.

Roark blinked in surprise as he witnessed the tension roll down his son's back. That was an unusual thing to witness. The last thing Roark would have ever said about his son was that he could calm down so quickly, even with Talisa's touch. Roark shook his head. "Annie is right. We should move this into the room."

"Pischk, listen to me. I won't leave you. Once I'm restored to a body, we will have our chance. Please try to not kill my dad in the meantime, though. We may need his help with the equipment to bring me back." Annie's soft smile shone out of the screen.

The growl returned to James' voice. "But Anne…"

78

Annie's smile shifted into a smirk. "We talked about this. Remember?"

"I know." James' sigh echoed his repentant look.

Once again the tension seeped from James. Roark knew the connection that occurred with mates. He'd felt it every day with Talisa, but to see it happen in James when his mate was trapped in a computer was uncanny. "We will figure it out. One thing at a time. First things first, we need to talk to Abby and Warren to explain what's happened. Depending on how Abby reacts to Warren's current tirade will determine how fast that conversation needs to happen."

"If I were a betting woman," Talisa started.

Roark couldn't resist a tease. "*If?* Pretty sure our first date was to a casino."

"Zip it, bub." Talisa wrinkled her nose in an attempt to hide her amusement. "Anyway, I'd say sooner rather than later. I'm still getting a handle on this telepathy stuff, but the amount of anger and rage coming off Warren isn't helping my focus. It's rather blinding."

"If Mom can calm him down that will help some, but I've never heard him that angry before. Of course, that could have been by design since Steele planted the memories." Annie's head whipped to the side. Panic etched onto her digital features.

"Anne?" James sat directly in front of the laptop. "What's wrong?"

"My Dad. Warren…he's trying to access the laptop remotely." Fear laced Annie's voice.

"James is the laptop connected to the network?" Roark moved to the side of the laptop to check the cables.

"No, the only thing that's plugged in is the power. She lost some during the flyover. We were afraid of Warren's other programs causing an issue if we connected to the network."

James looked up at his parents. The expression on his face matched the fear in Annie's voice. "How do we stop him?"

"I can hold him off for a bit, but I don't know how long. If he pulls the wrong piece of code it may kill any chance of bringing me back."

A fierce snarl erupted from James that shook the table in front of him. "No!"

Roark grabbed James' shoulders to hold him still. "James breathe. We're not going to let that happen."

"Sooner than later it is. Let's rally the troops and have this conversation." Talisa sighed.

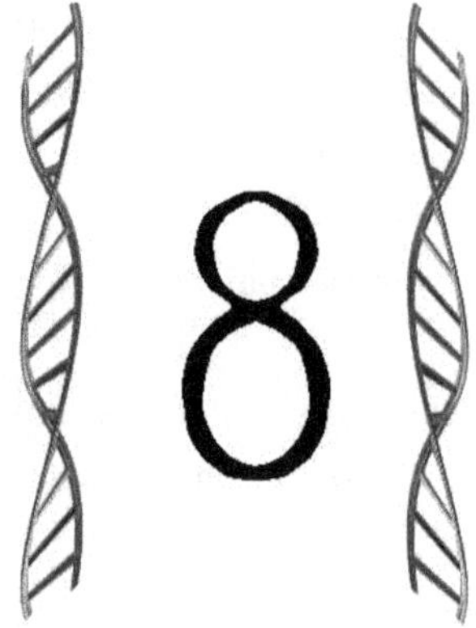

Abby stared at her reflection, feeling as though it were a stranger staring back. Water droplets from the shower she'd taken still clung to her hair and skin. In theory, a hot shower should have done her some good. She should be more relaxed, refreshed. The tenuous hold she had on her shields did little to aid in that endeavor. At the moment she would have sworn she had no shields at all, like the first day her gift had taken hold.

Every little emotion battered her in an endless siege. From every corner of the compound it never stopped, most especially from those she was closest to. Ethan's guilt, Charlotte's joy, Chance's sudden contentment, and then there was anger.

So much anger.

Everywhere.

In the instant she focused on the one emotion, every single iota of anger in the complex washed over her. Wave after wave eroded the flimsy grip she had on her ability to function.

Warren. She needed Warren. If she focused on him she would be able to pull herself together. Without much care as to how she actually looked she ran a towel through her hair and along her skin. She pulled on a buttery soft pair of yoga pants and a sweatshirt. They had been a gift from Warren on her birthday. He found them when they were scavenging for supplies.

Her fingers ran through her hair on automation to pull her curls back in a messy bun. Now that she was dressed she could focus on Warren and get herself under control. Or so she thought. Laser focus on Warren rewarded her with a tsunami of rage. The meager contents of her stomach revolted into the nearby trashcan. With a shaky hand she gripped the nearby table to assist getting to her feet again.

"Warren…" With the precarious semblance of control she had on her gifts she focused as much calm and serenity as she could pull together and sent it back in his direction. Another torrent of rage and hate slammed back at her. The calm she had sent towards him dissipated in tatters around her. Nothing short of someone holding her up would have kept her on her feet. The sudden fall caused her to cry out in pain as the floor came up faster than she expected.

"He stole her computer. That half-wit stole her damn computer." Warren stormed into their unit oblivious to Abby lying on the floor. "Who the hell does he think he is? She was our daughter, it belongs to us. And Tal and Roark helping him. They are working for Steele. All of them. He turned them."

Abby couldn't respond, the pain from the emotional onslaught and her fall stole her breath and clear thought.

"They think they can keep me from it but I can access it from here. They don't understand what I can do."

"Warren…" His name escaped her parted lips in a soft croak. "Please…"

"Then the nerve of her to try and make me think Annie was asking me to stop. Telepathy tricks. How do we know Steele didn't give her this telepathy to infiltrate us? I spent so much time searching for signs that Annie was sent here to hurt us that I didn't get to know her, and it was all them. It's something Steele would do." Warren grabbed a coffee off the nearby table ready to hurl it across the room.

"STOP!" Abby shrieked at the top of her lungs. Every particle within a ten-foot radius froze in place. Ragged breaths shuddered through her body. "Just stop…"

Warren's eyes widened but he made no other move, frozen mid-throw.

Abby reined in her unplanned use of her other gift causing Warren to double step and then shuffle to avoid hitting her. The coffee mug slipped from his fingertips and by some miracle didn't shatter when it landed on the chair next to him. "Please stop." Sobs wracked her tiny frame unable to hold it in anymore.

"Gail. What happened?" Warren rushed to her side and pulled her tight against him.

"No no no no no no…" With as much strength as she could muster Abby shoved against her husband's chest to extract herself from his grip.

"What's wrong?" The look of shock and rejection on his face broke her heart.

"T-the anger. T-too much anger. I can't handle it. Too many emotions." Tears cascaded down her cheeks at a steady pace. Her hands fisted in her hair tugging at it. "Please stop…"

"What do you mean? They stole Annie's laptop and won't let me have it." Warren growled.

Abby pressed her lips together in order to keep them from trembling to no avail. "Annie wouldn't want us fighting with our family like this."

"That is not my family." Warren snapped back.

"Tal was your family long before we met. We can talk with them like civilized human beings about Annie's laptop. But I cannot take the amount of anger and rage coming off of you." Another wave slapped her back causing her to dry heave.

"Gail...I..." Remorse danced across his face as he hesitated to touch her.

"I'm serious Warren. It's making me physically ill."

"I'll try baby...but they are going to give us that laptop one way or another."

Caiman paused outside Chaz's door. Despite the lack of interior decorating to the room, which had been at her orders, an awful lot of noise echoed out. The guards outside the room stared at the door like it might come flying off any second. To Caiman's keen eye, she noted they were trembling, despite their own Exceptional gifts.

She rolled her eyes. With a wave of her hand, she dismissed them. "Get the fuck out of here. You're useless."

"He should be in a cell, ma'am," one of them protested.

Caiman grabbed him by the collar, growling low. "His entire life has been in a fucking cell smaller than any we have here. Shut the fuck up and get out of my face. Tell James I said to never put such idiots in charge of *my* people again."

If he'd been trembling before, the guard now shook in fear.

Caiman released him without ever needing to thicken her skin or reveal a poisoned claw. The pair took off without another word from her. She scanned the hallway in hopes of finding Danny nearby, but he wasn't there.

She sighed, turning her attention to the door. The noise inside had ceased, likely because Chaz had heard her voice. She set a hand on the door but didn't open it yet. It would be better to give Chaz a moment to find her scent.

Approaching footsteps drew her attention from the door. Caiman smiled when she realized it was, in fact, Danny.

Danny had his uninjured hand shoved in his pocket; his features didn't raise in a smile to match hers. Her leaving seemed to have left a permanent scowl on his face, not that she blamed him. The situation he was about to walk into wouldn't help, but it couldn't be helped.

She took a deep breath. "He's been kept caged his whole life. Sold off for sexual favors to wealthy women, then returned for battle, prison, and then sold again. He doesn't understand freedom, even more so than I didn't understand it when I left Steele's command."

Danny glared toward the door. "You and he have…"

"Fucked?" Caiman eyed the door, then nodded. "He wasn't the only one sold off, if you remember. What better way to train us than with each other?"

Danny scoffed.

"You are my mate, Danny. He knows that. That's why he hasn't attacked the door, he recognizes your scent because it was on me when I went after Mom and Dad." She shook her head. There was no other way to explain, except to show him the man behind the door.

The door slid open the second she pushed the button. Chaz was nowhere to be seen, which was a feat in the nearly barren room. The mattress had disappeared from the bed. A flurry of cottony stuffing scattered across the room.

Elan sniffed deeply; his scent was everywhere. She closed her eyes to listen. A whisper of complaint from Danny had her set her hand on his chest. Chaz's quick breaths, quiet as they were, hit her ears over the small hum always present underground.

She nodded toward the closet and entered the room. Danny followed behind, silent again, his scowl unmoved.

"Cheetah. Aus!" In a disgusting display of Steele's opinion of Exceptionals, Chaz had been trained in German commands like many K-9 dogs pre-war.

The closet door slid open, and Chaz emerged on all fours.

"Hopp." Caiman gestured for him to rise. "You aren't a tool anymore. You aren't a prisoner, Chaz. Hier, now."

Chaz did as commanded. At her side, he eyed Danny carefully. His nostrils flared, then settled. "Your mate."

"His name is Danny." Caiman nodded. "He is my mate. Why have you destroyed your bed?"

"Too big." Chaz vibrated, but not with fear as his guards had, but tension and anxiety. "It's all too big."

"You had a forest at your disposal." Caiman frowned. "At times."

"Cage. Years." Chaz shook like ridding himself of the memory.

"Elan." Danny spoke finally. "He can't handle this."

Trust Danny's heart to see it. She knew it, but she didn't know what else to do. She turned to face Danny, but the moment she opened her mouth she noticed Chaz slinking away. "Bleib."

Danny's brow furrowed. "What?"

"I was telling him to stay." Elan frowned. "I was taught to be human; he was trained to be animal. Outside of being used for sexual fundraising efforts, where women wanted the animal, he has nothing. Being locked in here isn't any better than being locked in a cage at the compound."

"There's nothing else we can do." Danny leaned in close. "Maybe he's too far gone."

"Was I?" She met his gaze without faltering. "I was brainwashed, abused, and trained to destroy my own family. Was I too far gone?"

"He's an animal."

"He's an Exceptional." Elan lifted her chin in defiance. She got why Danny didn't like Chaz, but Chaz had been the closest thing she'd had to family besides Steele for years. "He is my family. I won't abandon him."

"Well, what do you suggest then?" Danny folded his arms across his chest. Every inch of him tense, ready for her to tell him something he wouldn't like. He wasn't far off, either.

"You and I have to help him."

Danny's eyes closed. "We have people for that."

"None of the people in this compound can help him, they don't understand." Elan touched his arm. "Plus they're all busy with those damn pods, and things they shouldn't be messing with, and finding Exceptionals and saving the world."

"Let me ask again." Danny's eyes opened to meet hers with laser sharpness. "What, exactly, are you suggesting?"

"He needs to live with us."

"You're fucking kidding me, right?"

The metal floor of her room was cool against Inessa's feet. The music from her earbuds flowed through her muscles, stretching and twisting them into familiar, graceful moves. For the first time in ages she was able to stretch, to move her muscles in the familiar moves of dance.

For now, she was in her small room since Chance slept nearby. It was just as well, her body whined from years of disuse. Soon as she was able to, she'd seek out the gym Chance had mentioned to stretch properly.

Mid-arabesque a shift in the room halted her in her tracks.

From the bed a spiral of colors from panic, confusion, grief and fear rushed over what had been Chance's sleeping form. In a heartbeat, admiration, and a touch of lust, faded the less appealing colors. She allowed her smile to show as she resumed third position and shut off her music. "Is everything okay Chance?"

"I'm not sure."

"Well, we know I'm enough to distract you. Thank you very much." With proper movements brought from years of training, she bowed low to him. Then, forgoing proper form she leaped out of her bow toward the bed. "Now tell me what you were thinking before you saw me."

"I'm not sure. I saw another battle, this one internal. Major changes hitting everyone here." Chance volleyed through emotional reactions to match what she assumed were his racing thoughts. They all flew by so fast it took her a moment to catch up. "I'm sure it was just a dream."

"You don't believe that. If you did, you'd still be asleep."

He rubbed his hands over his face. "What do you know of my mutations? Does your gift tell you things like that?"

"I don't get that. Emotions, sure. Connections, yes. Being able to tell your Exceptional ability with a glance, not so much." She shrugged. "Not that I mind. It's already pretty overwhelming. A daily acid trip without the recreational drugs."

A low chuckle emerged through the bubble of grey and black dampening his aura. "Charlotte has never put it quite that way before, but I suppose that's true."

"Trust me. I'm no angel. Before the infection swept through the world, I'd tried a thing or two. This has nothing on any of those." Heat flooded Inessa's cheeks at the admission. "I didn't like the drugs, and my focus was dance so I didn't do a lot, but it's enough to make comparisons."

"Trust me, there's no judgment here. Some of our herbs are sketchy by pre-war standards." Chance squeezed her hand. "Well, I have my affinity to plants, but there is a secondary mutation. It's imprecise and unreliable. I've never been able to get a real hold on it, but I have some precognitive ability."

"It's no wonder you haven't gotten a hold on it." Inessa frowned. "You don't want it. I imagine the war made you push it away pretty hard."

Chance lowered his gaze to the floor. "It's harder than the messages of the Spirits."

"Well, lover…I'd really like to dissect that further, believe me. However, there is a huge ball of anger heading our way. Perhaps you'd like to get some pants on while I answer the door. Somehow I get the impression this guy would use some security override if I didn't answer."

"Ball of anger?" A corner of his lip turned up in a cute little grin. "If I had three guesses and the first two didn't count, I'd say that was James."

"Oh, goody gum drops! I get to meet the carbon-copy-yet-total-opposite of Lucas? Yay." She did a little hop step to the door that drew another laugh from him. She opened the door partially at the first knock. Not even the glare she received in response to her smile could falter her relaxed mood. At least not yet. "James, I presume?"

James' dark eyes narrowed at her. "You knew it was me?"

"Well, I've met your brother. You look physically identical to him. But you, young man, are a pit of vipers compared to his cool spring."

"Yeah? Well live my fucking life and tell me not to be. I need the Chief. *Now.*" James' hand cupped the partly open door, his hand on the panel to force it open all the way.

She set her hand on her own panel to lock the door in place best she could until he overrode anything. "He knows you're here. Just relax."

"I don't know the meaning of the word."

Inessa giggled. "I noticed."

"What do you need, James?" Chance's tone had resumed its business-like nature in a heartbeat. His hand gently removed hers from the panel to open it fully. Though his face was stoic, calm, and back to his responsibility, his hand lingered on her back to let her know he was still with her as well.

"There's a lot of shit going on. Is your little vacation over?" James fairly vibrated with fury, and Inessa would dare say panic based on his aura.

"James. I am still your Chief." The strength in Chance's voice was enough to still the tense man in front of them. "Tell me what has happened."

"Sorry, Chief." James tipped his head, respect sliding across the burgeoning anger enough to shield it. Still, it remained under the surface, roiling and churning against the shield, looking for an outlet. "First off..."

Inessa quirked an eyebrow when his eyes cut to her. As if she had any doubt, he didn't trust her, he was out to make it as blatant as possible. "So, I'm to understand you're the one they send out to welcome Exceptionals into the fold? No wonder your numbers are so small."

"Inessa." Even though Chance's tone held a chiding note, humor flittered across him like a warm blanket. "What is it, James? Inessa has my full trust."

Somehow James kept his features perfectly still. There was no way to hide the blinding wave of shock that blacked out even his intense levels of anger and anxiety, if only for a minute. Like a comfortable shoe, it slid back into place. "Fine. You know Annie's not dead, and that she's in the laptop. Mom has her now, but is puzzling over how to make a stable clone. She just told me she isn't sure she can like she did with me because Annie isn't animal, she doesn't have the healing."

Inessa's mind went blank, shock washing over her this time. From the levels of grief through the compound, this didn't seem possible. She hadn't realized Annie wasn't dead. It wasn't something she expected Chance to tell her, odds are this was top secret. The prospects, though. To survive, only to die again?

"I know," Chance whispered.

James' fingers twitched at his side. A wave of deep grey grief hit him so hard Inessa stumbled back a step.

"Inessa?" Chance's hand supported her. "What is it?"

"Nothing," Inessa shook her head, "Really." She wasn't even sure James knew the levels of his affection for the woman in the computer, but she wouldn't embarrass him by revealing how deep it went. Even if it was contributing to his anger. "Go on. Please. Don't mind me."

"So why are you here now?" Chance's level head and calm demeanor did little to still James' yo-yo emotions.

"It's fucking Warren." A feral snarl raced out of James and was brutally harsh to Inessa's ears. "He's on a damn war path. Attacked me in my room."

Chance tensed. "Does he know?"

"No. He kept insisting I give him back the laptop. I refused, because it's not his to have. She isn't his to have." Red flared bright across James, his emotions for Annie like a lighthouse beacon. "Warren is trying to get in the computer, and in the process he could kill her."

"So we need to tell him, and fast. Is that why Tal sent you?" Chance ran his hand over his face. "Then we should—Inessa? What are you doing?"

Chance's use of her name brought Inessa's awareness out of James' aura enough to realize she now stood very close to James. One of her hands wrapped around his wrist, the other touched his neck. He stared at her like she'd sprouted another head. Inessa hesitated, staring back at him. "I-I'm not sure. I'm sorry James."

The hand he used to pull her hand from his neck didn't move brutally or fast, in fact it was surprisingly gentle. James shook his head. "It's okay. What were you doing?"

"James," she whispered. Cool blue had settled over his intense aura, ripples of white moving through it in a way she'd only seen in his duplicate. "Goddess, you're calm. What did I do?"

James' brow furrowed. He glanced at Chance. "Empath?"

"No. She sees auras like your sister. Inessa, can you manipulate those auras as well?" Chance's hands circled her upper arms to pull her back against him. "Is that what you did?"

"I would never do that, even if I could. Not intentionally." Inessa went over the previous few minutes in her head. Not once since her ability had arrived had she done anything like that before. "All I know is that he was so bundled up I felt like I had to do something. Anything. No one can survive on constant extremes like that. He'll burn out."

"Haven't burned out yet." There was a flash of a smile, but like he wasn't comfortable with it being there James wiped it away. He straightened. "We might have Charlotte check her out. I've never seen Char do anything like that, even though I'm sure she wishes she could tug a thread and detangle my chaos."

"Are we done talking about me like I'm not standing right here?" Inessa sighed. "Chance, before he gets angry again, tell him what you told me."

James' brow deepened into a 'V'. "What's going on, Chief?"

"It might have been a dream." Chance frowned. "I thought I had a premonition of a battle here. An internal one."

"Maybe it was this shit that's going on." James shrugged. "You don't get your premonitions too often, Chief."

"It threw him completely off. I don't think it was a dream either, because he was having a very different kind of dream from what I could tell. I hope it was starring me, at least…if it involved anyone else, I hope it was Tal, and that we were both there. Together. I've seen pictures, Tal is a looker. Combined, we must make a hell of a fantasy."

"Inessa." Chance's cheeks turned a delightful shade of red.

A sound she was sure was a rarity echoed through the corridor. The barking laugh of James came from deep in his belly. His eyes widened. "Where the hell did that came from?"

Inessa grinned. "Doesn't matter. When they made me, they broke the mold. Now, I think Chance needs to go talk with your family about this. If you think I can help, I'd like to go. I know nothing about science-y stuff, but I know emotions."

"I am going now. I'm sure you'll be there, Chief." James nodded to Inessa, and just like that he was running down the hall.

Chance finally let out a soft chuckle. "It's a good thing they broke the mold when they made you, Inessa. The world could not handle two of you."

"Damn straight."

Chance did his best to school his expression upon entering the conference room with Inessa. Rather than make comment on the obvious, he pulled out a chair for her. To be frank, the room looked like a divorce hearing. Each group clustered to one side of the room, and parts of those groups glared at each other.

Charlotte, spirits love her, sat more toward the middle than the rest. Despite this, her attention remained focused on James and the laptop in front of him. James wasn't saying a word or looking at anyone but the laptop that rested on the table, closed for the moment. Talisa and Roark stood behind their son, pensive and worried.

The opposite end of the table told a different story. For a brief moment if he could step outside of the scene, he could see the humor in Warren raging while James remained calm. Abby remained distraught, and with good reason, but at least she was not currently hysterical. He hoped that meant cooler heads could prevail.

"Let's see if we can discuss this like adults and come to an understanding okay?" Chance stood behind Inessa rubbing her shoulders with a gentle touch.

"He just needs to give us our daughter's laptop and I won't have to kill him." Warren growled.

"Warren." Abby hissed low. "We agreed to talk about this. Talisa will make him do the right thing."

A low growl that steadily rose in volume erupted from James. "You can try."

Chance raised his hands to silent both sides. He made it a point to make eye contact with both grumbling men. "Enough. No one is killing anyone. Now that being said—we all agree that inside these walls I am the final say. Do you both agree to abide by whatever decision I make?"

"Yes, Chief," James answered immediately. At least his sense of duty wasn't completely gone in the chaos and raised emotions.

"You can't be serious?" Warren flew to his feet. Fury made his features ruddy.

"Those are our laws, Warren. My first duty here is as Chief of this tribe and leader of the people here. Do you agree?" Chance set his hand on Inessa's shoulder to keep some form of contact with her. He couldn't understand this need to touch her, but it settled his nerves. They settled further when she rested her hand on top of his.

"Fine." Warren threw his hands up and fell back in his seat. "Who the hell is she?"

Chance smirked back at his friend. "She's with me." He nodded in Talisa's direction.

"Warren you have to know I wouldn't keep the laptop from you without good reason." Talisa glanced at the laptop and gave a subtle shake of the head that Chance barely noticed.

"Tal, I know Annie cared for James but there is no reason he should have that instead of us." Tears welled up in Abby's eyes. "Please just give it back to us."

"She is my *mate*!" A sound akin to a roar reverberated through the room.

"If she was your mate you would be incapacitated and writhing on the ground. You aren't. That means you were nothing but a convenient distraction that stole our last moments with our daughter from us. I'll be damned if you take the last piece of her no matter how small away from us." Warren snarled back across the table.

"She's not fucking dead, asshole!" James snapped back.

Silence fell over the room as Warren and Abby stared across the table in confusion. Chance blew out a breath ready to launch into an explanation of what they learned when Inessa spoke up.

"You really do know how to kill a room don't you, James?" A giggle escaped from their newest addition.

"Inessa…" Chance chided softly with a hint of a chuckle; his thumb trailed lightly along her shoulder. It wasn't exactly how he wanted to approach the situation. He could only imagine how they would handle the information.

"Tal, how could you? I thought you were my best friend. Why would you even entertain something so absurd?" Tears streamed down Abby's face. "I buried my daughter."

"Mom please don't cry." Annie's voice shook.

"That's just cruel. Using your newfound telepathy to trick us." A sob choked Abby. Warren pulled her close.

"Dad, stop it! Stop trying to pull code. You'll kill me." Annie's voice shifted from sadness to panic.

"They are using a computer program Gail. We thought you were our friends. Our family. This goes beyond anything Steele would have ever done." Warren dropped a kiss on the top of Abby's head.

"They aren't lying guys. I had a vision at the funeral. Charlotte sees an aura around the laptop." Chance gave Inessa's shoulder a gentle squeeze. "I'm sure Inessa sees it as well."

"Fascinating." Inessa's concentration shifted towards the laptop. "I've never seen anything like it."

"Oh God…" Charlotte's hand flew to her mouth. Her skin taking on a light green hue.

"Char?" Roark moved next to their daughter. "You okay?"

"I need—I need air. I'm sorry…." Charlotte pushed her chair back and bolted from the conference room.

"She's not okay. Very confused about something." Inessa frowned momentarily before focusing on the laptop again.

"James turn the laptop around." He waited until his second in command turned the laptop around. "Annie, can you explain it please?"

The image of the young woman on the screen nodded. "Before my body gave out, I had James bring me the laptop. I had a wild idea that I could essentially jump into the computer and if Talisa could create James with science, maybe she could help me."

"This is amazing. Her aura is shifting like any one of us." Inessa leaned on her hand tilting her head to the side, "She has threads all throughout the room. Very tied to this group."

"Who are you again?" Warren pursed his lips.

"Inessa. Pleased to meet you." Inessa grinned brightly.

"Is this really happening? I mean, if this is true, c-can you do what she's talking about, Tal?" Abby wiped the tears from her cheeks in an attempt to hide the hope now flickering in her eyes.

"I think we can. Roark and I are already working on it. We didn't want to say anything until we knew more in case it didn't work." Talisa wrapped her arm around Roark's waist.

"Do it. Bring our daughter back. In the meantime we'll take the laptop and you let us know when it's time for the transfer." Warren ran his hand along Abby's back.

"Warren, I don't think…" Roark started.

"You don't have a say in that, Roark." Warren interrupted.

"No." Annie's voice rang clear through the room.

"Excuse me?" Warren stood up again, glaring at the laptop.

"I'm staying with James." Annie's image glared right back at her father.

Chance sighed. "Alright, let's calm down. Annie wants to stay where she's been. I don't think she'd be adverse to visits but they are all working on the issue together."

"No offense, she's our daughter." Warren frowned.

"I said no." Anger tinged Annie's voice.

"Why the hell not?" Warren leaned on the table both fists pressed down onto it.

"You scare me. I feel safer with James."

The world dropped out from underneath Danny as the words passed Elan's lips. Live with them? Where were they supposed to put him? At the foot of their bed? The units everyone lived in were not that big. Couples all had one bedroom, bathroom, small kitchen, and living room. Two people were tight enough in there, but to add a third.

"I'm all for helping someone adjust after what he's been through but live with us? How is that going to work? We're all crammed in like sardines here as it is."

"I don't have all the answers Danny but he will lose his mind in this room by himself." Elan's wary expression tugged at his heart.

"Ya think I got them either? I just lost my damn sister, my mother is inconsolable, my brother has so much damn guilt he's giving me a fucking headache, I barely know which way is up, and now ya wanna move your ex in." He ran his hand through his hair gripping it tightly. The urge to pull it out sounded good right about now.

"Ex?" Chaz looked between the pair, confusion puckering his brow.

"It's not like we dated, Danny." A deep frown marred her beautiful face.

"I know that. But it's easier to think about it that way than what that monster made you do." Danny pulled her close and kissed her forehead. "Seriously though, how would this even work? We have no room."

"I don't know but I know we need to find a way so we can help him." Elan laid her hand on his forearm. "Please?"

"Damn it, woman don't give me that look. You know…" One eyebrow quirked up at the chime from the door. His eyes widened when the door slid open and it revealed Tori standing there holding a tray full of food and medical supplies.

"Oh, hey guys. I don't want to interrupt anything I just wanted to…" A squeak escaped from Tori as she went from standing in the doorway to pinned to the wall by Chaz. The tray she had been previously holding sat on the table.

Danny spared a brief glare in Elan's direction. He gripped Chaz's arm in an attempt to pull him off of Tori. "Chaz! Let her go now!"

Chaz gripped Tori's forearms and sniffed along her throat. "No mate."

A giggle escaped from Tori, "What is he doing? It tickles."

"Nein. Platz." A low growl rolled through Elan. Chaz stayed for a moment more but moved back to her side.

"Tori, you okay?" Danny checked over her arms and her throat for any damage.

"I'm fine, Danny. He didn't hurt me. Everyone is occupied so I wanted to see if our new addition was hungry or needed anything." Tori tilted her head to the side to meet Chaz's gaze as he avoided meeting anyone's. "I'm sorry. I didn't mean to startle you."

"A meal and a smile aren't going to get him to respond to you. I suggest you keep your distance unless you want to accidentally get hurt." Elan pursed her lips as she looked the younger Coleman girl over.

"I was just trying to be nice, Caiman. No need to get pissy about it." Tori rolled her eyes.

"He's not going to respond to nice so take your pretty, pretty princess mentality and leave him alone." Elan snapped back at her.

A low growl rolled through Chaz, but he made no move from where he stood.

"So glad you brought your sparkling personality home, Elan." Tori looked up at Danny and laid her hand on his forearm, "If you need anything let me know, okay? Mom isn't a hundred percent, but I can get away if you need anything."

"Thanks Tori, I appreciate it. Let us know if you need any help with Ariel." Danny ignored the growl that came from his wife this time as Tori left the room. "Was that necessary? She was just trying to help."

"Let me know if you need anything Danny." Elan replied in a mocking tone. "She needs to watch herself around my husband."

"Are you serious? Tori is like family and she was just trying to help. Right now we need to focus on how exactly we are going to move Chaz in with us. Our place isn't big enough. There is no way he can move into the unit we are in." Danny folded his arms across his chest.

"All I know is we have to help him. We're the only ones that can." Elan's frown deepened.

"Maybe I can ask the Chief if we could move in to one of the new two-bedroom units that were just built" He blew out a breath of frustration. The new units were in a different section of the compound. They were away from the rest of the family. The one-bedroom units were set up to be somewhat modular and let you connect them but the empty one next to them had been Annie's and he didn't know if he could handle that.

"Will you do that?" Hope lingered in his wife's eyes.

"Is he going to be able to handle having his own room in that unit if we do this? He tore this one to shreds. I can't live with what little furniture we have being demolished." He scrubbed his good hand over his face. "Chaz, what do you think?"

The other man stood there silent for what felt like an eternity when Elan answered for him. "He's not used to answering things like that, Danny."

"Well then he's going to have to start somewhere. You want to help him; we have to break through the programming. Chaz, what do you think?"

"She has no mate." Chaz said matter of fact.

"Who? Tori? No, she's not seeing anyone. I mean about moving in with us." Danny pursed his lips, a million thoughts running a marathon through his head. Could they even do this? Could they do this without anyone getting hurt? Most importantly, would his marriage survive?

"I'll do what Caiman says." Chaz still stood next to Elan, not moving a muscle.

"I'll talk to the Chief. I hope you realize what you're doing."

"You scare me. I feel safer with James." Annie's words settled the room into silence.

Warren's face went slack. He sank back into his chair without a peep. Beside him, Abby let out a singular sob before silence fell again.

Tal guessed Annie was about to speak again, so she took the lead before anything else would spark Warren back into his lather. "Why don't we take a break? Warren, Abby, I assure you that we are doing whatever we can to bring Annie back. Warren, I hope you'll help. We've retrieved some cryostasis pods from Steele's compound that might be converted to aide us in that endeavor."

Though some hope returned to Abby with a mentally whispered, *Please*, Warren only offered the smallest of nods. He glared at the computer, then James.

James' grip on the computer tightened, but he did not bristle under the glare. A sign his mate attachment was still working, though Annie was nestled in that very computer clinging to life.

Chance nodded to Tal, his hand still on the newcomer's shoulder. Tal couldn't help but smile at the closeness he displayed with this woman. He'd shown little interest in women since they'd been in high school, so focused on caring for his people he'd forgotten to care for himself.

Into the silence, Chance cleared his throat. "Why don't we agree to reconvene in, say two days? Will that be enough time for you, Talisa? Roark?"

Roark glanced at her in question. Two days was hopeful, but at least they might have made progress and managed to remove someone from the pods. She nodded in agreement. Roark also nodded, this time toward Chance. "We should have made some progress by then."

"Then let's do that. Abby, Warren." Chance turned to them. "If you'd like some time with Annie, I'm sure James wouldn't mind."

James tensed, but didn't argue with his Chief.

Warren lowered his gaze back to the computer. He gave one short shake of his head.

Abby bit her lip. It didn't take a telepath to see how torn she was by the situation. Her hand shook as she set it on Warren's, her tearful gaze steady on the computer. "I, um…" She cleared her throat. "I think we need some time to process. I'd like to see you, though. Annie. Maybe in a little while?"

Talisa couldn't see Annie from her vantage point, so she had no idea what the girl was feeling. All the telepathy in the world wouldn't let her hear the coding that now made up Annie's thoughts. Finally, Annie's voice responded, shaky. "You know where to find me."

The group broke up slowly after that. Inessa, the first to rise, leaned in to speak low to Chance. The man blushed in a way Tal had only seen him do when she herself had teased him. Tal slid past Roark to meet the pair, but Inessa slipped out before she could arrive.

Tal reached Chance's side, her gaze still on the door. "Pretty."

"Talisa." Chance's voice hedged on both humor and warning. "Be nice."

"Chance, look at me." She pressed her forehead to his when he did. "For many years I have longed for you to find happiness. I like her, and I don't even know her. You know why?"

Chance met her gaze evenly. "Why is that?"

"Because of how you look, think, behave around her. I don't know where she came from, but you are an impossibly better man around her. I didn't think you could get more perfect."

He scoffed. "Now you're being dramatic."

"Maybe, but it is what I do best." She chuckled and kissed him on the cheek. "I've missed you."

"Me too. Sorry you had to come back to this."

"It wouldn't be our life if it wasn't chaos." Tal caught sight of Warren and Abby leaving, Abby's gaze still flashing back to the computer. She sighed. "Excuse me. Keep my men busy for a few, please."

"Am I grouped in that?"

"Always, C. Always." Tal winked on her way out the door. In the corridor, she paused at the sight of Abby and Warren in an intense discussion. She turned away politely, doing her best to focus on her husband's thoughts so as to not listen in unintentionally.

A few minutes later, Warren stormed past her with a harsh bump to the shoulder that was definitely intentional as the corridor was plenty wide enough for the both of them.

Tal turned toward her friend, hesitating to give her a minute to gather herself.

When Tal approached, Abby tensed. Abby's shaking hands clenched into fists. "Just go away, Tal. Now isn't a good time."

"Abby." Tal kept herself calm as possible; her friend seemed on the brink. She could only imagine what the emotions of recent weeks had done to her. "I'm so sorry."

"Sorry? For what? For lying to me?" Abby's head snapped up, the fire of a thousand angers in her eyes, likely fueled from her own husband. "For comforting me when you knew my comfort was in a computer in the compound?"

"I didn't know how to tell you; I wasn't even sure if I could save her." Tal focused down the hall where Warren had disappeared. "I am sorry, even if you don't believe me, but there's something else. It's Warren."

"He has every right to be angry."

"I'm not saying he doesn't, but this seems to be more than that. Abby, I think there's something wrong."

"How dare you." The muscles in Abby's jaw twitched in her anger. "You don't even know us anymore. You were gone for a year. Working for that bastard."

"Against our will. We tried every day to find a way home."

"I honestly don't give a fuck. You don't know us anymore. So stop. Stop assuming. Stop acting like now that you're back we should worship you like the messiah returned. You're not the Goddess's gift to Exceptionals."

"Abby! Listen to yourself." Tal stared at her friend in shock. "This isn't you. Are you clinging to your husband for some sort of baseline for your emotions?"

"Leave me alone, Talisa. If you can save my daughter, great. Otherwise, just leave us alone."

"Abby." Tal stared at her retreating back in shock. Either the year really had changed Abby, or something was seriously wrong.

"Li?" Roark set his hand on her shoulder. "What was that about?"

"Whatever's wrong with Warren is affecting her. I think she's leaning on him like she always has and it's messing her up." Talisa lifted her gaze to meet his. "Without reading her mind, I can't be sure, though."

"That's why you were in here." Roark tapped his head.

"Safest place for me. Well, sort of."

"Sort of?"

"You have got an awfully filthy mind."

Roark chuckled. "In my defense, I spent a year separated from you by a mere sheet of glass. It led to a lot of fantasies."

"Boy, do I hope we have a minute to try some of them out soon."

"You and me both."

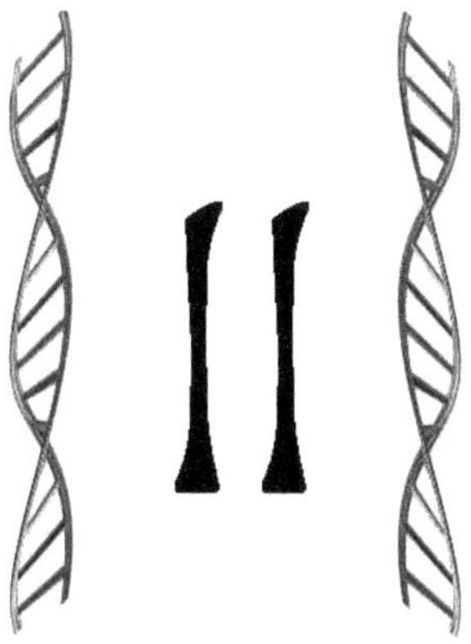

Lucas had the light in his quarters dimmed nearly all the time, preferring natural light to the harsh man-made lights. It didn't matter that the lighting had been designed to mimic natural sunlight, it still seemed harsh and false.

He made it a daily ritual to go to the surface, if only for half an hour, to get his fill of sunshine. Even on the coldest days, it restored his sense of center. While he tolerated the lighting throughout the compound, his and Kenzie's quarters were his sanctuary.

For the moment he'd made an exception and turned the lights up to full. Considering his guests ability to only see in light and shadow, it seemed appropriate. Neil had made his own way to the chair, at least, so that was something.

Lucas took the seat across from Neil, pondering his brother-in-law. The request had been simple enough, but Lucas worried about the repercussions. "Are you sure you want to see this?"

"Is it that bad?" Neil's hands, clasped tight in his lap, twitched as if to reach for his face.

"I didn't say that."

108

"I need to know what it looks like. I've been on my own for so long, and I can't look for myself. I want to see how bad the scarring is. I need to see what Charlotte sees."

"Well, that's the rub. Charlotte doesn't see what I see. To add more to that, I don't see what your average person sees." Lucas leaned forward. He tapped Neil on the knee. "You are family to us. In our family, in our people, the scars mean nothing. They mean even less to your wife."

"Inessa didn't once react to them or say a word about them. When I asked her directly, she said she didn't see them." Neil pursed his lips, "But I'm not an idiot. I know it's not easy on the eyes. I can feel it in how tight that side of my face is now. When I touch it I get a sense of it as well. I know it's bad."

"Inessa was not lying. Just like Charlotte sees your aura first, your physical the second. In fact, Inessa has become so entwined with her mutation that the physical visual appearance is only about twenty-five percent of what she factors in. Charlotte is not much different in that aspect." Lucas sighed. Neil was a good man, but stubborn, and Lucas knew when to fight and when to give in. "I will show you, but you must promise you will not make any decisions for your wife."

"What's that supposed to mean?"

"It means you do not get to decide that you are no longer good enough for Charlotte. She loves you. Remember how long it took the two of you to get past her fears. Do not go throwing yours in there now." Lucas frowned; relieved Neil could not see it. Neil and Charlotte had gone through enough in their lives, they didn't need more added to it now. "Are we agreed?"

"What if I promise to try my best? I can't swear until I've seen it."

"I think I can live with that." Lucas knew Neil had always been as good as his word, so he trusted him to make the right choices. "All right. Close your eyes. Try to relax."

Neil did as he was told, sitting back in his chair. In a heartbeat, the natural barriers that existed in everyone's mind fell away. Neil had never been a closed off person, so when he relaxed, those blocks all fell away. This made it easier for Lucas to slip into his mind.

After he'd established a link with Neil, Lucas sent him the images he could see before him. Neil, relaxed in the chair, scars lining his face. His eyes opened to reveal the unseeing white eye on his right side.

Shrapnel had torn across the right side of his face, leaving behind what looked like claw marks. As if he'd been mauled by a bear instead of being nearly blown to bits. Neil's hand rose to his face, running along the lowest line of scarring.

Bit by bit he moved up along his face, a small frown forming as he studied himself through Lucas' eyes. "Plastic surgery could fix the worst of the scarring. There isn't much I can do about my vision, though."

The realization struck Lucas. The root of Neil's fears wasn't how his wife saw him, but something else. "It's the vision you're most worried about, isn't it?"

"I was a doctor, Lucas. A damn good one, I don't mind saying." Neil's eyes closed again. Walls formed in his mind, nudging Lucas away. He was done seeing himself for now. "I really don't know what good I am to the team without it."

Lucas smiled. He'd withdrawn from Neil's mind without trying to get a read on his reaction to the image of himself. Lucas was pleased that his instincts to the real concern had been correct, that it wasn't about the physical. "Everyone has a purpose. I'm sure you'll find somewhere to work for now."

110

"I guess."

"Don't forget you're married to another amazing doctor. Maybe during off hours the two of you can come up with a way to restore the sight to your one eye." Lucas rose. "I'm sure we'll figure something out."

"I hope so. I hate feeling useless. Glad as I am to be home, I want to be able to contribute in some way."

"I think you can be useful right now." Lucas crossed to his herb cabinet. "Charlotte is heading this way. She appears to be upset and confused."

Neil frowned as he stood. His fingers barely touched the chair before he stepped forward. "She's upset? Has something else happened?"

"Charlotte." Lucas opened the door for her. "Neil's in here with me, keeping me company while Mackenzie visits with her mom."

"Neil?" Charlotte ran into the room without hesitation. Her arms wrapped around Neil tight as the first tears slipped down her cheeks.

"Charlotte. Baby, what's wrong?" Neil held her close. "What happened?"

"I'm okay. I think. It just caught me off guard." Charlotte sniffled against her tears. "It's not anything I ever expected."

"Why don't we go back to our room? You can tell me everything." Neil kissed the top of her head. "You'll feel better once you talk about it."

"I probably will." Charlotte kept her arm around her husband's waist. "Lucas."

"Your secret is safe with me, Charlotte. Get some rest, talk it over with your husband. You can deal with it tomorrow once your head is clear." Lucas smiled as the door shut behind them.

Mackenzie was due back soon, and she always struggled after an afternoon with her mother.

Ariel, Mackenzie's mother, still struggled with her husband Joe's death a year after the battle that took him. No one was surprised by the turn of events. Joe and Ariel had been as close as his own parents, possibly more. He was certain that if his mother had been left behind, she would still be as lost as Ariel.

Lucas dimmed the lights again. He went into the bathroom to draw a hot bath, which he sprinkled some herbs into. By the time the candles were lit, Mackenzie was home. Before she'd gotten two steps into the room, Lucas wrapped her in a hug. "I have drawn your bath."

Even through her tears, her cheeks lifted in a smile. "You always know what to do. Thank you."

"Do not thank me too much. It was not an unselfish move."

"How so?"

"Because I plan on joining you."

She laughed. "I thought that was a given."

"I suppose it is. How was your mother?"

"Better. Relatively speaking, of course."

Lucas cupped her cheek. "Even baby steps move you forward. We have to believe she is on her way back."

"I didn't tell her about your parents. I wanted to. It's happy news, but for her it might not be. It could set her back. To know that they survived when Dad…" Mackenzie's eyes watered as she held his gaze. "Was that wrong of me?"

"No. She will find out eventually, one way or another. For now, you are only trying to protect her. When you think she is ready, we can tell her together." Lucas gave her a soft kiss. "Now come, my wife. It is time to relax."

"That sounds like the best idea I've heard all day."

"Annie...I..." Ethan raked his hand through his hair. Nerves kept his gaze focused anywhere but on the laptop. Guilt wound his vocal cords in tight knots. He'd thought that since she was dying, he wouldn't miss her if he didn't get to know her. He'd been so wrong. Still now, he didn't know how to say it. "I don't know where to start."

"It's okay, really. I understand. It's not like any of this was the best situation. We all got thrown for a loop." The digitized image of Annie was so clear it might have been a video chat. "We'll figure it out. I just want to have my big brother back. Much as you were always a pain, I missed you."

Ethan spared a glance at James, who sat nearby. Not necessarily sulky or angry, just present in a weirdly calm way. Ethan shook off the distraction, his attention back to Annie quick as it had faltered. Guilt welled again, and he rubbed his hands on the top of his legs like he could erase the emotion with the action. "I wish I had those memories. All I know is I want us to have a relationship."

The smile that graced her features carried the warmth of understanding. "I get it. Trust me, I really do. There are things that I remember so clearly, but when I compare them to what I see now—well, I become well aware they are little more than implanted fantasy."

"What do you mean?"

"Oh, I remember clear as day all of us getting into trouble on occasion. You two creating mischief, carrying me along for the ride—or sometimes I was the one creating mischief myself and you were trying to rescue me."

An odd sense of melancholy over the memories she carried hit Ethan. He couldn't help but match her almost playful grin. Until it faded quick as it had appeared.

"I don't remember ever being scared of Warren. Not once." She played with a lock of hair; a shimmer of her tear barely visible under the red curtain of hair. "He was our dad. He loved us. I never for one second thought he would hurt any of us."

James leaned forward in his chair, touching the edge of the computer. "Anne."

"I'm okay, James." She reached toward where he'd touched the computer. Then as if realizing she couldn't reach him, pulled her hand back again.

"Dad wouldn't hurt us. I mean, honest. I've seen him angry but nothing like what you're describing." Ethan leaned back, trying to grapple with what Annie and James had told them about. "Maybe he's just being protective."

"He spent more time trying to prove I was a threat than getting to know me. Once that wasn't possible anymore, he blamed it all on James. I just wanted my daddy."

"I wish I knew what to tell you, Lil Bit. I tried to talk to mom before I came here, but she wouldn't let me in."

Annie's head snapped up, her eyes wide. "What—what did you call me?"

"Uh…" Ethan hesitated, unsure at her reaction. Even more, the low growl from the man beside him made him uneasy. Speaking of protective, he didn't doubt James had that in spades. "I said, I mean, I called you Lil Bit. I didn't mean anything by it. I swear. It just sounded right."

The monitor went black without warning.

"Anne." James shot to his feet. "Anne, where did you go?"

114

"Annie?" Ethan rose to his feet, concern pressing into his chest. "What happened? Where did she go?"

"You think I fucking know?" James all but vibrated with tension, the low growl of earlier growing at her disappearance.

The screen flickered several times, drawing Ethan's attention away from the hovering threat of pommeling from James. "Annie?"

A grainy video flickered to life on the screen before them. Annie couldn't have been more than a teenager. She stood behind a table, a large cake in front of her full of lit candles. An atrocious fuzzy pink tiara sat on her head. On one side of her stood his parents, on the other stood himself and Danny.

"Well, that's weird," Ethan muttered. On the screen he and Danny wrapped up a horribly off-key rendition of *Happy Birthday* to absolutely no cheers but their own.

"You two sound horrendous." Annie's protest lilted with laughter. She nudged Danny in the ribs, shaking her head.

Ethan's own voice echoed from the screen. "Come on, Lil Bit. Blow out the candles already so we can have cake."

The image froze then, Ethan kissing his sister on the cheek. The image flickered away, replaced by Annie again.

She smiled with an apologetic one-sided shrug. "Sorry about that. I probably should have warned you first, but I honestly didn't know if it would work."

In unison, both men spoke, "What was that?"

"That was one of my implanted memories. I was mad at you for years over that stupid tiara." Annie smirked at Ethan.

"I was just thinking it was hideous," Ethan acknowledged.

"It really was."

James cleared his throat. "Anne? How did you do that?"

"I'm part of the computer, aren't I? I thought if I could make you see me on the screen, why couldn't I do the same with what's in my head, so to speak."

"Brilliant." James appeared to be impressed and proud. Looks Ethan hadn't seen often on the fierce man's visage.

Annie, for her part, blushed under the compliment. "No. Logic."

Any argument dissipated at the sound of the door chime. All three looked toward the unexpected sound, but James took the initiative to cross to see who was there. The more familiar appearance of an angry frown creased his features. "It's your mom."

"Oh, well." Anne's tone took a bitter note. "I guess she can stand to look at me now."

The door slid open to reveal Abby. Her hands wrung together, her hair mussed, and dark circles under her eyes. "I was hoping to speak with Annie."

Ethan rushed to his mom's side, worried over her appearance. "You don't look so hot, Mom. Come on, have a sit down. Talk to Annie. She might help."

"How did you find out about this Ethan? Your father and I hadn't said anything yet." A deep frown puckered his mother's forehead.

"Dad was raging down the hallway on his way to his office. Half the family section of the compound heard him. I came to ask James what was going on. Finally, been getting to know Annie." Ethan rubbed his Mom's shoulder.

"That's not your sister. I mean partially. But we don't know what's been influenced. Your Dad said he's not sure. He's doing some research." Abby pressed her lips together in a thin line.

"Mom what are you talking about? No one has influenced me. This is me." Annie protested.

"I haven't made Anne do anything against her will or that she didn't want to." James growled at the accusation.

Abby rolled her eyes, "Like mother like son. Awfully convenient that you didn't tell us right away and our daughter wants nothing to do with us."

"Mom. It's Annie. Just talk to her." Ethan pled with Abby. "Why would you think Annie wants nothing to do with you?"

"She was very specific when we all met. She wants to stay with James." Abby's voice quivered.

"Because Warren is scaring the crap out of me. Apparently you don't see it but the way he's acting is exactly why I asked Talisa and Roark not to say anything about me being in the laptop. Mom what if they tried this and nothing works? I can't stay in the computer indefinitely. What then? You have to mourn me a second time? I was trying to spare you the pain." Annie sighed. "I have other reasons for wanting to stay with James, but no one will understand them."

"Because he's making you do something. He stole your last moments with you from us and he's trying to steal you now." Abby's chin jutted out defiantly.

"No. Once again, that was me and not James." Annie sighed, barely concealing an eyeroll. "This isn't you talking. It's Warren. Those are his words."

"Wait, what? Hold up." Ethan held up his hands in desperate confusion. "What on earth are you guys talking about? What on earth did I miss? How is it our parents think their best friends are out to hurt them?"

"That's a long story," James muttered. "Drop it for now."

"Mom could barely function before my body gave out, much less after. I was doing what I could to protect her." Annie let out a long sigh. "There's so much more than that, but I should point out that when James is close the pain is almost non-existent. It's a pretty big incentive to stick by my mate."

Abby touched the edge of the laptop. "Annie. Your father—"

"Correction. Your husband," Annie interjected. "I think he's made himself quite clear, and I will not be a possession to be fought over."

"He loves you." Abby sniffled. She swiped at a tear on her cheek, her hand trembling. "He just wants his little girl back."

"I was never his little girl, remember? Even if he remembered like I did, he has a funny way of showing it." Annie reached forward again, only to pull her hand back with a frustrated grunt. "Mom, look. I love you, I do. All this hostility, though? It's not you. I know it isn't."

"Wait a minute." Ethan couldn't help himself when his brain latched on to something Annie had said. "Annie, you said *is*."

James turned to him; his confusion clear. "What in hell are you talking about?"

"My brain just caught up, so much going on. Annie said the pain *is* almost non-existent when you are close." Ethan knelt to meet his sisters gaze. "Lil Bit, spill."

"Nothing you need to worry about, Ethan." Annie cut him a warning look, full of venom any animalistic Exceptional would be impressed by. "I'll be even better if Talisa and Roark can pull this off."

Abby stared at the screen, wide eyed, pale. Her hands shook. "Annie?"

"Don't worry about it, Mom. Worry about Warren, since his word means more than mine right now." Even Annie flinched at her own biting tone, her gaze downcast.

"I, um, I should go tell your father how you're doing then." Abby rose, her hands clutched tight together. The next words erupted louder than necessary and choked. "I love you, Annie."

"I love you too, Mom." Annie's tone carried no further malice, she simply sounded tired. Her gaze remained downcast while Abby backed away.

James waited until the door closed behind Abby. "Anne? What's going on."

"I'm fine. I promise. Right now worry about my parents being possessed." Annie sighed.

"Someone wanna tell me what happened to our mother?" Ethan looked between the screen and James. "If she stays that angry, we're screwed. She's the rational one."

"No shit, big brother."

Charlotte remained steadfast in her spot on the couch, against her own will. Neil had insisted he could take care of her, and that he remembered where everything was. She wanted to help him so bad, to make the cup of tea herself so he wouldn't injure himself. Such a thing would make him feel inadequate in some way, though.

She knew he didn't have to prove his capability to her, in the end. It was his own measure he was taking at that time. His memory and care against the scars of his loss.

"It's almost ready." Though she'd been watching his every move, the sound of his voice started her.

"Take your time, baby. I'm in no rush."

With careful measure, his fingertips danced along the counter to where he'd left the mug. He dropped the teabag in, dipping it a few times for good measure. With it in hand, he headed toward the couch. Along the way, his lips moved with what she assumed was the counting of his steps. "Here you go."

"Thank you." As soon as Neil stopped in front of her, she took the mug off his hands. She leaned into him the moment he sat, relishing the feel of his arms around her again.

His fingers traced along her arm. The familiar tingle of his soothing her nerves tickled her skin until she felt even calmer than before. "Do you want to tell me what happened?"

After a few sips of her tea, she set the mug on the table. Without missing a beat, she sank back into his embrace. The soothing dance of his fingers along her arm resumed. "You remember when I explained all that was done to me as an infant?"

"Of course I do. They kidnapped you and Elan. While she was kept and trained as a perfect soldier, they decided to mess with you. Altered your gifts somehow and that is why you have four. That's also why Chance is your father as well as Roark."

"Right. Three parents."

"Right."

"Three parents, but four gifts." Despite the soothing nature of his touch, Charlotte's gut twisted. She hoped he got it, that she didn't have to spell it out for him.

"That means the possibility of four parents from a DNA perspective I suppose. I've never been one for DNA, though. I'm a cutter."

She tried to laugh to cover the tears welling. "Yeah. I know."

"Charlotte." He nudged her temple with his nose before placing a soft kiss there. "Talk to me. Let me help."

"You're helping more than you know."

"Then tell me."

"The fourth is here. She's here. My mother or whatever is here." She blurted it out before she could help herself or censor it in any way.

"Hm?"

"I saw it. The other woman I'm connected to. Is here. Now. In this compound."

"That's good news, isn't it?"

"If she buys the whole explanation sure. I don't know why she didn't say anything. I mean I see the ties, the thread that holds us together. Hell, I see the thread between James and the laptop Annie is trapped in."

"A thread between James and the laptop? Have your parents had any luck?"

"Nothing yet. I couldn't handle the auras in the meeting. I can usually keep it in check and dial it back for big groups like that but Uncle Warren and Aunt Abby's auras were so chaotic and then I saw the thread and I guess the shock threw me off and the rest overwhelmed me." She scrubbed her hand over her face, "Sorry I'm getting off track."

"Baby, it's okay. You've had a few surprises thrown at you in the last few days." His arm tightened around her shoulder pulling her close. "You are allowed to be a little frazzled."

A shaky breath danced across her lips, "It's Inessa."

"Inessa? As in the woman who helped me get here?"

"Yes. Inessa is biologically speaking my other mother."

"I don't understand. Why didn't you see it in New York? Why would it show up now?"

Charlotte grabbed the mug off the end table. She clasped it in her hands as she stared down into it. "I was still learning to control all four of them then. I saw threads but I was working on other patients and I never met her face-to-face. You told me about her after the fact."

"Inessa is very easy going. I think she will listen."

"You want to know the crazy thing?" She couldn't help the snort that escaped. "Yes, the crazy thing that's part of the story about your wife that has four biological parents."

Neil chuckled and dropped a kiss on the top of her head. "We both know things are a little insane down here. But what's the crazy part?"

"Pops has taken a liking to Inessa. From what I heard, before the meeting they were spending some quality time together. Before I got sick to my stomach he was smiling. I mean a real smile. His aura was practically dancing. He seems happy." One shoulder rose in a shrug. "Well as happy as you can get under the circumstances."

"Those are all good things though, right? He hasn't been happy in a long time."

"It is. If you listen to Mom tell it, he hasn't been happy like this since high school. It's good for him. I'm just confused. I mean Mom, Dad and Popsicle have been there for as long as I can remember. I don't know how I feel about this." A tremor ran through her and she was beyond grateful when she felt the soothing impulses from her husband to counteract it.

"You are more than entitled to be confused. No one expects you to start calling her Mom or automatically become close with her."

Charlotte rested her head on his shoulder with her eyes closed for a few minutes. She let the fact that Neil had made it home and had his arm around her calm her. "What if she wants nothing to do with me? I mean she could want to pretend I'm nothing to her."

"I don't think Inessa is like that baby." His chin rests on the top of her head. "I don't think Chance would be with someone like that. He's a pretty good judge of character."

"I know he is but what if this affects them? He's my other father. I don't want to cause any problems for them." She shook her head, "I can't think about it right now. It will drive me crazy."

"You can't avoid it, Charlotte."

"Not avoiding it baby. Just nothing I can do until I talk to Inessa." Her fingers danced along his arm with a feather light touch. "How was your visit with Lucas? Did he show you?"

"He did."

She felt the tension rise in his body as well as the sudden shift in his aura. "And? Or do you not want to talk about it?"

"I feel useless."

"The last thing you are is useless. I know if you weren't here right now, I would have driven myself insane with this stuff with Inessa."

"I mean for the team. I was a brilliant surgeon, damn it!"

"You still are a brilliant surgeon. Once Annie is taken care of I can focus on you."

"What do you mean focus on me?" Anger spiked in his voice which in the past had been an odd occurrence. Due to his mutation his emotions tended to run as cool and even as Lucas'.

Charlotte shifted in his arms to face him. She ran her fingers through his hair. "What bothers you more? The physical aspect of it or the fact that it limits what you can do as a doctor?"

"That's not a fair question." He snapped back. Red pulsed through his aura.

"It's not fair or you don't want to answer it?".

"Charlotte." His voice held a warning tone she rarely heard. It almost sounded like James. "With Lucas' help I was able to see what it looks like. I can't even see you anymore."

The mug ended up discarded on the end table again. She pushed on his shoulders and straddled his lap. "You see me just fine."

"I can't see you at all. Nothing more than a shadow."

124

With one of his hands in her own, she brought it up to her face. "You still see me." A smile danced across her lips at the feel of his fingers dancing along her face.

"It's not the same."

"Isn't it?" Her own fingers traced the line of his jaw moving upwards towards the scars. She didn't pull away when he tensed up. Instead she leaned in and kissed along one puckered ridge.

"Charlotte." His hand shot up and grabbed her wrist.

"Neil. I love you."

"I love you too. That's not the point."

"My point is this." She brushed her lips across his. "Right now I'm tied up helping Mom and Dad with bringing Annie back. We kind of have a deadline with her. But once we find the answers there, if you want, maybe we can find a way to restore the sight in your one eye."

"Lucas mentioned something similar." The red had retreated some in his aura but not completely.

"Maybe Lucas can help show you how I see things. I can't guarantee it won't make you nauseous though."

Neil's hands slid down to grip her hips. "Maybe. When do you need to go back to work?"

"Mom told me to take a break. Suggested I lay down. Apparently I looked a little green. Care to join me?"

"Best offer I've had all day."

"Right this way then."

A low chuckle hit Tal's sensitive ears from the direction of the door. Roark's voice filled the lab space, though he spoke low. "Just what do you think you're doing?"

"I'm working. I told Char she's not allowed back in the lab for a couple of days while she and Neil have some time. The meeting this morning was rough on her, which seemed odd for her." Tal glanced his way. "I think she's just stressed."

"I meant." He approached quick enough she couldn't react before his hands settled on her hips, his body pressed against her back. "What do you think you're doing working without me?"

"Oh." She turned just her head so she could meet his gaze. "I thought maybe you needed a break as well. Besides, I'm the one that managed the stable clone, not you."

"Ouch."

"Well, it's true."

He smacked her ass just enough to sting. "There's plenty other I can do, my brilliant wife."

"Good point. Why don't you look into the details on those two animals we have in the pods?" Tal focused on the screen to her left, her fingers dancing across the keys for that computer. She turned her attention to the right computer, where her computations, for a possible clone, were running steadily.

"What about the girl?" Roark set a laptop on the counter across from her.

For a moment, Tal flashed back to their captivity, their mirror stations behind the wall. A shudder passed through her so hard she had to press her hands against the counter to stop it.

"Li?" Roark's hand settled on hers, warm and sure. Nothing separated them, and the solidity of his touch brought her back to reality.

"Sorry. Flash of PTSD, I think." Tal let out a long, slow breath. She flipped her hand in his so she could hold on. "We've been so busy; it's been easy enough to brush it aside most of the time."

"You want to work on this somewhere else?" Roark's brows furrowed. "Would that help?"

"Psychologically? Probably. Scientifically? It's best to have what I need in front of me in case I get an idea. I'll adjust. I may just have to touch you a lot to remind myself we're not trapped apart from each other any longer."

"I don't think I will ever complain about you touching me, woman."

"Pig."

"Pig, perhaps, but you love me for my mind."

"Hence why I tolerate the pig." Tal chuckled. Comfortable again, she pushed his hand away. "Get to work, you brilliant boor of a man. Let me focus."

"Still don't know how you focus with two computers at once."

"All your brilliance can't make you ambidextrous." Tal winked. She ignored his stuck out tongue. "And you could, if you tried. I have two very different projects running. Annie is over here, the girl over there."

Roark followed her vague wave toward the computer on her left. "Anything yet on either?"

"Not nearly enough on Annie. Even without that defective basal strand, I can't keep the strand strong enough to withstand the Exceptional power she was gifted with. It's like it was forced on her, not naturally born."

"Might have been. We are talking about Steele."

"Don't I know it?" Tal rubbed her hands over her face. "I have to do this for her, for James. For Warren and Abby, even if they are being bat-crap-crazy right now."

"You aren't responsible, Li. Steele is. Remember that."

"Steele may be a brainwashing bastard that forced me to use my skills for bad, but that doesn't negate the fact that it was my skills that did this." Tal tilted her head to pop out the tightness forming. "I managed it with James. It isn't impossible. I managed it with you and I, our extra mutations should have broken us down."

"Do you know why you love me?"

"Instinct."

"Ouch."

Tal smirked, peeking at him through her lashes. "What? We're mates, we just didn't understand it before the change."

"You're really running on thin ice."

"Fine. I love you because you're brilliant, a good dad, and a fucking fantastic lover."

"All very true," he acknowledged. "You forgot that I could cut through that blinding intelligence in your brain that sometimes clouds your own common sense."

She paused, her fingers hovering over both keyboards. All attention focused on Roark. "What do you see that I missed?"

"We're animal."

"Right."

"With animal alterations comes…" he let the words trail off.

The simple, undeniable truth hit her so hard, she closed her eyes against the simplicity. "Faster, better healing abilities. Our bodies, down to our DNA, makes corrections for damages."

"Bingo."

"Hot damn, I do love you."

128

"You'll have to prove it to me again real soon." He kicked her under the table gently. "Even if I have to drag you from the lab because you're lost in your computations."

"By my hair?"

"Like the caveman I am."

"If done right, that could be so hot." She grinned to match his low laughter.

A ding from the computer on her left stopped their mutual laughter dead. They both turned their attention to the computer as another series of dings set off like a string of firecrackers had sparked to life.

Tal turned her full focus on the results that kept springing to life.

"What is it, Li? You get some familial hits for the girl?"

"A shit-ton of them." As she flipped through the notices, her hands grew cold. How could any of that be possible?

"What part of the country? Do you think there's family to dig up?"

"I—yeah, you could say that."

"Li?"

"Fucking hell, Roark. She's family."

"What?" He sped around the table to her side. She flipped through the notices again so he could see for himself.

"She's family. To us."

"Who does she belong to?" Roark took over the keyboard, his fingers flying across the keys. A deep sigh erupted from his lips. "She's not ours, not directly. If we'd had another kid we didn't know about I would have ripped Steeles' balls off and fed them to him."

"Get in line. She's not ours, but she's — look, she's a grandchild to us."

"Who's her—"

Another screen popped up; final results displayed across the screen clear as day to them both.

"Fucking hell," Roark muttered. "It can't be."

"Elan. It's Elan's daughter."

"Who's the father?"

"Unknown."

Roark pinched the bridge of his nose. "It's not Danny?"

"No match to any known Exceptional. Danny included."

"They aren't going to handle this well."

"No fucking shit, Sherlock."

Neil paused at an intersection in the corridor. If he turned right, he knew he'd be on his way back to his and Charlotte's quarters. Where the compound had changed, he'd been able to use the computer's guidance to get from point A to point B well enough on his own.

He knew Charlotte worried about him, though he'd survived well enough over the past year with only minimal help. If he weren't so happy to be home, he might be bitter about it, but he couldn't deny how glad he was to be back.

Then again, that hadn't stopped him from using his special ability to urge Charlotte to sleep before he'd left the room. Guilt flared over the act, but Charlotte had been exhausted. Between the stress of Annie's brief life and near-death, as well as her parents return, and his own, he didn't think she'd slept well in weeks.

Based on everything that had happened in recent weeks, Neil knew his own problems were likely low on the priority list. His wounds were healed, and though he could no longer see, he wasn't laid up, in pain, or about to die.

That made him low-priority in the war.

Knowing it didn't make it sting any less. He wondered how long he'd have to go on without doing what he felt best at.

Hell, if he had any skill in DNA himself, he'd work on solving the question of if they could create an eye for him. Sadly, his specialty was surgery, and he'd never taken to learning what Charlotte's family was so deep into.

A twitch in his hands made him draw them close. They'd been so out of practice for so long, even if he could get his sight back, who knew if they'd even work like they once did?

The faint echo of music echoed through the metallic halls, so faint anyone walking down the hall probably didn't hear it unless they were listening for it. Neil tilted his head, sending a little extra stimulation to his own ears to pick up the tune better.

A classical piece his mind noticed immediately. His brain turned it over trying to remember the days when he would listen to such music as he worked in the operating theater.

"Prokofiev," he whispered soon as he recognized the tune. The piece was from the ballet, *Cinderella*. When he'd been in school, it had been one of his favorites.

He let the music lead him down to the left, through unfamiliar hallways. One finger glided along the wall with each step to keep him from wandering into anything unexpected.

He rounded another corner, where the music became louder. The piece progressed, and the closer he got to the source, the more curious he became.

A door slid open beside him unexpectedly, letting the music stream out clear as a bell. He cleared his throat for attention, but no one replied.

The music echoed through the room that now seemed cavernous by the way the sound carried. He stepped inside, still doing his best to keep one foot on the wall. "Hello?"

No one replied. The music continued on, a piece familiar to him. The dance Cinderella did with a broom, pretending it was the prince. At times funny, and touching, he'd always enjoyed the moment in the ballet.

"Oh!" The voice interrupted the music with a sharp suddenness that intruded on Neil's memories of the last time he'd seen the ballet years before. After a small clatter, the music ceased. "My goodness, Neil. You startled me."

"Sorry. I tried to say hello, I think the music drowned me out." Neil immediately recognized Inessa's voice. He smiled. "Were you performing?"

"Hardly." She laughed, but the tone was bitter. "Do you know how long it's been since I stretched these muscles? I don't even have pointe shoes. I was just…I don't know. Trying to do something, I suppose."

"Then you were rehearsing, though there is no upcoming performance."

"I suppose. What are you doing in this part of the dungeon?"

"So morose." Neil frowned. Even in their weeks searching for the compound, she hadn't sounded quite so down. "I thought you were adjusting well here. You've made friends."

This time Inessa's laughter held a lighter note. "I suppose that much is true. I do enjoy Chance's company. I just feel rather useless for much of anything besides showing him a good time. Ugh, good gravy I sound like a kept whore."

Neil snorted at the surprising mix of sweet and bluntness of her statement. "Inessa."

"Sorry. It just struck me."

"It's been striking me for a while. Not that I feel like a whore, of course."

A small, warm hand settled on his shoulder. "I can only imagine, my friend. You, however, have family here. Roots, of sorts. You're far from useless. What good is a dancer to these brilliant people who've survived such dark things?"

"You're more than a dancer, Inessa."

"You're more than a doctor, Neil."

"But I'm not." Neil sighed. Once again, his hands twitched at his sides. "I mean, I am. I'm a husband, and I have a wonderful wife. Surgery was all I did. I can't even contribute any knowledge here, myself. There are quite a few capable medical specialists in this place."

"Oh!"

Inessa's hand had disappeared from his shoulder, and she'd become so silent he couldn't be sure where she'd gone. "Inessa?"

"It's probably crazy," she muttered close by.

"What?"

"Okay, bear with me on this. If it's crazy, please don't laugh at me."

"I promise."

"Okay." She took his hand. "I used to be a TV-whore. I watched while I stretched in my apartment, walking to rehearsal, stretching, any time I could I was watching all sorts of craziness. Including medical shows. ER, Grey's, and the like."

"Um," Neil hesitated to correct her. After all, he'd promised not to laugh. "You do know those were shows, and real life is different."

"Of course, but the idea that struck me came from one of those. It's sort of what I was doing here with *Cinderella.*"

"Which is?"

134

"Muscle memory. It's been quite some time since I performed *Cinderella*, and I'm terribly out of shape, but my muscles remember the moves."

"Okay."

"I remember seeing one of those doctors in a skills lab doing something the same. He was doing some sort of stitches with a laparoscope with his eyes closed."

"That's just part of an operation, and no offense but you're a dancer, you aren't likely to kill someone if you fail."

"True." She squeezed his hand. "But you haven't operated in ages, and you probably feel rusty. Doesn't this massive nightmare of a place have some sort of skills lab for all those doctors they have prancing around this place?"

"They might."

"Okay, so let's go. We'll see what you can do."

"I don't know about this, Inessa." Neil hesitated to allow her to drag him anywhere.

"I don't know much about anything anymore, Neil. One thing I do know is that you aren't useless, and with all these brilliant minds around here, they'll find a way to help you do what you do best again. I can't let you rust away in the meantime."

"It could take ages. I'm low priority here."

"Not to me you aren't."

Charlotte startled awake to stark silence. No warmth in the bed beside her, no gentle snoring. "Neil!" She blinked a few times to get her bearings. Had it all been a dream? No, it couldn't have been a dream.

Within a few minutes she managed to gather her wits to find her own threads of connection. One by one she peeled them away until only her husbands remained. Strong and clear, it veered off into another area of the compound.

The minor heart attack she'd given herself on waking to find him gone subsided. Just as she had pushed aside the other threads, she allowed them to trickle back into her awareness.

Among them came the same thread that had caused her to feel overwhelmed in the conference room. She paused at the sight of it and held it in view for several minutes.

There stood only one way to deal with the situation—to face it head on.

She untangled herself from the bed sheets. After a quick minute to straighten herself up, she trailed after the thread in question. Halfway down the corridor, she paused. Maybe direct confrontation wasn't the best way to handle things.

"Charlotte?" Chance's concerned tone weaved its way into her thoughts. He walked up behind her silent as anything, but she knew he was there before she saw him. "Are you okay?"

"I'm okay, Pops. I'm just…" She pursed her lips, unsure how to truly answer the question. Of course, Chance knew better than anyone what it was like to learn he had surprising parental ties to her outside of normal means.

"You left that meeting rather quick. Were the auras too much? Inessa mentioned that Abby and Warren were pretty intense." He draped his arm across her shoulder, comforting as always.

"Uncle Warren needs a valium. Or maybe a good kick in the ass." She blew out a breath, glad to have his chuckle cover it. Avoiding things wouldn't help her situation in the slightest.

"Funny you should mention Inessa, though. She actually is why I left the room like I did."

Chance turned to focus on her. His forehead puckered in concern. "Inessa? Really? Is there something wrong? Should I be concerned? Did you see something wrong about her?"

"Only if you think her being my other mother is wrong." Charlotte cringed at the blunt manner she'd spit it out. That hadn't been her intention, exactly.

"I'm sorry. She's a what now?"

"She's connected to me somehow. That's the only explanation that I can come up with since I've never really met her before. I heard about her from Neil but that day was so chaotic I wasn't paying attention to things like that. Just who needed medical attention the most." She worried her lip between her teeth, half expecting him to tell her she'd lost her mind.

"Well, that makes things more interesting then, doesn't it?" The concern remained, brief streaks of orange and violet flickering with his usual blue and white aura.

"I don't expect her to take on a parental role or anything like that, but she should know. I mean, she should already, or should if she doesn't. Oh, I don't know. I wanted to find Neil first, then talk to her." She gazed down the hallway toward the direction she'd been heading.

"Find Neil? Why should you need to find him? I figured he would have been with you after the meeting."

"He was, but he knocked me out. I have sorely missed his ability to relax me, but we're going to have to have a chat about making me sleep, and then upping and disappearing on me." Charlotte cast a wry smile her father's way.

"Well, why don't we go find him and then we can look for Inessa and talk to her about it. I would like to think she trusts my opinion on the matter." Chance steered her down the hallway.

"Oh she's wrapped around you like a bow on Christmas present. At least from what I can see."

"We enjoy each other's company, but I don't know if it's that serious yet." Chance protested, albeit a weak one.

"Right Popsicle...you know you can't hide that stuff from me, right? Neither of you may realize it but you two are as connected as James and Annie are."

"I'm not saying I don't believe you, it's early though."

"The threads don't lie." Charlotte pulled Neil and Inessa's threads into focus. Both of them veered down the hallway towards one of the medical labs. "Huh."

"Issue?"

"I think they are together." She inclined her head towards the hallway to the left, "This way."

"They did travel here together."

"Not worried about anything like that Dad." The pair made their way down the hallway to the lab. "They are in there. Both of them are very focused on whatever it is they are doing."

Chance walked into the lab without any announcement so the pair in the room didn't know they had company. "What are you two up to?"

Neil jumped and the tools in his hand clattered onto the table in front of them. "Chance. I supposed we should have asked to use this lab in case anyone needed it."

"Why would you need to ask baby?" Charlotte walked in next to Chance. "I was just looking for you. I woke up and you were gone."

"And you were worried about me wandering the compound alone?" Bitterness latched on to Neil's tone a murky grey sliding through his aura.

138

"God no…" Charlotte started.

"I don't think that's what she meant. Whatever made Charlotte seek you out has her downright anxious but not about you." Inessa interrupted.

"I wanted you with me when I talked to Inessa." Charlotte laid her hand on top of his. A sigh of relief escaped when he pulled her close and kissed her forehead.

"I'm sorry." The whisper danced from Neil so low she almost didn't hear it.

Charlotte lifted her free hand and ran it through his hair and let her fingertips dance along his temple. She brushed a light kiss on the tip of his nose. "Don't apologize."

"Well now that the excitement is done with. You wanted to talk to me Charlotte?" Inessa had moved next to Chance.

"Do you prefer blunt or easing into something?" Charlotte asked the other woman.

"I'd say just rip the band aid off. No reason to drag it out. I won't bite you I promise." Inessa smiled as Chance wrapped his arm around her waist.

"If you say so." Charlotte leaned into Neil grateful for the waves of relaxation she felt running along every nerve in her body. "You're my mom."

"I'm sorry, what?" Inessa looked at her as if she had grown another head. "That's not possible."

"There's a lot that is possible and we never would have thought. Dad a little help here." Charlotte focused on her second father in an effort to not throw up from the rainbow aura swirling around Inessa.

"Dad? I mean I see the thread between the two of you, but I thought James was your brother which would make Talisa and Roark your parents." The confusion etched deep into Inessa's expression as well as her aura.

Chance pulled Inessa close. "Short version is Charlotte and Elan were kidnapped when they were infants right after they were born. General Steele did experiments on Charlotte and altered her DNA. He combined the DNA she already had with mine and one other person."

"So she has more than two gifts?"

"Four actually," Neil cut in this time. "She handles them all quite well. We never did figure out how Steele's scientists managed to balance them since a normal body can only handle two without severe consequences, but he did."

"I have Dad's animalistic tendencies with his healing and Mom's fire with Pop's plants and then the auras and threads like you do. I know it sounds insane, but trust me I've been living it my whole life."

"Charlotte that's just not possible. I've never had children or even come close to having children. We really aren't that similar." Inessa looked shell-shocked.

"You mean besides the blue eyes and the fact that I have your mutation." Charlotte ran a hand through her hair. "Sorry I'm tense."

"I can tell you believe it. I can see that you all believe this is the truth. Even Chance isn't questioning it, but I don't see any connection."

"I can run the DNA comparison to prove it if you want, but I can see the connection clear as day."

Inessa shook her head before Charlotte finished her sentence. "I don't have connections to anyone."

"I beg to differ. You have a pretty strong connection with Popsicle there. You have one with Neil, too. Bonding through what you went through. What do you mean no connections?" Charlotte clenched her jaw to rein in her smart mouth, a gift from her mother.

Perhaps she was spoiled in some weird way. After being forced to live underground and everything they'd been through, accepting the impossible was the norm. Wasn't the fact that they were Exceptionals at all example enough of how the impossible was possible? Chance had accepted her without question or hesitation. He'd always treated her like a daughter and loved her as if she'd always been a part of him.

Then there was Neil. While she didn't begrudge the connection between Inessa and her husband, she had just gotten him back after a year. She wasn't ready to share him yet, especially seeing the joy whatever they'd been doing had caused him.

The pair had traveled together through the country and all the dangers therein. A bond was bound to form between then. Because Inessa had brought her husband back, Charlotte would always be grateful to her, but to deny what she could see with her own eyes?

"Charlotte? Did you hear me?"

Charlotte blinked a few times, now realizing that Inessa stood directly in front of her. "I'm sorry, what? I guess I got lost in my own head."

Inessa tucked a lock of hair behind Charlotte's ear. "I think this is throwing both of us for a loop."

The younger woman pulled back with a grimace. "This is why I never have to do psychotropic drugs. Damn is that what I look like? How do you not lose your lunch?"

"Trust me the lunch we had earlier is threatening to come back up." Inessa grimaced along with her.

"I don't have a lunch to come back up so I may be lucky in that aspect."

"Char you were supposed to relax and take care of yourself." Chance chided with a smirk.

"I did relax Dad. Lots of relaxing with my husband. He knew exactly what I needed." She brought Neil's hand up to her lips to kiss the back of it.

"To be fair I gave her some tea and then we went about relaxing." Neil chimed in with a smile.

"Some things I don't need to know about. Married or not, you are still my daughter." Chance chuckled.

"They took a blood sample when I first got here if you want to run the sweep. I think I just need some time to digest all of this." Inessa managed an uneasy smile.

"Thank you for listening." Charlotte released her hold on Neil and hugged Inessa.

"We'll talk more about it soon, okay?"

"I'd like that. For now I think I'm going to take my husband for some more relaxing."

"Charlotte." Her name came out of Chance's mouth half chuckle and half growl.

"Love you too Dad."

Annie watched James sleep through the camera on the laptop as she had every night since her death. The machine never strayed far from him and even now his fingers rest on the keyboard as he slept. It killed her to watch him at night and see him twitch or tremble from a dream or the inherent programing that resided in his DNA and not be able to do anything about it. As much as it could affect a soul trapped in a laptop.

The odd thing was she still felt pain. Or at least what she perceived as pain. Her entire being went from a physical body to a bunch of ones and zeros in a machine. The few times Warren had attempted to access the laptop it felt like white hot lightening shooting through her very being. Now watching the man that had been deemed her mate fret in his sleep she reached out despite knowing full well she had no way to touch him.

"Rest well my Pischk. Spirits give him strength."

Everything went black. She could no longer see through the camera. Had he shut the laptop? A flyover maybe? Was this the end? Did they forget to plug her in? No matter how many times they said that it never sounded right.

"What is going on?" Not that anyone could hear her.

"Follow the light, <u>Kwëlaha</u>." A deep rolling timbre echoed through the pitch black space she now resided in. A thin beam of light trickled from her feet extending through the darkness, widening the further it travelled from Annie.

"I'm not ready to go. I don't want to leave him." Despite the apprehension at words they still held a comfort to them.

"Nhakeuchswochwen."

"Tell him…" A tear rolled down her cheek pondering what to say next. "Tell him he did everything right."

"Kwëlaha, it is time. He will know."

Annie took one step onto the beam with a shaky breath. "Why do I suddenly have the urge to sing 'Follow the Yellow Brick Road'?" One foot in front of the other she approached the light. Not sure what she would find on the other side. Would there be peace with no pain? Or would she be considered an abomination and punished for her very existence?

The light blinded her as she neared the end. Suddenly the light disappeared. In its place, a large field with a wigwam in the middle of it. When she turned around she expected to see the tunnel she had exited and instead it was more of the field.

With no other logical place to go she approached the wigwam. Her fingers glided over the woven rush mats that had been attached to the frame. She closed her eyes and let the cool breeze wash over her, amazed at the feeling of not once ounce of technology around her.

Technology had always been a huge part of her, but here without it an innate sense of peace washed over her. Everything else fell away and lifted an immense burden off her shoulders.

"I will gut anyone who enters my sacred space." James' voice carried from inside the wigwam.

144

The sound of his voice enveloped her like a warm blanket. Annie took her chances and pulled back the flap at the front of the wigwam. "I get the whole tall dark and angry thing but gutting? You sure you want to do that with me?"

James sat in the middle of the wigwam next to the fire, his legs crossed. His eyes stayed screwed shut. He refused to look at her. "You are a trick. A punishment for my failure."

The feeling of being wrapped in a warm blanket had been swapped for a punch in the gut. "James look at me." She approached cautiously not wanting to startle him or end up with his knife in her gut.

"I may have been unable to save my mate, but you will not torture me this way." His eyes remained closed.

"Pischk, please." Annie knelt in front of him. "I am no trick, Ehoalan."

A brief sharp shake of his head was the only response.

Annie reached up and tentatively smoothed back a braid from in front of his face. The gasp that escaped was inevitable once she touched him. To feel him again. To feel anything again. Tears welled up in her eyes as the tips of her fingers danced along his temple. "James Logan Nashuk you have never failed me."

James remained tense but silent. She brought her other hand up and cupped either side of his face. Annie leaned in and pressed her lips to his in a soft kiss. His hands shot out and gripped her arms, fury on his face. "I said you will not trick me this way."

"James, I am no trick." She looked around the wigwam. "I'm not sure what this is but for me it's either the end and the Spirits are letting me say goodbye or something else entirely that I don't quite understand. All I know is the voice said Nhakeuchswochwen."

"Go in hope?" His expression softened and he truly looked at her for the first time since she had arrived. "Anne?"

"There he is…" She pressed her forehead to his. A tremor ran through her at the thought that this was their goodbye. "I don't want to leave you."

"Don't talk like that." He shook his head. "If this isn't a trick, I don't think it's goodbye. It can't be. Mom and Dad are working on fixing all of this."

"What is this place anyway?" Annie glanced around the wigwam again.

"It's a sacred place to commune with the Spirits in our dreams."

"So, I'm in your dream?" Annie's forehead knit together. "I don't understand. I was watching you sleep."

"Stalker much?" One side of James' mouth pulled up in a sexy smirk that made her heart flutter.

Annie caressed his cheek, "It's not like I can go for a walk or actually sleep at the moment. I miss dreaming."

"Guess it's a good thing you ended up in a meditation dream and not any of my other ones. That might have been embarrassing." He chuckled although it sounded somewhat hollow.

"Afraid I'll find out about all your other romantic prospects?" She teased with a coy smile on her face.

A low growl rumbled through James' chest. Before she could react, he had her on her back. He hovered above her. The fierce expression on his face stood out in stark contrast to the gentle way his fingertips trailed along her hairline and down her cheek. "You are my mate."

Annie wrapped her arms around James' neck and pulled him closer, not a hint of fear in her soul. "Yes I am. I want all the things I saw in the visions. I want that life with you."

"I would not stray from you." His expression settled into something still serious but not as intense.

"I know. I will always be able to count on you." Annie leaned up and captured his lips in a slow searching kiss.

The growl that rumbled through his chest now was far from predatory. He held her close to him but made no move to push things further. A shaky breath escaped as they parted. "They are going to fix this Anne. I swear to you. You will be whole again."

"And then we can be together."

Elan did her best to hide her amusement at the situation before her. Not only did she rarely let anyone see she *could* laugh, but Danny would be gravely insulted at her laughter over the scene.

Chaz buzzed about the hallway on full alert. With a burst of speed, he'd run to one end, then back to the other. At each point he'd stop to sniff out the situation. Elan knew it was just his way to adapt to so much space, but it was an odd sight for a normal human.

The funniest moments came when innocent bystanders tried to walk down the hall. Chaz would appear at their side so fast, that nearly all of them dropped what they were carrying, tripped, or jumped against the wall.

Chaz was good enough to catch anything dropped, but still. She could understand Danny's burgeoning annoyance.

For his part, Danny would let out a sigh of frustration every time Chaz took off in another burst of speed.

He muttered under his breath. "You're the one that said he doesn't understand human. Can't you leash him?"

Elan lost hold of her control for just long enough to let out what she'd embarrassingly qualify as a chortle. "Really? A leash?"

"Wait." Danny paused. The frustration left his features as he turned to face her. For the first time in a while, his features softened into a look of pure love she hadn't seen since before the war. There was no hint of his usual frustration with her, or the situations at hand. For a moment, he seemed to even forget about Chaz nearby. "Did you just laugh?"

Elan couldn't hold his gaze, happy as she was to see him look at her like that again. She had to fight the urge to thicken her skin to hide the rising heat in her cheeks.

"Elan Chenoa Johnson." Danny's finger hooked under her chin to draw her gaze back to his. A warm smile lit his features. "You did laugh. I can't remember the last time I heard you laugh."

"I can't remember the last time you looked at me like this." She wanted to turn away but stood strong to soak up the rare moment of peace. "Maybe we're going to be okay?"

"Maybe we just might." He grinned as he placed a quick, harsh peck on her lips. "If you think you can smile and laugh more."

"I'm a soldier, Danny."

"Not in our bedroom, you ain't."

"Are you sure about that?"

He narrowed his eyes but couldn't hide the smirk on his features. "I thought we'd agreed that's the one place I'm in charge."

"Caiman. Super Soldier. Warrior. In charge. Alpha." Chaz's face pushed in between theirs. "In charge."

Elan should have been as frustrated as Danny; she knew. But the way his features twisted into the same sort of frustration she'd seen on her own father's face once when he'd drawn the short straw and been the one left behind in charge of a nursery of Exceptionals.

Perhaps she should have scolded Chaz for interrupting, or apologized to Danny, but none of that happened. Laughter bubbled to the surface despite her fight to keep it tamped way down. First, a scoff, then a bursting guffaw.

Before she knew it, she was bent over laughing so hard her stomach hurt, causing her flesh to thicken in response to the twinge of muscles she'd so rarely used.

Danny stared at her wide-eyed for several minutes. After a minute, the corner of his lip twitched, then the other. Low laughter emerged until he'd joined her in the full throes of laughter.

Chaz dropped to the floor, poised under Elan, studying her intently. His brows knit together, head tilted to the side. "Caiman hurt?"

That sent Danny into another fit of laughter, and Elan had to re-double her efforts to collect herself. "No," she tried to assure Chaz even as she struggled to regain her breath. "I'm not injured. Not even a little right now."

Danny managed to gain some sort of hold on his laughter, little bursts of a chuckle emerging every few seconds. "There is something wrong if he thinks your laughter is caused by pain."

"Yes, well." Elan let out a few more bursts of her snickers as she slowly regained composure. "He's never known what I look like in pain, except for my skin. Of course, he's definitely never seen me laugh before. Not many people have."

"Too bad. You're even more gorgeous when you do." Danny wrinkled his nose. "Oh, my cheese-o-meter went off on that one."

"Yeah. You think?" Elan took his hands. "I was thinking. I know you don't want to leave your family. What if we ask if Ethan and Ilana will move down one room? Or take ours, and we take theirs? The room next to theirs is that Inessa woman, and she's spent all her time with the Chief anyhow. Plus, there's another room across the hall. Either way, maybe we can merge two rooms somehow instead of moving."

"Laughter and compromise? I'm gonna have to write this day in the record books." Danny smirked.

"Smart ass." Elan swatted his arm. The laughter faded in an instant, her hackles rising with a sense of danger. Damn her happiness, it had thrown off her senses.

No, Chaz had flipped to attention as well. His teeth bared to reveal razor-sharp fangs. A low growl rumbled through the hall.

"Elan?"

Elan held up her hand to Danny, eying down the corridor. "Chaz. Pass auf."

"Stop," Danny chided. "He's not a—"

"Shh." Elan tilted her head, trying to make sense of the rising hum of the tech around them. "Such!"

At her command to search, Chaz raced away from them too fast to be seen. In three seconds flat, he returned to her side, poised to attack. "Angry one."

"Well, that could be anyone," Elan muttered under her breath.

"What's going on?" Danny spoke quietly.

"My spidey-sense tingled." Elan could have cursed her continued clinging to the humor of earlier. Then again, they were in their own home. She should be allowed to have some level of relaxation from duty. "Chaz sensed it too, or I would have passed it off as overcompensating for my laughter."

"Ya got issues."

"I'll never argue with that—shit. Is that your dad?" Elan blinked as the lights went out along the corridor. She braced her arm across Danny as her eyes adjusted to the dark. "It is."

"Dad?" Danny called out into the darkness beside her.

The lights over their head clicked back on. Elan had to blink against the flash of blindness. The growl beside her let her know Chaz had to do the same.

"Dad, what are you doing?" Danny pushed Elan's arm down.

"The bastard killed her. Again. I'm going to return the favor." Warren's face twisted with fury as he glared at Elan. "Get the fuck away from her, Danny. Their whole family is poisoned by Steele. She is probably the one that brought it all on us."

"What? Are ya crazy? It's Elan, Dad."

"I know exactly who it is." Warren's hand slammed against the wall. A burst of energy shot through the corridor. A panel right near Elan burst open with a surge of electricity so harsh she flew backwards.

Her skin thickened, but not in time to block the rush of electricity through her system.

"Fuck! Dad, what the hell?" Danny's features appeared over her, twisted in concern. "You okay, babe?"

"Buzzing, and not in a good way," she muttered.

A door down the hall hissed open, another explosion sounded, and a feral yell.

"Fuck me," Elan muttered. "Chaz, *fass*."

A light brush of wind that blew her hair in her face was the only indication Chaz had listened. A clamor of noise rang through the hall. Elan pushed to sit, grateful for Danny's help as her body continued to fight off the burst of electricity. By the time they rose, the lights were still out, but there was no missing the white bundle cocooned from the ceiling.

Elan sighed. "Pass auf."

"Elan? What just happened?" Danny rubbed her arm.

"I don't think you want to know, Jimmy?" Elan moved forward, stretching out the last of the shakes with each step. "You okay in there?"

"My head." James grunted response came out over the crackle of electricity. "Fuck. Anne? Anne, tell me he didn't get you."

"I." Annie's voice was faint. "Don't know. What happened?"

Elan frowned. "Chaos. What else?"

"Warren." James growled.

"Out for the count," Elan assured him. A few seconds later, the systems appeared to reset themselves, and alarms blared through the halls. Elan pressed her hands over her ears at the cacophonous noise.

Outside the door, Danny stared at the tightly wrapped comforter hanging from the ceiling, only a foot with a fancy shoe poked out near the top. "Dad?"

"Inessa?" Chance's voice, rich with concern, poured over her like a soothing bubble bath. "Are you okay?"

That's when she realized she was lying curled on a very cold floor in the corner of a room dark as midnight. A shudder coursed through her as panic seized her heart tight in its vice. Her throat closed off; screams filled her ears. Explosions. Bright red panic filled her vision, laced with oily black streaks of death.

"Inessa." Chance's voice yelled over the noises that might just have been in her head. Strong arms wrapped around her. "I've got you."

The panic eased enough at his touch that she found herself able to gulp in a deep gasp of air. The lights flickered back on, sirens blaring throughout the complex. Inessa gulped down air and made an ineffective attempt at pushing him. "Go. Be Chief."

"Talisa can handle this one. I'm not going anywhere until I know you're all right." He kept his arms tight around her. With a few movements, she found herself secure on his lap. "I know a panic attack when I see it. We're no stranger to them around here."

A tremor passed through her again and pillowed her head against his chest in an effort to hide her embarrassment. "It will pass."

"Of course it will. I'm still not going anywhere."

Once the sirens stopped their blaring, Inessa's ears rang with the blessed quiet. She kept her eyes shut so she might keep everything away for a while longer. Last thing she needed right then was to see whatever chaos was going on outside the room they were in.

"What was it? Can you tell me?"

"Same as before. New York, the battle, death everywhere."

His hand smoothed along her back gently, soothing her easily with a touch. "It started before that though. The lights going out may have triggered it to take you back to New York, but you started panicking before that."

"I did?" Inessa tried to focus past the immediate memory of terror. Before that they'd been where? The skills lab, with Neil and Charlotte. Charlotte told her they were related, more than related, there was a mother-daughter relationship.

Inessa had soothed the young woman, but as soon as they'd left, the truth had again reared its ugly head. No matter what Charlotte said, there was no connection. No connections at all.

Her breath caught in her throat again. "Oh."

"What is it, Nessa?"

She lifted her gaze to Chance's, studying his kind eyes quietly. This man hadn't doubted Charlotte, would he doubt her? "I'm really confused. I'm not—I can't be—it's just not possible. I can't be Charlotte's mother. I'm not connected to anyone."

"I don't know about that." Chance brushed a tear from her cheek. "I know we've only known each other a couple of days, but I think we're pretty connected already. You heard Charlotte; she sees our connection too."

"I don't." Not that she wanted any connections, anyhow. After what had happened during the war, she couldn't bear it. Her stomach churned violently, her hands shook so hard, she clenched them tight. Her lungs constricted until breathing became laborious.

"Talk to me. Breathe, and talk to me."

She stared at the beads around his neck rather than meet his eyes. "No one is connected with me. No one has been for a long time."

"Was it always like that? Or did you used to see connections to yourself?"

"I don't remember."

"I think you're lying." Chance tucked a finger under her chin to lift her gaze to his. "Tell me. What happened?"

"The same thing that happened to everyone. I have no more reason to be upset than anyone else. It's selfish."

"Please. I want to understand. Explain it to me."

In order to explain, she would have to go back there. Just the idea of it made her sick. How could she ever go back there? See it all again?

"I'm right here. I'm not going anywhere. No one should have to carry whatever it is you're carrying by themselves. Please, help me understand. Help me to help you."

She dug into the reserves of her experience to put on a stage smile, despite the burning in her eyes from suppressed tears. "I'm the one that makes others feel better. I can handle anything."

"Even you need a break. You need release as much as any person." His fingers brushed a lock of hair from her cheek. "I want to help you."

"You don't need to fix everything, Chief." Her voice cracked in an embarrassing fracture in her wall. Despite her protests, the memories bubbled to the surface.

"No, I don't. I even can't. But this I *want* to do. For you."

The kindness and understanding radiating from him poked a big hole in the dam she'd built so the grief burst forward. Every freed emotion exploded into a sob she couldn't contain. "I used to. You're right. I used to."

"Have the connections?"

She nodded rapidly, trying to stop acting like a blubbering fool. "Yes. I tried to explain it to you earlier. I just don't like talking about it."

He kissed her gently, the simple action soothing some of the tremors. What that didn't soothe, his constant reassuring touch aided further. Warm hands rubbed along her cold arms. "The attack on the city?"

"I could see so many people dying. Slow deaths, instant deaths. Dark lines of black streaking across the pure reds of panic. Each light as it faded into nothing." She lowered her gaze as tears broke free. To try to keep them at bay, she chewed on her bottom lip. The pain made it easier. "Those hurt, broke my heart, gave me nightmares—but they were nothing."

Somehow his fingers worked their way into her fisted hands. Thumbs soothed along the tense palms, sending soothing waves along her arms. "I can't begin to imagine what that was like for you."

"Those connections Charlotte can see, that I can see in others, they are so beautiful. Have you ever seen them? You should ask Lucas to help you see them. Indescribable beauty."

"Maybe I'll ask."

"Until you watch them die." The tears she'd fought so hard against spilled over like lava on her cheeks. "I could physically feel them weaken. I had to watch them shrivel to nothing as I lost someone I loved. Someone that was family to me. They wilted like flowers, so many of them just disappeared into the rubble."

She pulled away from the comfort of his hold. Before he could catch her, she was on her feet. She crossed the room to where the false window projected an image of acres of farmland swaying in an invisible breeze.

The memories flowed back like it was yesterday. Her hand extended to the non-existent one she saw only in her memory. When she realized she was reaching for a ghost, her fingers curled against empty air.

"The whole time I lay pinned under that beam, unable to help one soul. I couldn't even help Jacques. He was two feet away from me, and I couldn't help him."

"That's not your fault."

Inessa snorted. "Tell yourself that, Chief. You, who blames yourself for everyone else's death. You, who spends hours in meditation atoning for the non-existent sin of being unable to protect all of your people."

"Inessa."

"He was my partner, Chance. We practiced every day for two months for that ballet. We had to be connected for us to be able to partner in a way that had critics raving and audiences pouring in. And we were. Deeply." She clutched her hands to her chest when her heart reached out again as if to find him. For a moment she could still sense him there.

Crossing the memory into reality, Chance's arms wrapped around her.

"I could reach out with my hand and barely touch his fingers." Again, she stretched toward the memory. "But it didn't help. I could see him work through anger and denial, bargaining, hear him pleading with God in four languages. The whole time the tie that bound us grew weaker. I could see him, feel him die. After the dust settled all of my connections were gone beneath the rubble. I'd lost them all to the battle, to that moment when Jacques died. Everyone I loved was dead."

"They are still there," his tone remained quiet, but warm. The gentle brush of his breath across her neck kept her rooted in reality. "There's one right here if only you were willing to see it."

"I don't think I am."

"Hey." He turned her to face him. A soft smile crossed his lips, tears of understanding sparkled in his eyes. "I know the thought of losing them again is hard, but you can't give up on love, on life. Life is full of connections."

"It's not giving up. It's easier this way. When I'm not connected, I can help others easier."

"But you are already connected. Refusing to see it doesn't make it less true, and it won't make it any easier on you if you lose someone you love again. Or someone that's connected to you."

She stared at their joined hands, unable to meet his gaze again without her own tears spilling forth.

"Look now, right now. Between us. Can you see it there? I know it's there. I feel it." Chance lifted her hand so it settled right over his heart. "Right here."

"Why do I need to see it? Why do I have to open myself to such pain again?"

"Do you really want to live the rest of your life missing a piece of yourself? That's what you're doing. You're leaving a part of who you are behind because it might hurt you."

Through the haze of tears blurring her vision, something glimmered into view. She blinked a few times in surprise, certain it was her own tears that caused it. Yet, it remained there after she'd blinked away the tears. Her lips trembled when she recognized the shimmering, colorful thread for what it was. "I see it."

"Is it strong?"

"No. Not yet."

"Then I guess we'll have to build on it." He pulled her close and captured her lips in a slow kiss.

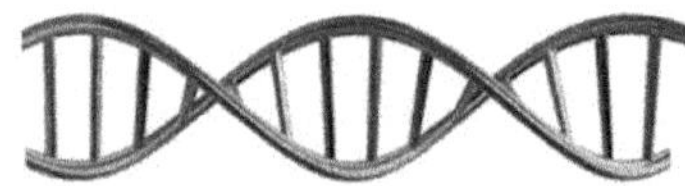

Danny stood in the hallway staring up at the comforter that now hung from the ceiling. He hadn't really talked to his parents at length since Annie's funeral. While he understood they were grieving the loss of Annie, the man he just saw in the hallway was out of control. Why the hell did he want to kill James?

He folded his arms across his chest as he continued to stare up at his father's current restraints. "What the damn hell just happened? He's lost his damn mind. I ought to kick his ass for what he said about you and your family babe."

Elan huffed out a breath blinking her eyes a few times. "I don't know what's going on with him, but he was out for blood."

Chaz for his part stood below the cocooned Warren and occasionally reached up to swat at it.

"He thinks James did something to me to make me want to stay with him." Annie's voice sounded a little stronger but not back to herself.

"That's all well and good sis but that sounded like a rampage against their whole family." Danny shook his head. "Don't make no damn sense."

"He's lost his mind Danny. Mom isn't much better. Ask Ethan. It was weird when she came by to visit." Annie sighed, "I don't know what to do but I'm not going with him."

"Mom too? Damn she's the rational one." Danny blew out a breath.

"Ethan said the same thing." Annie's voice evened out.

"Well if Ethan sees something is wrong…. wait a damn minute! What the fuck?" Danny walked into James room and looked around. "How the hell am I having a conversation with my sister?"

James shifted the laptop for Danny to see the screen. "Anne, your brother looks like he's going to throw up."

"Well it's not like we've had a chance to tell him or your sister anything yet. Hell your family is so big I can't remember who knows and who doesn't." Annie's image on the screen smirked.

"Babe!" Danny called into the hallway. "Why does your brother have a program that acts like my sister? This is weird bro. I mean like really weird."

"What are you talking about?" Elan moved into the room just enough to see the screen. After a minute, she stared at her brother. Her eyes grew wide. "That's why you didn't have a fucking reaction. She's really in there? She's in the fucking computer."

"Something like that." James nodded. "Mom and Dad are working on making her a body so that she can transfer back. Warren won't get it through his head that she's not a possession."

"So wait Dad's pissed because James has your laptop?" Danny took a moment to glance into the hallway. "Chaz, stop punching him in the head."

Elan chuckled low. At his look she held up her hands. "What? Your dad just tried to kill me and now he's a stuffed cat toy."

Danny pinched the bridge of his nose as he muttered. "I don't know how this living arrangement is going to work."

"Living arrangement?" James's eyebrow quirked up.

"Chaz is moving in with us." Danny said with a tight smile.

"Aren't all the units on this side the same size?" Annie asked with a skeptical look on her face.

"Yeah, we talked about moving into the new section that has two bedrooms." Danny pulled Elan close and dropped a kiss on the top of her head. "Elan mentioned seeing if Ethan and Ilana minded moving so we could convert one of her rooms but with everything…. Chaz, stop."

Elan looked out into the hallway again. "Chaz Platz!"

"Wait did she say Warren is a cat toy?" Curiosity ran through Annie's voice. "Could your parents hurry up and fix me? I'm missing too much."

"Anne." James chided with a smirk on his face. "We will be together soon."

"I know." She sighed. "Hey Danny, take my unit. It's between you and Ethan. Convert it. Not like I had a lot in there."

"You sure sis? Where are you going to live when we get you back?" Danny focused on the laptop in an attempt to ignore Chaz running up and down the hallway again. He loved his wife and he could do this for her. For them.

"With me." James interjected. "We were talking about it before Warren went bat-shit again."

Annie nodded, "I don't want to go back to that room. I mean there is nothing wrong with it I'd just rather be with James."

"Thanks sis. We appreciate it." Danny signed and looked at the cocoon now starting to swing outside the room. "I think he's waking up. He's going to be even more pissed."

"James why don't you take me down to the lab to see how your parents are doing. Being near him right now makes me nervous. I can't retaliate if needed and that jolt he gave me hurt like a bitch." A deep V etched into Annie's forehead.

"He's not going to be happy with any of us sis." Danny rubbed Elan's shoulders, "He may be my father, but no one is going to hurt my wife."

"What in the world is going on out here?" Abby's voice filled the hallway. "Warren? Warren who did this to you?"

Danny stepped back into the hallway. "Mom he attacked us. He tried to kill James and Elan."

"Your father is angry and rightfully so Daniel. That family…"

Danny grabbed his mother's shoulders and shook them. "Mom do you hear yourself? You are talking about your best friend's kids. We all grew up together. You were in each other's weddings. I'm pretty sure with the way you guys used to talk you slept with Tal, but I have no proof."

"Danny eww…." Elan smacked his shoulder.

"That family," Abby continued, "They stole your sister from us and now they are stealing my boys."

"Stole us? We're adult and can make up our own damn minds. Elan is my wife. James is helping Annie. You and Dad are the ones that are alienating everyone."

The cocoon shook violently from the ceiling but stayed attached. Whatever Chaz had used proved to be effective.

162

"Your father and I were kept in the dark about your sister's real fate." Abby lifted her chin in defiance.

"Quit your bitchin'. Neither of ya thought that I might want to know that my baby sister was trapped in a damn computer. Neither of ya did a damn thing when Elan was gone. Ya know who checked on me? Ethan. James. Lucas. Charlotte. Not my parents. I'm not whining about it I'm just statin' fact." Danny's fists rolled up slowly into tight clenched fists.

"Daniel." Abby pursed her lips into a frown. "We were busy with your sister."

"Right and they were busy trying to figure out if it could even be done before they got anyone's hopes up." He pointed towards the still swinging cocoon. "Tell your husband to stay the fuck away from my family. He's lucky I don't have Chance lock him up for attacking us."

Elan laid her hand on Danny's arm "Babe…"

"I'm serious. He needs to leave Annie and James alone and he needs to leave us alone." Danny wrapped his arm around Elan and pulled her close again. "Annie's given us her unit so we will be moving some stuff into it for Chaz. We have things to do."

"Annie's unit. You can't have that." Abby shuddered.

"Annie gave it to us."

"You can't have it."

Danny let go of Elan and gabbed Abby's shoulders. "Do you hear yourself Mom? Seriously?" He shook his head. "I can't do this. Chaz. Hier." He walked down the hallway without another word leaving Warren hanging from the ceiling.

Chance once again stood in the middle of the conference room. This time he pinched the bridge of his nose in hopes of warding off the developing headache he felt creeping in behind his eyes. A tight smile tugged at the corners of his mouth at Inessa's hand on his arm.

"What's the point in all of this Chance? You're just going to side with them anyway?" Warren snapped from his spot at the table.

"After the stunt you pulled yesterday Warren my patience is thin. I understand you are hurt and upset but you attacked members of this tribe. You are damn lucky no one was seriously injured." The tone of Chance's voice left little doubt that he meant business.

"You saw what they did to him" Abby interjected. "They had him tied up and stuck to the ceiling and were hitting him like a piñata."

Chance did his best not to chuckle at the memory of how they had found Warren when Abby came to get him for help. "I get it. You are upset. But he could have seriously injured Elan and James and he nearly killed Annie. Technically Warren should have been tossed in one of the containment cells but we've allowed a little bit of leeway considering the nature of the situation."

"We're allowed to be hurt and angry. They stole our children from us." Abby glared across the table.

"You have every right to feel what you feel, but this is getting out of hand. All of a sudden you both hate our entire family because we followed Annie's wishes." Roark at least made an attempt to have a civil conversation with their friends.

"You had no right to make that decision." Warren's eye narrowed with his fists clenched on the table.

"I have every right to make decisions for myself." Annie glared from the computer screen.

"You are our daughter." Warren leaned forward on the table.

"I am my own person. If I wanted to delete myself that would be my choice." The computer screen flickered before it settled back to normal again.

"Anne…" James leaned forward; concern etched his face.

"I'm okay. Warren did some damage to the laptop. We just need to keep an eye on the fan, maybe scrounge up another one to fix it." Annie reassured him. "Mom you really have to stop using Warren for your emotional baseline. You are not acting like yourself. The two of you have already done a pretty good job of alienating two of your children. And Ethan is already on the fence after the way you acted the other day when he was visiting me."

"I can't believe you would say something like that. Are you just trying to be cruel?" A sob ripped through Abby's chest.

"Damn it Mom! Warren almost killed me." Annie yelled from the computer. The volume increased despite no one touching any buttons.

"I thought you were gone for good." Warren's voice dropped to just above a whisper. "I wasn't searching for anything. Just making sure the laptop was still functional and you were all right and there was no degradation. Then you were just gone. I couldn't sense you at all. You were gone and I never got to make things right."

"And trying to barbeque Elan and James seemed like the best way to make it right? Do you understand how much pain you caused? James and Elan heal but my soul still aches. Not to mention you yanking James and I out of a shared vision and the near migraine you gave both of us." Annie glared in Warren's direction.

Chance straightened up at Annie's statement. "Shared vision?"

"Yes Chief. Initially I thought it was the end but the Spirits were gracious enough to give us some time together." A brief smile graced Annie's face on the screen.

"But what happened?" Abby asked with a shuddering breath.

"That's between James and I." The smile on Annie's face disappeared.

"We have a right to know." The anger that had drained from Warren's voice slammed back into it.

"Why the hell would you think you have a right to know what James and I talked about?" Now Annie looked confused.

"Because I am your father." Warren slapped his hands down on the table as he shot to his feet.

"Maybe if you fucking acted like it we wouldn't be having this conversation." Annie snapped back.

The headache spread to the base of his skull. Chance squeezed his eyes shut tight.

"Chance" The concern in Inessa's voice made him open his eyes.

"I'll be fine." He managed a weak smile down at the woman that had quickly become a central part of his life. "Let's get back to the reason we are here. I believe Tal and Roark have an update for us."

"You would be just as upset if it…" Warren started again.

"We need to focus on getting Annie back right now," Talisa interrupted. "Warren we are close to needing your help with the pod we brought back. Can we count on you to assist us in bringing your daughter back?"

The man standing across the room from them deflated like a balloon as he fell back into his chair. "Of course. What kind of monster to do think I am?"

"All right then. Warren why don't you coordinate with Tal and Roark on the pod and getting things set for Annie's return to a physical body. We can meet again in a couple days if you would like as well." Chance folded his arms across his chest hoping this would be the end of this meeting and he could deal with the pain in his head.

"James give it to them." Annie looked pensive on the screen.

"Anne are you sure?" James leaned forward to make eye contact with her on the screen.

"Positive." She paused while James slid a thumb drive across the table. "Maybe this will help you understand where I'm coming from. I have over 20 years of memories that were implanted in my head. They aren't all perfect. We were by no means the perfect family. My father was stern when he needed to be but he never raised his voice. He certainly never screamed at us to the point of scaring me where I thought he might physically hurt me. Above all else, he never used his gifts to harm his best friends or his daughter-in-law."

"Annie what is this?" Abby leaned forward and picked up the drive.

"It's my memories. They come across more like home movies."

Chance looked between each end of the table. Warren remained silent with Annie's gift and explanation. "Tal keep me updated on your progress. I'm going to take something for this headache."

"I will, Sani."

"Talisa, stop." Abby tugged her arm free from Talisa's hand. "I don't want to talk to you."

Talisa ignored the way Warren snapped to attention. She'd merely been pulling her friend to the side of the room in hopes of a quiet conversation, but the protest had poked the bear. Rather than make the man get up off his seat, she raised her hands in surrender, not that she intended to do anything of the sort.

"Abigail," Talisa spoke quiet enough to keep under the current of low conversation in the room. At a mental request to her husband, Roark raised the tone of his voice in his conversation with James and Inessa, who kept casting a concerned glance toward the door Chance had disappeared behind. "I am still the one remaining matriarch of this tribe and can force your husband behind bars to separate the two of you if I need to."

"I'm not Lenape. Your position means nothing to me, you deceptive, pushy bitch."

"Well, I never will deny being a bitch." Tal sighed. "I didn't want to do this Abby, I promise."

"Do what?"

Tal did her best not to cringe at the mere idea of what she was doing. Considering how the matter had escalated, the safety of the entire tribe was at stake. Without allowing herself another thought on it, she touched on her new gift of telepathy to breach her friends mind. The moment she found the source of Abby's emotional connection to Warren, Tal created a shield of sorts between the two. Abby would still be able to sense Warren, but she'd be able to rely on her own emotional core again.

Abby blinked rapidly a few times, a flash of fury crossing her features before the tension in her shoulders sagged. Her hand reached for Tal's forearm as she swayed a little. "Woah."

"Easy." Tal set her hand on Abby's, letting her friend readjust. "She's fine, Warren. Just a little tired."

Warren slowed his approach, but still eyed Tal suspiciously. "What did you do to her?"

"Nothing," Abby said quietly. She lifted her gaze to meet Tal's, the fury of their past few meetings long gone. After a small nod, she turned to her husband. "Tal didn't do anything. I just got lightheaded for a second."

Warren's features mellowed slightly, which Tal knew thanks to her current position in Abby's mind. He frowned but didn't protest.

"I was just going to ask Abby to help me with a few equations Roark and I were struggling with." A blatant lie, Tal knew Abby could probably guess as much. Tal and Roark rarely struggled too hard when they worked on a problem together.

She hoped Abby would go along with the ploy, after all she had her reasons.

"I thought you could come with me, Warren." Roark approached the group. He didn't trust Warren one bit, but he knew Tal had her reasons, which she'd expounded to him quite thoroughly the day before, after the incident with James and Annie. "Take a look at the pod we're hoping to convert. We've taken the person out of it and put them in a medically induced coma so you could have access."

Warren hesitated.

"You said you wanted to help," Tal reminded him a gentle tone. "This is for Annie. This is for your family."

"Fine. Abby, why don't you come with me?" Warren held out his hand.

"I'd like to see the formula, honestly." Abby did take his hand, but thankfully didn't back down. "I'll understand it better than what you're doing. Plus, it's our daughter's life I'll be looking at, while you're preparing to help bring it about."

"Great." Tal pulled Abby along behind her. "We'll be in the lab. You boys have fun."

Abby followed along behind her, not saying a word for several minutes. Once they entered the quiet of the lab, she stopped short. "I don't know if I should be really pissed at you or really grateful right now."

"Don't worry, I'm pissed enough at myself. I sure never wanted to do something like that against someone's will, but you both were out of control, and about to lose all of your kids." Tal set her hands on Abby's shoulders. "You're my best friend, Abby. You thought I was out to take your children away from you. Me, Abby."

Abby's brows pinched together; tears sparkled in her eyes. "What is going on?"

170

"A whole lot of fucked up nonsense. What else would it be in our lives?"

A short laugh slipped out of Abby. "That's encouraging."

"It's not, but do you know what is?"

"What?"

"Somehow, we always manage to dig our way out of the fucked-up nonsense."

Inessa stood in the open air of the neglected suburban neighborhood that rested above the underground tunnels. A light breeze blew across her face, and she turned toward it. Her eyes closed, she took in the quietness of the moment, and every bit of sun she could allow to soak in.

Though no sound hit her ears, the sensation that someone approached crept into her awareness. Of course, it could be any number of the guards that patrolled the area in regular course, but she thought it could be the person she actually asked to join her.

She opened her eyes to take a peek behind her and smiled at the approaching form. "Chance. I'm glad you came."

"Why wouldn't I?"

"Some burden of responsibility that you've lugged on your back and in your soul for ages."

"Ha ha."

"I'm not kidding." Inessa brushed her fingers along his forehead where the dark waves of a headache still burgeoned against his usual calming tones. "Did you know there is such a thing as too much grounding?"

"I did."

"Did you ever stop to think that in order to cope, you've been doing just that. Grounding at every turn, when you already live within the earth?" She slipped her hand along his arm to take his hand. "Come with me."

"Is this more of your prescription?" A teasing light tone edged into his words. "Because we don't have to be out in the open for that."

Inessa laughed. "No, we don't, but it can make it more fun in the right light. Still, that isn't why I asked you to come up into the open air. Here, she's right back here."

"What? Who?" Chance stopped short once they rounded a small house. Inside the garage stood the horse she'd arrived on, well cared for with hay and feed. A makeshift stall had been created, not that she needed the encouragement to remain. "Oh."

"I know there are a few horses scattered around here, but she is a good one, Shiksa is. She carried me across the country to find this place. I think she's bored here in this garage all day." Inessa stroked the horse's soft nose. "And you need to run for a bit, remember what freedom is."

"Inessa, the gesture is kind, but—"

"Nope. No arguments. I checked with Talisa, and she agrees. She said something about how now that she's back you don't need to be everything all the time anymore. Something about a matriarchal society and how you might be the girliest man she's known, but you still don't qualify." She smiled when he chuckled low under his breath. "I was right, she is hot and funny to boot. If we ever cross paths in your fantasies or dreams, I want to hear about it."

Warm lips pressed to the crook of her neck. "Now you're teasing."

"A little." Inessa turned to face him. "Now go. Have fun, run free for a while."

"I can't."

"You can."

"We don't know what's out there." He frowned, his gaze falling on Shiksa again. "It isn't safe."

"You'll receive plenty of warning if something happens. Trust me."

"I do." He said the statement emphatically, and it seemed instinctive. His aura showed he meant every word. Still, he hesitated.

"Go. I'll be here when you get back." Inessa pushed him to the horse until he swung up onto Shiksa's back. "Remember, if just for a little while, what it's like to be free."

He leaned down long enough to grant her a quick kiss before he urged the horse out into the open. Though he hesitated to look back at the neighborhood, Shiksa took off before he could change his mind.

Inessa smiled at the way his whole being lightened within moments. "You have him?"

"I am the Guardian," a young girl said simply from a nearby tree, her wings extended to catch the breeze.

"He's not the only one that needs to lighten up around here, Ilana."

"War changes people, Inessa." Without another word, Ilana flew into the air. In moments she'd disappeared into the low cloud cover that lingered even in the bright sun.

For several minutes, Inessa stood in silence until Chance's aura was faded enough to barely be seen. This time when she sensed someone approaching, she knew it was someone uninvited, but not unwelcome. "Charlotte."

"That was good of you. What you did for him."

"He is a good man. He deserves it. Hell, everyone does after what we've been through." Inessa turned to face the young woman that had claimed to be her daughter.

Charlotte clenched her hands together, her aura a swirling mass of joy, worry, and indecision. Though her gaze remained on the distant point where Chance was riding free, somehow her attention also seemed focused on Inessa. "I was just wondering…"

"Charlotte." Inessa took Charlotte's hands in hers. "You are a brilliant, caring young woman. You model your parents and Chance very well."

"And you," Charlotte offered with a bit of hope brightening her aura.

"I need time. This is a lot to process for anyone." Inessa brushed a stray lock from Charlotte's features. "I'm human."

"You're an Exceptional." Charlotte's brow puckered. "We all are."

"Yes, but I am also human. I was raised human. By human parents. When my gift came, it didn't change my physical appearance like some. Once I got used to the constant acid trip, I was able to be human, and nothing more. I didn't fight in the war; I didn't grow up knowing that these crazy things could be possible."

"But they are. This is the truth. I see the connection."

"A connection I am just learning to see again. I haven't seen my own in a long time." Inessa squeezed Charlotte's hand in her own. "In one day, my world blew up, everyone's did. I took a long time to heal, and then knew I had to find a place I could belong again."

"And you have?"

"I think so, but I still need time." Inessa looked down between them to try to see the thread Charlotte spoke of. Still, her heart blocked what might have been a beautiful connection. "In a few short days I've found this compound and gotten involved in a family that has lived the impossible for so long they don't remember what normal is any longer."

"I don't know what that means."

"I know." Inessa lifted her gaze to meet Charlotte's again. "You are a beautiful young woman, inside and out. The sort that I would be proud to call a daughter, if I understood any of this. I have never had a child; I don't even know how this is possible as I'd never met your family before the battle in the city."

"The registry—"

"Charlotte. I know you are excited and hope for nothing else than for me to embrace you as my child, but I need you to hear me now." Inessa took a deep breath. "I, me, I don't understand any of this. I have never lived with the impossible, and you have from the day you were born. I need time to process, to understand all of this."

"So—you don't want me to bother you?"

"I want you to give me time to process. I am happy to know you, to be your friend, and to get to know you beyond what your aura shows me. I'm not asking you to avoid me, nor am I asking you to give up hope. I'm just asking for you to let this measly human figure out how to live the impossible."

"I think I can do that." Charlotte smiled. "As long as you don't say that the connection isn't there. I'm getting tired of people telling me I'm wrong all the time."

"I'm not saying it's not, I'm just saying I haven't seen my own in a long time, and it's going to take some time for me to heal enough to see them."

"Okay."

"Good."

"And Inessa?"

"What?"

"You are no measly human."

Inessa chuckled. "I feel like it around here."

"No. You're not. Even if you weren't an Exceptional, what you do for Popsicle makes you pretty damned amazing."

"Well, that part is easy. He's pretty damned amazing."

"I'm glad you at least see that."

"It would be hard to miss."

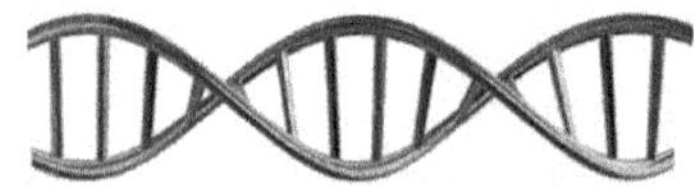

Roark stood back a distance from the man he'd once called his best friend. Nowadays he'd just call him bat-crap crazy. He hoped Talisa had better luck with Abby than he could hope to have with Warren. The man may have been looking over the pod as promised, but his running commentary was nuts.

"Fucking mess. All of it. Turn our kids against us. Destroy our daughter. Could have fixed her if they didn't waste time with these damn pods." Warren growled as he slammed his hand down on the top of the pod.

"Easy Warren. I know you're pissed but don't take it out on the equipment. We need that to bring Annie back." Roark laid his hand on his friend's shoulder.

Warren shook off the hand in one quick snap. "What the hell do you know? Knocking on the top isn't going to destroy it, for fuck's sake. Knocking in James' face though—that may help the situation. Why don't I give that a try?"

Roark pinched the bridge of his nose. How he'd love to unleash his complete frustration on his friend. Release his inner animal. Instead, he reined it in. "Why don't we focus on the real issue right now? We need to outfit this pod so that we can bring your daughter back. We're running out of time here."

"We wouldn't be running out of time if you had come straight back and not wasted time with these pods. I wouldn't have had to mourn my daughter, comfort my distraught wife, and lose all of my children to your traitorous family."

"Jesus, Warren do you even hear yourself? I mean seriously. Listen to what you're saying. We are your best friends and have been for years. We were captured and tortured for the last year by that maniac. We came home to a shit storm. The last thing we ever wanted was for you to lose your daughter or your family."

"Well that's what fucking happened." A vein pulsed in Warren's forehead.

"Did you ever think that the way you are acting might have something to do with it?" Roark took a few steps back.

"The way I'm acting?" Warren spun on Roark, "You and your family caused this. I have every right to feel the way I do."

"Steele caused this. This damn war caused this, but you can't blame us just because you don't like how things turned out. You pissed off Danny by attacking Elan. You scared Annie by acting like this."

"You son-of-a-bitch. I'm not going to let you all drag my family down. My own daughter is calling me by my first name." Warren seethed in front of him, fists clenched at his sides.

"Because you scared her. Come on man, think about it. Did you watch the memories she gave you? Don't you want the chance to have a relationship with her?" Roark folded his arms across his chest. There had to be a way to get through to him.

"What do you know? You two just popped out a football team of kids and left." The other man leaned on a nearby table with his clenched fists.

"Yeah cause Tal and I wanted to be practically burned alive by a bomb and forced to spend the last year in hell." Perhaps there was no getting through to him. If he could get his help actually making the adjustments they needed to the pod, he would be happy. Anything else would have to come after that.

"We've been in hell here so don't make it sound like you had it harder."

"I know I keep saying this, but do you hear yourself? I spent the last year behind a glass wall where I could see my wife but never touch her. Separated from our children and our friends. You are the one alienating your friends and family. Not me. I get that you are angry but you need to show it some other way. You keep this up you are going to destroy your relationship with Abby."

"You have no idea what you are talking about." Warren lunged at Roark with a right hook that missed completely in his anger.

Roark sidestepped easily and swung his arm around the other man's neck. He locked him in a choke hold just tight enough to keep him in place but not enough to knock him out. "Warren calm the hell down. You have two choices right now."

"What?" Warren growled as he struggled against Roark's grip.

"I knock your ass out and when you wake up it will be in the containment cell next to Lucy. Or two, you cut this shit out and help us bring your daughter back, so that if you extract your head from your ass, you might salvage your family." Roark's grip tightened around Warren's neck. "Up to you. But I'm not going to fight you. Annie has limited time left for us to save her."

"Let me go." Warren growled through clenched teeth.

"Promise to behave?"

"I said I would help. I won't let her die again." Warren glared at Roark once he was released.

"Good. Let's get to work then."

"Tal, what the hell happened?" Abby leaned on the lab table. Sprawled out before her were pages of sketches and equations in Tal's sharp, precise handwriting. She scanned over them out of habit, though she knew they weren't the real reason they had separated her and Warren.

"I wish I knew. All I do know is you were so tied into Warren's emotions that it had your own emotions twisted up in knots. I've never seen you like this, not even after you first got your gift." Tal leaned back against the table next to Abby.

"I'm so sorry. I was horrid to you. The things I was saying, I can't even…"

Tal set her hand on Abby's when the words trailed off. "Stop. You don't have to apologize."

"I was so destroyed when Annie died." Abby closed her eyes, the sadness creeping up again. This time she recognized it as a normal emotion, nothing as extreme as she'd been through so recently. "I thought Warren would help me get on kilter again. He's always been a rock."

"Understandable. I do the same with Roark while I'm figuring this out." Tal tapped her forehead. "It's natural to do that."

"Except in my case it was apparently a horrible idea."

"So it seems."

"I just don't understand why."

Tal shook her head. "I don't know. Something is going on beyond all of this with Warren. I wish I knew what it was so we could fix it, but that may have to wait until we get Annie back."

"I would love if we had time for both. Warren keeps getting more and more angry." Abby wiped at her tear. With her head now mostly clear, she had a small flicker of realization. "I think the day I nearly passed out from his anger is when my own control became so muddled."

"That's a good possibility. He may be the computer guy, but he may have overloaded your circuits in this case."

"Maybe." Abby let out some of her tension with a long sigh. "I don't know how to fix things with Annie. Or Danny and Ethan for that matter."

"Why don't we start small, then?" Tal gave Abby's arm a gentle squeeze. "James, come on in with Annie."

James did as he was bid, though he didn't appear completely at ease with the situation. One eye remained on Abby while he plugged in the laptop. He stepped back a smidge, but well within range of the computer her daughter resided in.

Abby couldn't blame him and held no ill will toward him for it. She'd been awful.

Annie flickered into view on the screen. She also eyed her mother critically, her head tilted slightly. "Talisa tells James that you're feeling…better."

"I'm starting to, with a little help from my friend." Abby squeezed Tal's hand gently in thanks. When she reached toward the laptop, she noticed her hands were shaking. "Baby, I am *so* sorry."

Annie appeared to be determined to keep her anger for a few seconds, but it quickly dissipated into something more relaxed. "Really?"

"Really. I don't know what happened. There's something going on with your dad, and it threw me for a loop. We'll figure out what it is and help him."

"It's going to take a lot more than that for me to forgive or ever be okay with Warren. My entire short life was manipulated by Steele, and I won't allow it anymore. I'm not anyone's possession. Not even James'."

James made a noise that almost sounded like a real laugh. By the time Abby had glanced his way, his face sat neutral and quiet.

Abby shook her head at the oddity before turning back to Annie. "I know. I do. I'm sorry. I just want you back. All I want is for you to be safe and happy."

"Wait." James stared Abby down with intensity, but not much anger. "You believe it's really Annie now? You don't think she's a trick anymore?"

"I do. I can't say exactly what happened, except I was tied into Warren pretty tight. I did it out of pure desperation, to keep myself from losing it. He's always been my rock before." Abby swiped at a tear on her cheek. She didn't miss James' nod of understanding. "I can only apologize from now until eternity."

"You don't need to apologize that much." Annie smiled at her, with only a little hesitation in the action. "Actions will speak for themselves."

Talisa set her hand on Abby's arm, a warm, reassuring touch. "Warren is looking at the pod now. The calculations appear solid. We're closer than we were before to bringing you back. Why don't you guys relax for a while and we'll let you know when we're ready."

Annie brightened at the suggestion that they might be able to bring her back soon. "Will you come see me later, Mom?"

"Of course I will. So long as you'll have me. I still need to stop by and apologize to your brothers, but if it's okay with you and James I'll see you both later." Abby smiled at her daughter. "I do love you Annie."

"Love you too, Mom." Annie waved in the moments before James picked up her laptop.

James gave her a brief nod, carrying the laptop from the room.

The moment the door closed, Abby could no longer contain her amazement. "He loves her. I mean, he *truly* loves her."

"I know." Talisa stared after the pair. The smile she wore held a mix of sadness and pride. "They became connected extremely quick, especially for a pair only half animalistic. None of this was expected when Warren dispatched the retrieval team, that's for sure."

"I had become so accustomed to the tangled mess of James' emotions before they picked up Annie. It threw me off the first time I felt how much he cared for her. He didn't even realize it at the time."

"Roark and I told him he could push through the anger and he could be more than that."

"I was so caught up in having a daughter all of a sudden and wanting to get you guys back here I didn't take the time to see how it affected him. I'm sorry for that." Abby leaned her elbows on the table and put her head in her hands. "How much did I mess up being so tied into Warren's emotions?"

"Abby, stop!" Talisa ran her hand along Abby's back. "Everything will work out as the Spirits intended. We have to believe that."

"I'm trying to believe that. I'm worried about Warren. I don't sense it as much since you put up the block but whatever is going on with him has him so twisted and angry. It scares me." Abby looked up at her best friend, fear evident in her voice.

"We will bring Annie back and we will figure out what is going on with Warren." Talisa's attempts to soothe Abby's fear and worry were noted, but ultimately not entirely helpful.

"Annie gave us that disk with her memories. I'm afraid to watch it." Abby closed her eyes with a sigh. "What if I can't be the mother she remembers?"

"You can't." Talisa held her hand up at the gasp that escaped from Abby. "Hear me out. The memories that Steele programed were a near perfect childhood. Warren never yelled. He took what he knew about you both and gave her enough to look for you."

"I guess you're right." She pulled the hair tie out to free her curls, only to pull her hair into another messy bun. "Why don't you show me these equations so I can feel like I'm doing something productive."

Talisa pointed to the papers on the table. "This is what I've got so far. Sorry. I feel safer working with a pencil and paper still. It's hard to shake the feeling of constantly being monitored every second of every day."

Abby instinctively sent the warmth of reassurance to ease the flash of panic in her friend. "No worries. Let's just see if I'll be of any help."

Inessa walked down a random hall, music blaring in her ear buds. She hoped to find a quiet place to listen to music and forget about auras for a while. After nearly two years on her own, with only random occasional company, the constant influx of the compound was giving her a headache.

It was a headache caused by the wonderful beauty of company, but a headache nonetheless.

When she'd left her quarters, she'd been certain she could find the hot springs again, or perhaps one of the future levels of the compound Chance had dug out, but now she had a distinct feeling she was lost.

She turned in a circle in an attempt to re-align herself to where she was. There was the computer in the wall she could ask like some weird Trek throwback, but she was determined to figure it out.

On her next circle, she took notice of the auras behind some large, thick doors in front of her. She recognized them from the conference room. Roark and Warren, and they were both drawing closer. She could ask them, but she'd rather figure it out on her own.

Right before she could turn away to round the corner, something odd caught her attention. A weird flicker in Warren's aura made her stomach churn so hard she thought she'd throw up right here. The doors slid open before she could make her exit.

She clicked off her music at Roark's quizzical glance.

He paused, as did Warren. His aura was friendly, curious, but on guard. Over her or Warren, or perhaps both, she couldn't be sure. "You all right there, Inessa?"

"Yes, just fine. I wanted to take a walk, get a break from the chaos for a while." Inessa pulled the buds from her ears, doing her best to avoid looking directly at Warren.

"Can I help you find anything? It's been a while and this place has expanded since I've been here, but I'm sure Warren could help you out." Roark glanced at the man beside him. "Right?"

"No, no. It's fine, really. I can ask the computer like the guests on the Enterprise do." She grinned at her own joke, relieved that Roark chuckled as well.

"Can we go now? I thought we were saving my daughter, or is that not a priority when a pretty lady comes along?" Warren's fists clenched tight, his dark glare on her.

"I…" Inessa found herself staring again, despite her best efforts to avoid looking directly at the ball of anger. Once again, his aura blinked away, then fractured into a million pieces before reforming. It all happened in a split second, so fast she might have missed it if she hadn't been looking. She wished she hadn't been. Her stomach turned so fast, she doubled over.

"Inessa?" Roark's hand touched her shoulder. "We should get you to the clinic."

"No." Inessa forced herself to straighten. The influx had to have thrown off her senses was all. Or all the thoughts of old sci-fi TV shows had her brain in a weird place. She swallowed back the bile. "It's been a weird week for me. I'm sure it's nothing, I just need some peace and quiet."

"Are you sure?" Roark scanned her features thoroughly. His surprising calmness, despite the edge of feral that rimmed it, soothed her mind from the weird sight she was now sure she'd imagined. "I'd hate for Chance to kill me for leaving you alone if you're ill."

"Not ill. It's just been a really long week. Promise." Inessa smiled bright as possible. "Now go. Do. Save the girl. I'm going to find some quiet for a while."

"If you're gone too long, I'll send out the search party. And by search party, I mean Chance." Roark winked, but stepped back next to Warren.

"I'm fine. I need a couple hours to decompress is all." She waved them away and slipped around the corner to avoid any further chance of seeing what she was still determined had to have been her imagination. Down two more halls she finally found the doorway to what would be the new expansion.

She slipped through the door, down the stairs into the quiet. LED lights gave a soft glow to the earthen steps so she wouldn't slip, but otherwise it was calm and quiet.

When she turned the final corner to the length of hallway, she tripped. A stumble, fall, and roll brought her back to her feet. She spun fast to see what she'd tripped on, stunned to find a person there she hadn't seen on her way down the steps.

Little by little, the aura grew out of the still form, until Ilana lifted her head, her eyes blinking slowly. She rose to her feet, eyes wide. "Inessa."

"Ilana. I'm so sorry. I didn't—wait, I didn't *see* you. How is that possible?" Inessa had never known anyone to be invisible to her before.

"I am the Guardian," Ilana all but whispered. "Or, I was. Am. I don't know."

"Is everything all right?" Inessa set a hand on Ilana's arm. "What's wrong?"

"What's wrong?" Ilana laughed coldly. "There is war, people are dead, the world is forever changed. Our people are fighting to save a girl in a computer, while Warren has lost his damn mind, everything is on its head, and you ask me what's wrong?"

"Yes. Because I'm not talking about them, I'm talking about you."

"I am the Guardian."

"Ilana."

"I have to go. It's time for patrol." Ilana raced up the earthen steps, so silent Inessa wouldn't have been sure she'd left if she hadn't watched her aura disappear into the others above her.

"Well, I'm really winning today." Inessa sighed, dropping to the ground. She rested her head back against the wall, placing the ear buds in her ears.

Maybe if she took the time she'd wanted to, her head would be back on straight. Maybe then the weird shit would stop happening.

Then again, in the world of the people she'd just joined, she couldn't be sure that was possible.

Tal worked in the peaceful silence of the lab. Only the hum of the machines running experiments touched her consciousness. Stray thoughts of others tended to disrupt her in bursts and flashes, as well. Seeing as she hadn't yet fully trained herself to keep them out, it was an unsurprising, if annoying interruption to the peace she wanted to enjoy.

Still, it was good to be in relative quiet for a bit. She'd sent Abby to get some sleep, in quarters that she didn't share with her husband. Somewhere in the compound Warren toiled away at the instrument panel that would turn the cryostasis pod into a chamber where a human could be created. Roark remained with their conflicted friend to be sure his focus remained where it should.

In the silence, she knew someone stood nearby, watching her. Though they could move in utter silence, and block their mind from hers, she'd spent enough time being watched to know when someone was nearby.

"Lucas. I am not comfortable being watched." Tal set down her pencil, an uneasy sense keeping her from putting too much information from her head into the computer. Whether it was Warren's state of mind, or years of manipulation by Steele, she didn't know for sure. Perhaps it was both.

"I apologize." Lucas bowed his head in contrition. "I did not wish to interrupt you."

"Even before I had this new addition of voices in my head, I always knew when my children were near, Lucas. You can't sneak up on me, no matter how silent you can be." Tal smiled to lessen any potential sting of her words. "Also, your concern is unfounded."

"I do not believe it is. Your telepathic ability is still new, and untrained."

"I'm a fast learner."

"I would not deny such a fact." Lucas stepped closer. "But you are doing too much."

"As always." Tal took her sons hand in her own. "You are sweet to worry, but I'm fine."

"You will overwhelm yourself, taking on so much so fast. Telepathy can be taxing on the body as well as the spirit." He set his hand on hers. "You have been using it non-stop since you obtained this gift. For many things beyond the norm."

"It isn't something you can shut off."

"You can rest, though."

"I do." She frowned when his brow creased in disbelief. "I have a sanctuary. Whenever it is too much, I turn to your father. He is so familiar to me, that it is like a dip in a refreshing pool. I promise you that."

"You have not rested since you have been back here. It has been one crisis after another."

Tal fought against the grin, but finally unleashed it. "It's what made me feel at home. When have our lives not been chaos?"

"You were held captive."

"I am well aware." Tal yanked her hand free from his, lowering her gaze so as to not unleash an angry glare he didn't deserve. "I was the one there, along with your father."

"You were held captive."

A sharp, dark pain hit her in the gut. "I am aware."

"You have not—"

"I dealt with it every day for a year, Lucas." Tal lifted her gaze. "I am home."

"Home is not what it was. We are all changed, in small ways or big ways."

"I don't need a psychiatrist, son. I'll deal, I always do."

"I know you will, but you should not be doing it apart from your place of rest." Lucas stepped aside, to reveal Roark in the doorway.

"You're supposed to be with Warren. Abby is in our quarters, if he finds her…"

"Warren is being supervised. Lucas told me I was needed here." Roark stepped into the room, a quizzical glance at their son. "What's the deal, son? She looks fine."

"As do you, but neither of you has been able to spend time coming to terms with your release. You have been going non-stop since your return." Lucas smiled. "I have reserved you two slots at the spring, and I expect you to use that time well."

"Wait." Roark leaned close to Tal. "Is our son trying to help us hook up?"

"Ew." Tal wrinkled her nose. "That's a little weird, even for our family."

Lucas laughed. "I was merely trying to give you time alone without the non-stop chaos. I made no suggestions on what you do with the time. Although if I had it would have been to talk, not as you suggested."

"We've been talking non-stop since the telepathy," Tal pointed out.

"You were held captive." Lucas took several steps back toward the door. "For a year, you were held captive. You are now free."

"But are we?" Roark frowned. "We still live in hiding."

Lucas didn't respond. In fact, he was gone.

Tal met her husband's gaze, a soft sigh slipping out like a whisper on the wind. "He's got a point. It's been much easier to be busy."

"We haven't had time alone yet. Not real time alone."

"It feels like a waste of time, when there is so much to be done."

Roark glanced around the lab. "What do you have running?"

"I'm testing some cell fusion to see if that will help the cloning process."

"How long?"

Tal smiled despite her attempt to be frustrated. "A couple of hours. That little brat read my mind. I really need to get better at this."

"Want to practice on me?"

"No."

"No?"

"Nope." Tal tugged on his hand. "I'd rather go to the spring."

"Woman after my own heart."

"That's not all I'm after."

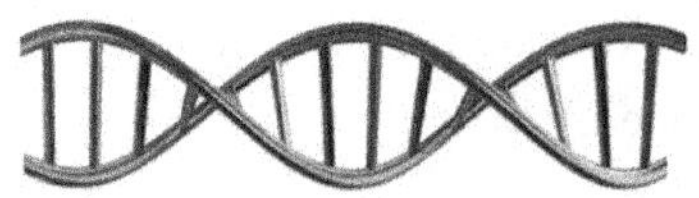

Charlotte looked over the printout in front of her taking notes on the pad next to it as she did. Occasionally she glanced across the table at Warren working on the pod that would help bring Annie back to life.

His grumbling across the room had become incessant. She didn't need to examine his aura to know the amount of anger that poured off of him. Every nut and bolt he'd adjust had been followed by a cut down or attack on her parents and the rest of the residents of the Exceptionals compound. At one point he blamed Lucy for not telling them this would happen to Annie when she first arrived.

"Did they leave you in here to babysit me?" Warren snarled in Charlotte's direction.

"You know it. Drew the short straw and everything. But since straws are hard to come by these days, we used twigs." Charlotte punctuated her statement with an eye roll. "I'm working on something for Neil actually. I thought I could pick your brain while you worked on this since you are always multi-tasking. But since you appear to still be in cantankerous-asshole mode I guess I'll pass."

"Just like the rest of your damn family. The only thing we should be worried about is bringing back Annie. We wouldn't even have to worry about that if you had just saved her in the first damn place." A clang reverberated through the room that could only have come from Warren slamming another tool down on the pod.

"Let me know when you're done with the pod so we can do that. The preliminary tests are running already to ensure everything goes smoothly. Aunt Abby helped Mom double check the calculations so the pod is the last thing we need. Forgive me if while we wait for all of that to finish that I research if there's a way to restore my husband's sight." Charlotte scribbled a few more notes.

"What's wrong with Neil's sight?"

The anger receded just enough in Warren's tone that she was curious enough to examine his aura. Unfortunately looking up not only made her nauseous but added a million questions to her already growing list.

Green feathered out from the center of the myriad shades of red that had become an ever-present staple in Warren's aura. Pink and violet spiked out only to be strangled out of existence by another layer of deep red that extended from the outside of his aura as if it existed all on its own.

"He's blind. When the attack on Indiana happened, he was there and injured. We're lucky he's alive." When she concentrated on his aura again the green pulsed out again for a brief moment before his entire aura blinked away. It came back into her view as if a rock had shattered a pane of glass and immediately resumed its swirl of red fury. Bile rose in the back of her throat.

While she didn't want to push the woman, Inessa would be the only one that had any grasp on what she just witnessed. An aura had never done anything like that before. Once she finished babysitting Warren, she would have to seek her out.

"Neil's a damn good surgeon. We can't afford to lose that."

Despite the minute hit of concern in Warren's tone Charlotte didn't bother to study his aura again to confirm if it was genuine this time. "He's an amazing surgeon. It really bothers him so I was hoping we could figure out something to help him."

"I don't know about the medical side. Robotics is an option but we would have to send a team out to scavenge for parts.

Abby helped with mine. She might be willing to help." Warren continued to tinker with the pod.

Charlotte chanced another glance across the room. "Thank you. I appreciate any help you both can give us. How's the pod coming?"

"I'm almost done. How long until the simulations are done? I need Annie back from James." Warren's grip on the tool in his hand tightened.

"We all need Annie back, Uncle Warren." Charlotte slipped off the stool towards the man that had been family to her since she'd been born. It was a gamble but she wrapped her arms around him in a loose hug.

"He stole my daughter from me." Anger and grief rolled off the man in waves.

"She'll be back soon and you can tell her how much you love her." Hopefully the adage of getting more flies with honey worked in this situation. Her hope was that if she appeared sympathetic it would calm him down some and dissipate at least a little of the animosity.

To her surprise he hugged her to him. "At least you understand that Annie belongs with us and not your brother Charlotte. No one else understands."

Charlotte held herself still despite the desire to recoil back from him at his statement. Her mother was right. Warren had gone bat-shit crazy. "Only another hour or so and the tests should be done and we can review the results. I believe Mom was really close on figuring out how to keep Annie's cells from degrading again."

Warren cleared his throat and took a step back. "Then I should finish up on the pod. Thank you again for understanding, Charlotte."

196

"Uh, sure thing Uncle Warren. I'm going to go back to my research on Neil while we wait on the test results."

"Of course. Bounce things off me if you need help." Warren flashed a brief smile in her direction. His aura on the other hand shoved back any hint of compassion and stayed a deep red tangled mess of ire and irritation as if the layers battled each other.

A conversation with Inessa was needed as soon as possible.

"Alright where are we with everything? And where is everyone? Besides James, I know where he is." Chance scanned the meeting room with his lips pursed as he took in the change in roster. What had previously been Warren, Abby, Charlotte, and James had been drastically reduced to just Talisa perched on Roark's lap.

"Charlotte is keeping Warren on track since we are running short on time with Annie. Warren is working on converting the pod and Abby is resting in our quarters." Roark ran his hand along Talisa's back.

RB stepped into the room with his head bowed. "My apologies Chief. The perimeter sweep took longer than expected."

"It's fine RB. We have a skeleton crew at the moment. How are things looking out there?" Chance massaged the back of his neck. The ride Inessa had set up for him helped but tension still lingered in his neck and shoulders.

"Nothing to report from the sentries. Night Hawk made sure we were well prepared. There have been a few questions about our newest addition, but I have informed them that Caiman will introduce him when she feels the time is right."

"We'll leave that decision to Caiman. I don't want to push the issue. They are still working on getting him settled." The door slid open again to reveal Abby. "I thought you were resting."

"I was…I did. I need to feel productive even if it's just a briefing. I need to be around other people to recalibrate my sensors so to speak. Well people that aren't my raging husband." A ghost of a smile graced her lips.

Talisa chuckled from her spot on Roark's lap, "Charlotte is with him now. They are almost done with the modifications."

"Abby how are our medical supplies doing? I know we are running low on herbs. We're growing what we can but it takes time. I'm hoping I can get down there and speed up the growth soon." Chance leaned back in his chair taking a sip of the tea Talisa had made him before she mentally prodded him again.

"Not great. We were low already when Annie got here." Abby held her hands up, "I'm not complaining that we took care of my daughter, but I don't know what you guys are going to need in order to bring her back. Everything is low, even things as basic as aspirin."

"Kajah, do you have what you need or do we need to get a scouting party out sooner rather than later?"

"We'll need to take some blood from Warren and the boys since they match Annie's blood type and then some hair follicles from Abby and Warren. Beyond that we'll do the rest in the lab. We need to map as much of Annie's original DNA without the destructive parts so we don't change her too much." She sipped her tea once she finished.

"So, we're good?" Chance's forehead knit together in confusion. "You had me up to blood and hair. Beyond that you lost me."

"Too much science for you, Sani?" Talisa smiled at Chance from behind her cup.

"You could say that."

"We can wait until after Annie is back but not much longer." Abby tucked a loose curl behind her ear. "Then maybe we can figure out what is going on with my husband."

"I asked the Spirits for one crisis at a time but they seem to think we can handle more than that." Chance blew out a breath of frustration. He inclined his head towards RB in a nod. "Thank you RB. Let me know if anything comes up."

"I will Ravenhawk." RB bowed to those in the room again before he strode out of the room.

"Do we have any idea what crawled up Warren's ass other than Annie dying and his sudden intense hatred of James?" Chance pushed on his knees as he stood up and made his way over to the counter. He pressed his palms down on to it staring at the wall.

"I wish I knew, Chance." Abby sighed with her own frustration. "Nothing I've been doing has gotten through it. There's a rage in him right now that I've never seen before. Quite frankly it scares me."

"What I saw in his brain was nothing like the man I've known all these years. Something is definitely off." Talisa added to the worry of the group.

"So what do we do about it? He's got Annie scared to death. He's attacked James twice, Elan once. I've already put him in one headlock. I don't exactly want this to escalate. Especially not once we start the process of bringing Annie back." Roark added to the dogpile of problems that centered around one man.

"Annie was so upset after her visions that she would have rather James killed her than hurt anyone here." Chance folded his arms across his chest as he turned around and leaned back against the counter. "This…I just don't get it. He went from wanting to find you guys and bring you home to screaming that you've been compromised by Steele to anyone that will listen."

Abby laid her hand on Chance's arm. A wave of calm emanated from the woman. "As much as I want my husband back to himself, we need to get Annie back. We have to try to tackle one thing at a time."

"One day at a time. One thing at a time. One minute at a time. And we wonder why we are so far behind."

Inessa peeked through several crock pots lined up along the counter. Chance was off doing chiefly things, so she'd done her best to keep busy and out of the way. Now what she needed most of all was food. The odd aura-related events had taxed her, then there were her activities with Chance himself, and the vigorous workout she'd made herself go through after the last bit of oddness with Ilana.

Sustenance would be welcome, if her growling stomach gave any indication. However, being so hungry led her to some pretty massive indecision. Everything looked and smelled so good, she wondered if she should just play eenie-meenie-minie-mo and be done with it.

"The venison stew is the best, I promise." Charlotte interrupted Inessa's train of thought. "It was my grandmother's recipe. She taught me before the war took her."

The wave of grief off the young woman was so powerful, Inessa couldn't help but give her a quick, warm hug. "Well, then. I will have to try it."

Charlotte smiled briefly. "Sorry. It hits at the weirdest times."

"Grief always does." Inessa dug for a way to change the subject. The past few days had dredged up memories she didn't care to face in such a public place. Even as they got their food and found an empty table near the wall, more people entered to grab food. The tables became a scattered mix of human and Exceptional, and a melting pot of races. "So much has been going on with your family, I've almost forgotten this is a sanctuary for so many."

"Currently there are one hundred fifty-six, outside of my immediate family. Only seventy-eight Lenape survived, us included. The rest are folks we've saved all across the continent. We've been in touch with similar branches of hidden Exceptionals in other countries too."

"I'm relieved to know other countries are still striving to survive and build on what happened. So many of the places I stopped on my journey here, many had forgotten other countries had been as badly affected."

Charlotte paused with her spoon half to her mouth. "Who did you lose in another country?"

"My grandmother in Poland. It was so difficult to get word in or out of the country, especially being an Exceptional—but I knew."

"You saw it."

Inessa pushed back the rush of grief and bile. She blinked rapidly to avoid tears. Damn, no matter what she did, she couldn't avoid mention of what she'd gone through.

"I've seen it too. The entire tribe, my grandparents." Charlotte stared at the stew with a dreary frown, her shoulders sagged. "Even from New York I saw it happening. If I hadn't had Neil and my parents, I don't know if I would have gotten through it."

Inessa didn't respond. She probably should have used the moment to bond with Charlotte, but her churning stomach led her away from the subject. "Well, this place gives me lots of chances to see weird things I've never seen before. Two in the past twenty-four hours alone."

Charlotte blinked before offering Inessa little more than a blank stare.

No matter that the subject change had thrown Charlotte, Inessa plowed forward. "There was your sister, Ilana. The girl had no aura whatsoever. I fell right over her. Shocked the shit out of me. I've never seen that before. She's your sister, have you seen it?"

"I, um. What?" Charlotte shook her head, waves of confusion and hurt slipping across her aura before she settled into plain confusion. "I'm sorry, you threw me with the subject change. What do you mean, no aura?"

"I mean none. Zero, zip, zilch. I was going down into the fresh tunnels for a little peace and quiet. Normally auras guide my way even in the dark, but there was absolutely nothing from down below, I had to rely on the LEDs—and fell right over Ilana because she was there, but emitting no aura whatsoever."

"That's insane. Ilana has an aura."

"Clearly, I've seen it. In that moment, or those moments? There was nothing." Inessa thought back to the moment and her utter confusion. "It was so odd to see, or rather not see, I suppose."

"Are you sure you weren't just distracted?"

"I'm sure. I was a little distracted, I suppose, but I had to pay attention because the tunnel was dark, lit only with those little lights. I would have seen the big, shiny aura long before I tripped over her if it had been there."

"True." Charlotte dug into her stew again. The change in subject appeared to have reignited her appetite. "I can't imagine that. I swear I've never seen such a thing."

"Hm. I'll have to keep an eye out for it to happen again. So odd." Inessa tried again to figure out what it could have meant. Such an odd thing to happen. She'd seen Chance in meditation, and though his aura lightened and became purer in such moments, it didn't completely disappear. She'd never doubted the Spirits were real in moments like that.

Charlotte's voice broke through her musings. "You said there was two?"

"What? Oh. Right. Sorry. The other was Warren." Inessa had to pause for Charlotte's aura had spiked so hard at the name. Shock, confusion, excitement mixed into a vibrant flash of light. "What is it Charlotte?"

"Nothing. Go on, please." Charlotte leaned forward; her food ignored as her full attention settled on Inessa. "Tell me."

"Okay, then. His aura—I'm not even sure how to explain it. It fractured like a pixelated image on a computer. No, wait. First it flickered, then disappeared, then it exploded into the pixels before it reformed. All of it happened in a split second, made me nauseous really."

"Oh. My. Spirits." Charlotte sat back, dropping her head into her hands. A low chuckle filled the space between them.

"I'm confused. What's going on?"

204

"Nothing. I was just afraid to talk to you about it. I wasn't sure how you'd take it. If you'd think I was crazy. I saw the same thing." Charlotte whispered the words, but she might as well have shouted them for the impact they had on the conversation.

The silence lingered for several minutes between them. A round of loud laughter from a table across the room shook Inessa back to the present.

"What was it?" Charlotte lifted her gaze, studying Inessa quietly. "I was already worried for him; he's gone off his rocker. Is this what that looks like?"

"Is that what Lucy looks like?" Inessa shook her head. "You know what insanity looks like. Everything is more real and intense for them. Everyone is different, but I think we've both had the misfortune of seeing a lot of insanity thanks to the war."

"More than our fair share," Charlotte mumbled in agreement.

"This was something different. It might be affecting him and causing his current state…or it may be a result of his current state. I have no idea. It worries me. It makes me think he's broken."

"Damn straight he is."

"No. I mean really broken."

A slight vibration in his fingertips startled James awake. He blinked at the LED clock on the wall. "Fucking hell. Why did you let me sleep that long?"

Annie's chuckle slipped freely from the computer's speakers. "You were snoring, a cute little kitten snore. I wanted to enjoy it."

"Lies," he snarled. He rubbed the sleep from his eyes.

"I could play you a recording, you know." Annie's image crossed her arms across her chest. "Or I could save it for when you really piss me off."

"That's bound to happen at least once a day for the rest of our…"

"What? Lives? Tall, dark, and depressed isn't as attractive as tall, dark, and angry on you."

James shook off the melancholy best as he could. She wasn't wrong, but that didn't stop him from snarling in her direction. "You shouldn't have let me sleep so long. We only have a limited amount of time. If my mother doesn't get this handled…"

"I'm fine."

"That's a lie."

"I'm fine," she repeated.

"Lie."

"I've got time."

"Not much better." James eyed her on the screen. "Tell me the truth."

"I really don't know. I just know I wasn't meant to be here."

"And it hurts."

Her eyes grew tight, but she didn't dispute him outright this time.

"I'll check with mom."

"That won't do you any good. All you'll do is piss her off. Let her work." The image on the screen flickered before showing a feed inside the area they'd converted into a lab. Talisa and Roark were both bent over the former cryo-chamber. Annie's voice echoed out again. "They've been at it all night. Aunt Tal seemed pretty excited about an hour ago. I took it as a good sign, except she still hasn't tried to reach you."

"There's a lot of hurry up and wait in this gig."

Annie's visage reappeared; her brows furrowed in confusion. "What?"

"Something Mom used to say all the time when she was both trying to get me to help her and tell Dad why I'd be no good at it. There's a lot of hurry up and wait."

"That's helpful." Annie sighed heartily.

"Exactly." James flopped on his back to stare at the ceiling. He'd been cooped up in the room too long, but he wasn't about to leave Anne. Not with her nutcase dad wandering around the compound ready to attack at any time. His last attack had cost her time, even if she wouldn't admit it outright, he knew that's why she was worried now.

"Penny for your thoughts."

"Currency is worthless now."

"Fine, kiss for your thoughts."

"Can't kiss me in there."

"I can when I get out of here."

James closed his eyes, not willing to let himself dream of that time. He'd rather err on the side of caution in everything…especially in this. The thought of her not getting out, though. Fuck, if that didn't just rip his guts open better than the sharpest knife could.

"You've been in here too long. Trapped in this room, because of me."

"Not because of you." James rolled to his side to see her better. "I fucking suck at waiting, Anne. That's just all there is to it."

"Well, I'm not too happy about it, either."

"I know. Fucking hell this sucks ass. I can feel you slipping away, even if you won't admit it. What can we do?"

"I could show you the video of you snoring like a kitten."

A chuckle rose despite his frustration, and her mock-innocent fluttering eyelashes didn't help him hide his amusement. "You're a little smartass, you know that, right?"

"Proud of it, too."

Before he could respond, the door slid open. James flew to his feet, on his guard for the next attack from Warren, but instead his own mother flew into the room. Her hair flew out behind her, her eyes alight with excitement. "It's time. I think it's time."

"What? Really?"

"Do you want to question, or do you want to come?" Talisa laughed as she held out a hand to him. "Come on. Bring Annie. Hi Annie."

"Hi Aunt Tal. You're really done?" Annie spoke as James picked up the computer. He would have shut the screen, but he liked seeing the grin on her face. "I thought you might be close."

"I had a feeling you were spying." Tal wagged a finger at the screen. "No matter now. We aren't one hundred percent sure, not that we could be in this situation, but I think we've got it."

"Just one question." James eyed her sideways. "Why didn't you call me telepathically?"

"What?" Tal's eyes widened. "Fuck. I was so excited I forgot about it. I just ran. I'm sure your dad is standing there staring at the empty space where I was standing in utter confusion."

When they got into the room, Roark was leaning against the chamber instead of staring in confusion. He grinned at his wife. "Eager beaver should have been your name."

"You said that on our honeymoon, too."

"*Ew,*" cried Annie from where she was. "Ugh. Can you bleach our brains after that?"

"I'm with Annie on that." James set Annie's computer on the counter.

"Sorry. I get frisky when I'm excited." Tal set her hand on the chamber Roark still leaned against. "This has never been done, so we're gonna have to figure it out as we go along. Annie, you're the only one that knows how you got in there—do you know how you're going to get out?"

"Same way I got in, I suppose. You'll have to have me on that thing." Annie leaned sideways as if she could see in the chamber. "How do I look, James?"

"You'll see when you get out. That's less important than this working." Tal took a deep breath. "All right. Let's get Annie on here. Don't try to move until Roark and I say, okay?"

James set the laptop on the chamber. Despite Tal's avoidance of the subject, he peeked into the chamber. Annie's features sat inside, no bit of life in them. Her hair seemed darker, but otherwise she appeared the same. "What are we waiting on?"

"Not everything is in place. Once it is, Annie is free to go home." Tal tapped a few keys on the side. "I haven't told your parents because we aren't one hundred percent sure. I wouldn't have told James, but you're inseparable."

Annie hummed softly. "I see why you wouldn't. I'm glad he's here, though. Just in case."

James tensed. "Anne."

"You never know is all." Annie smiled at him. "How do I look?"

"Perfect."

"Pixels are amazing that way."

"It's not your pixels I'm looking at."

"Now it's my turn to have my brain bleached," Roark muttered.

Tal chuckled. "I'd say young love, but we haven't stopped and we're ancient."

Abby fidgeted in front of Danny and Elan's door. Worry about her apologies being rebuffed kept her from hitting the panel. The smell of cinnamon wafted from the pan she balanced in one hand. Perhaps it could have been called a bribe, but at this point she'd resorted to the comfort of baking to soothe her nerves, so she might as well make use of it.

She wiped a sweaty palm on her pants. Her nerves would be the end of her. She had to just push the button. So she did, immediately hoping it wasn't a mistake.

"Ma?" Danny's voice came from down the hall instead of from the room. "Did you need something? Wait, is that…do I smell…you made strudel?"

"Danny I…I wanted to apologize." She held up the pan towards her son. "I brought a peace offering."

"That's like a week's worth of egg rations and other stuff. How did you find apples this time of year?"

"I did some bartering."

"Won't your husband be pissed you did that?"

A frustrated breath blew out between her lips. "Danny I'm not here for your father. He will have his own apologies to make. I'm here for me. May I come in?"

"Yeah, I guess. It's just me anyway. Elan is in the training room with Chaz." He punched the code in the door panel. He gestured her through first. "After you."

"You guys redecorated?" Abby set the strudel on the table in their living room.

"Looking for decorating tips, Ma?" Danny blew out his own frustrated breath. "Tea? Lucas dropped some off earlier."

"Tea is fine. Thank you." A miniscule part of her wanted to bark back at him for his sarcasm but once the war had become full blown the majority of them used it as a defense mechanism. "Is Chaz settling in okay?"

"Not great to be honest. Kinda feels like the poor guy just went from a smaller cage to a slightly bigger one. He hasn't torn up his room too bad this time. Being closer to Elan seems to help." Danny shrugged setting a mug of water and a tea bag in front of her along with two plates. "You heat it up quicker."

A pang of sadness pulled the corners of her lips downward. Abby placed her hands on either side of the mug concentrating on the molecules inside. They raced around inside the mug colliding at an increased rate until steam rose from it. "Annie was even quicker than me."

"So what's goin' on? I can't remember the last time you made strudel. Something else gone to hell?"

"Just what I said. I wanted to apologize. With everything that happened I had a lot of trouble keeping myself straight emotionally. I made the mistake of connecting to Warren emotionally. I thought it would help keep me on an even keel. Boy was I wrong." Abby blew on the contents of the mug before she took a sip.

"Well what the hell crawled up Dad's ass? I mean he tried to kill James and Elan. He could have taken Annie out of the equation permanently with his little stunt. I'm not gonna apologize for Chaz turning him into a piñata." Danny served them each a piece of the sweet confection.

"To be honest…I wish I knew. He's so blindingly livid and I don't know when it started. When your sister first got here he was convinced that she was a spy and he needed to find out what her mission was. By the time he accepted that she was his daughter it was just in time, but he got angry at the littlest thing."

"I don't get why though? I mean I know Ethan and I weren't exactly the perfect big brothers to Annie when she still had a body but we're trying now." Danny shoveled a heaping spoonful of strudel into his mouth.

"To her you were though. James gave us a flash drive with her memories on it. In her mind you and Ethan were Gods. The perfect mix of sometimes annoying but always protective big brothers. You taught her how to drive a car. Ethan taught her how to hunt with a bow. I'm glad you are working on your relationship with her now though." Abby picked up the fork Danny set out with the plate and picked at the confection in front of her.

Danny chewed what he had shoveled in his mouth and laid his hand on top of hers. "Ma I don't gotta be an empath like you to see you are not doin' good."

"I swear I taught you better English." A small chuckle escaped. "I'm not doing well. I've been avoiding your father. His violent moods, quite frankly, make me physically ill. I don't know what is wrong with him. I wish I did. I wish I could help him and make it all better, but I think this one is beyond even my capabilities."

"You are gonna drive yourself nuts Ma if you don't stop tryin' to fix all of us. They'll stick you next to Lucy if you keep it up. How about you let us take care of you instead of you worrying about us?"

"Don't you have enough to worry about with Elan and Chaz? I understand that Chaz is a full-grown man but it is almost like you are dealing with a child of your own." Abby finally took a bite off her own plate.

"That would make him your grandkid. Not sure how that would go over." Danny chuckled. "Let us help. Tal and Roark are working on Annie's body. James is keeping Annie safe. I think Ethan and I can help our own mother. Dad…I don't know there. But he's gonna have to make his own apologies."

Abby laid her hand on top of her son's. "I don't think Chaz wants me to treat him like my grandchild, but I appreciate you and your brother wanting to help. We'll get through this like we always do. As a family. And when we figure out what is wrong with your father, we'll deal with that too."

"Do you want us to call your parents down here Annie?" Roark knew none of them really wanted Warren present with the way he'd been acting.

The image of Annie on the screen shook her head. "I appreciate the offer Uncle Roark but Mom is already having enough trouble with her shields. If something sets Warren off again it could seriously hurt her."

"Your brothers?"

"They have their own stuff to deal with." Annie released a sigh that could have been frustration or worry, or both. "Either way, James is the only one here that really knows me."

"Fair enough." An odd mixture of sadness and rage jolted through him. The intense desire to rip Steele apart limb by limb resurfaced. The psycho inadvertently put James through a similar torture that he and Talisa had gone through in the compound. Being able to see and talk with the other person but not touch them wore on both of their spirits. He made a mental note to mention it to Talisa once they had finished everything here.

*We'll make sure he gets through it.* Talisa's voice floated into his mind. Her newfound telepathy could be handy. *Just as we did.*

*He's close to breaking Li. This has to work.* He met her eyes from the other side of the pod.

*I can't believe that the Spirits would grant her visions of a life together or access to James' Spirit dreamscape without reason.* Talisa's hopeful tone smoothed over the jagged edges of his anger.

*You're right.*

*I always am.* A coy smile played across his wife's face.

Roark compared the printout on the clipboard in front of him to the readout on the side of the pod. So far everything matched up and in theory, Annie could jump into this new body the same way she jumped out of the dying one. "Everything looks good here, Tal."

"Is it ready now?" The inherent growl that always been a permanent fixture to James rumbled through his chest.

"Easy, James." Roark clapped his son on the shoulder despite the fact that he knew it did little to calm him. Talisa always had better luck with that. Annie on the other hand, her voice switched James' anger off.

"James, let them take their time. They need to make sure everything is right." A sad smile marred Annie's features.

"But your pain…" James' fist clenched at his side

"Is manageable." Annie's voice drifted from the computer.

Another squeeze to his son's shoulder did less to calm him than a few minutes ago. If they stopped to try and calm James down it would delay the process even more. He met Talisa's gaze across the pod. "Ready to bring Annie's body out of stasis."

"Turning her core temperature up." Talisa tapped a few keys to start the process.

The converted pod sprung to life, each panel lit up with vital signs and data from the occupant inside. "Basic functions are good. Heartbeat is normal." Roark moved to the other side of the pod with Talisa.

"It worked?" Impatience strangled the hope in James' tone.

"Give it a minute James. We need to make sure everything is good to go, and we'll tell Annie to jump in." Roark attempted to reassure James.

"Annie, can you see the connections we gave you? Will that work?" Talisa ignored their son's impatience.

The image on the screen nodded. "I see them, Aunt Tal. Clear passage straight to the brain."

"I'm going to count backwards from ten and then you have the go ahead to merge into your new body." Talisa grabbed on to Roark's hand.

Roark squeezed Talisa's hand back, but his eyes never left the panels. Each readout pulsed in front of them in a cycle of information. Blood pressure, heart rate, and most importantly, any degradation.

"Ten…" Talisa started the count down.

"James…" Annie's face on the screen looked stricken.

"It's going to work Anne." James laid his hand on top of the pod.

"Nine…"

"Pischk…" Annie's pixelated hand pressed up against her side of the screen.

"I'm going to be right here when you wake up." Fear wormed its way through the façade of faith on his face.

"Take your time, Annie. It will be fine." Roark smiled at the woman trapped in the computer. His attention went right back to the readouts.

"Eight…"

"Ehoalid, ahoalan janewi…" Annie's Lenape had improved beyond just the basics.

"Seven…"

James' breath caught in his throat. A look crossed over his face that Roark had only seen reserved for Talisa. Not that he had doubted it, but Annie truly was his son's mate.

"Six…"

"I love you too, Kwëlaha." The words tumbled from James' lips barely above a whisper.

"Five…"

"Shit…stop the count down." Roark tapped the keys to scroll through the data from the pod. The clipboard in his hand went flying across the room. A roar of anguish rolled up through his toes. He spun and punched a nearby filing cabinet. "Fuck!"

"Roark are you sure?" Panic jumped into his wife's voice as she scrolled through the same data he had just reviewed.

"Positive." The word filtered through his gritted teeth.

"What happened? Why did you stop the countdown?" James tensed up ready to fight, his usual response.

"The body's degrading." Annie's voice answered the question for him.

"NO!" James' yell shook the pod.

"We will try again." Talisa cupped their son's cheek in an attempt to keep James from giving in to the anger and despair.

"She's running out of time." The growl from earlier twisted into a snarl.

"James Logan Nashuk." Annie's voice cut through the space between the before Roark could say anything.

"Anne…" The snarl dissipated like a puff of smoke.

"They will figure it out." Annie whispered.

Roark shook his head in amazement as the tension drained from James' expression and body. Even trapped in a computer Annie could calm his son's nerves just as well as Talisa could calm his own. "We aren't going to let you lose her James. We'll get right back to it."

"You both need some sleep, Uncle Roark." Annie interrupted.

"Anne…they need to fix this."

"They will, but not if they continue with no sleep. They were up all night." Annie's pixelated eyebrow rose on the screen.

"You will do just fine with this family, Annie." Roark nodded, "She's right though. At least a nap and then we will rebuild the formula from scratch. Figure out where the strand is falling apart."

"Please hurry." James whispered.

Roark gave James' shoulder a gentle squeeze. "We're not going to let you lose her son. I promise."

Tal lay still in the tall grass, her gaze fixed on the clouds rolling by. Once upon a time in her life she'd enjoyed this nonsense. Now it just annoyed her. What right did the skies and weather have to be so beautiful when the world was falling apart?

She could already hear Chance telling her she was being too hard on herself for the failure of the first attempt. On the same note, she could hear Roark cursing about his own failings while telling her she hadn't made them.

The two fools would do everything to protect her, even though she'd never needed an ounce of protection.

She'd come outside to avoid it all, instead she couldn't stop thinking about it out here either. For all the good her jaunt did, she might as well have stayed inside the lab the rest of the day.

Still, after so long in Steele's custody she had missed the sun. She closed her eyes to soak in the warmth, to let the gentle breeze drift across her skin. If she tried hard enough maybe she could transport back in time and space to the reservation of her youth.

She relaxed enough to drop her shields; a rush of voices entered her mind so fast it almost took her breath away. Rather than fight, she let them wash over her like the wind across her arms. The brutal rush became whispers that passed by like the winds across the prairies of her youth.

Once in a while a stronger thread would break through, only to die back down. The voices of her family were clear as a bell and easy to grasp for a moment, while others were less interesting to her.

*Is all well?* Lucas, more adept at this telepathy thing than she was must have picked up on the distressed thoughts she couldn't quiet for the life of her.

*Is it ever?*

*Fair point.*

*I'm fine. Trying to get my head on straight before we try again. Failing, but trying nonetheless.* Tal opened her eyes again to face a cloud shaped like a duck if you looked at it from a certain angle and squinted.

*Shapes in clouds should not be so difficult.*

*Tell that to my brain.* Tal managed to find a smile. *Go back to your day. I'm just trying to remember how it feels to be outside. Maybe enjoy it, even.*

*You did once.*

*I loved the freedom of time to enjoy it. It feels superfluous now.*

*We all need such things from time to time. Enjoy.* He slipped from her thoughts as quickly as he'd entered.

The silence surrounded her again, to the point of annoyance. Silent didn't suit her. Action, motion, doing something for the cause. Something. Anything.

Before her own cursing could erupt in her head, someone else's did. Elan's. *Fucking hell.*

Talisa sat up abruptly.

"What the fuck?" Elan stepped back a pace, her skin turning gray and scaly before her foot made contact.

"Easy, Elan. I heard you coming."

"Bullshit."

Talisa tapped her temple. "Not walking, in here."

"Again. Bullshit."

Tal stared at her daughter, waiting for the gray protective skin to fade.

"I can block telepathy."

"Better than anyone, I'd wager. However, you are my daughter, and sometimes you project. Usually when you're swearing, just like your dad."

A flicker of a smile twitched the corner of her lips before Elan stilled her features again. Her Caiman flesh softened back to human again. "Well, life's shit. There's a lot to swear about."

"I hear that." Tal tucked her legs close. "What has you wandering in the sunshine?"

"I could ask you the same thing. I expected you to be holed up in the lab forever until you brought Annie back or she kicked it."

"Classy."

"Super soldier."

"Doesn't mean you have to be an ass. We've discussed this plenty."

"I've gotta stick with what I'm good at."

"So like your dad."

"He says I'm like you." Elan didn't meet Tal's gaze when she said this, instead using her claws to shred several tall blades of grass with precision.

Tal couldn't deny her own pleasure at Roark saying such a thing, but she knew it wasn't something Elan wanted to hear. Their relationship had always been rough. The girl had always gotten along better with Roark, from the moment they'd finally found her.

"So why aren't you in the lab?"

"I don't know. I've been locked in a lab for over a year. I thought maybe some sunshine would do me good. I'd hate to end up as pale in flesh as Abigail."

This time Elan did smile. She flopped onto the grass beside Talisa. "Welp, I guess the only way things could get worse at this point is a Steele attack or Annie dying."

"Well…"

Elan's head spun toward her fast. "What? What have you heard? Do I need to get RB to gather the troops? We all know James is useless right now."

"No. That isn't what I'm saying. I'm saying it's not the only way things could get worse." A flash of guilt hit Tal that she'd said nothing yet. Even though they'd agreed to wait on the Annie situation, she also hadn't had any time alone with Elan.

"True. The possibilities are endless. I've analyzed a lot of them. They're pretty unlikely."

"Elan."

"Stop. It's Caiman."

"Elan." Tal set her hand on her daughter's. "We need to talk about something."

"What now?"

"The pods we brought back."

"I told you it was a mistake. You didn't listen. What is it? What happened to them?"

"Well, you know we had to open the one to convert it for Annie." Tal flinched at how fast Elan shut down her brain in preparation for whatever Tal was about to say.

"Yeah. So?"

"We chose the youngest as we thought her easiest to keep in stasis without the unit. Before we released her and moved her into our modest stasis unit, we ran the standard tests."

"Stop rambling and get to the point, Talisa."

Though neither of them was looking at the other, Tal felt as though Elan's hard gaze bore down on her. The girl nearly vibrated with tension that somehow didn't appear on her flesh as of yet. She'd learned quite a bit of control in the year Tal and Roark had been gone.

"Now you're delaying."

"No, I got lost on a train of thought. The genetic screen showed a very unexpected result. The child is related to us, to our family."

"So the asshole manipulated our genes again. What's wrong with her?"

"Nothing. As a matter of fact, she appears to be human—and your daughter."

At first there was no reaction, not in body or mind. The moment Elan jerked away, Tal's mind burst open under an assault like she'd never felt.

Torrents of not just words, but high-pitched shrieks flooded her mind so fast she had no time to throw up any shields, and all rational thought flew from her head.

By the time Lucas had helped her regain control without wasting time to ask what exactly had happened, Elan was almost out of sight. Risking the appearance of humans or military, Talisa threw a wall of fire hard and fast to block her daughter, hoping she was in human flesh at least long enough for Tal to have a running shot at catching up to her.

Somehow, luck was with her enough that the young woman stopped completely. Tal had enough time to reach Elan, where she found her staring at the wall of fire even as it disappeared.

She snarled under her breath. "That was a stupid fucking risk. You've got everyone on alert now, and we'll be lucky as shit if there isn't a patrol nearby that caught that heat."

"It will be fine."

"We're not that lucky."

"Elan."

"Don't." No matter the anger in her voice, Elan still didn't move. "I told you. It's Caiman, and what you said is impossible. I was a child."

"A child who was raped repeatedly…"

"It's impossible. You ran all sorts of tests. I never had a baby. I would have poisoned it myself if I had one while there. This shit needs to die with me."

224

"There are other ways for children to be born, especially with Steele's resources."

"It isn't possible. I'm no mother."

"It's more than possible, and you are."

Elan's eyes closed, the stillness that had taken her over now complete.

Talisa ran her hands along Elan's long, dark hair gently. "She's in stasis, but perfectly healthy. I could wake her."

"Don't you dare. Leave it be. I won't have it. If I thought I could get there without any of you knowing it, I would finish it."

"Elan."

"If it's mine, you have to listen to me. I don't want it to be taken out of stasis. Ever."

"You haven't even tried to—"

"Ever. And no one is to know."

"She's family."

"*It* is *nothing*."

Inessa didn't quite know what to make of the current state of things. This whole dinner had been Charlotte and Chance's idea. Yet, the two were so morose there'd been very little conversation.

To be fair, Neil had made several valiant attempts. Despite his lingering depression over his injuries, she could already see the world of healing being home had done for him. She knew he would never be the same man she'd met at the beginning of the war, but then again that was a common theme in the world these days.

She knew the first attempt with Annie had been a catastrophe, but she hadn't expected there to be this much of an impact on her two hosts. Though the whole family unit they lived in had a sort of symbiotic existence, this was quite a heavy mood to wade through.

If it were just her and Chance, well, she'd have a few ideas on how to solve his state for sure. They'd be quite fun, even. No, they'd be immensely pleasurable. The mere thought gave her a little shiver of pleasure.

226

Charlotte's gaze lifted. The first flash of anything but the morose muted tones she'd been carrying erupted across her aura like a wave of magic.

Nessa raised her eyebrows at the silent, unspoken question of what had caused her change of mood, hoping against hope the girl would take the bait.

Instead, Charlotte released a sigh before returning to the apparent monumental task of pushing the food around her plate with her fork.

Frustration burst from her lips like air from a balloon.

"Nessa?" Chance's brow furrowed as he lifted his head at the sound.

"Nothing. Nothing." Inessa waved his curiosity away. The depression rolled across the room like a wave. She'd imagined this dinner as awkward for so many reasons. Perhaps because it was like she and Chance were—what? Something, anyway. Going steady? She wasn't even sure what they called it before the war, much less what it could be called now.

Either way, that could have made it awkward.

Charlotte's hoping to continue a familial bond of some sort could have made it awkward. Neil could have started telling stories of the ripping of flesh from his face by bombs.

Definitely could have been awkward on so many levels.

This, however?

Not the awkward she expected. Every bit of conversation Neil had attempted, or herself even, had fallen like a lead balloon.

What was worse, is that she had always been able to spark life to the deadest of conversations.

This was crazy.

She let the bite of mashed potatoes she'd picked up slide off her fork onto the plate. It fell with the quietest *splat*. She scooped another forkful, only to let it drop again.

A wicked thought crossed her mind quick enough that she almost didn't catch the giddy hit to her aura before it erupted. If she were to manage to do anything without anyone being the wiser, she'd need to keep her emotions in check. The new challenge was almost exciting. She'd never met another like her, so she wasn't entirely sure she knew how.

She let the thought cross her mind several times, carefully testing the rush of humor she felt every time. Either Charlotte's distraction was utterly complete, or Inessa was able to keep herself in check enough to not be detected.

On the switch from her fork to a spoon, Charlotte glanced up again. Whether the action, or Inessa's excitement caught her attention, Inessa couldn't be certain. She took another bite of potatoes, trying to be nonchalant.

This time Charlotte was slower to lower her gaze. She studied Nessa for several long minutes before finally giving up whatever quest she was on.

Inessa took the opportunity to move as fast as possible. She scooped up some potatoes on her spoon and expertly aimed and released them at Charlotte before the girl knew what had happened.

Charlotte's wide eyes didn't even blink as the potatoes sat on her forehead. Her mouth wide in an 'O', her own fork balanced between her hand and the plate precariously. For the moment, her aura remained sort of static with shock.

"Nessa!" Chance sat blinking at Charlotte, his aura fluctuating madly between humor and surprise, never settling on either too long. "What was that about?"

"What?" Neil's brow furrowed. "What did I miss?"

"You missed," Charlotte muttered, wiping the potatoes from her forehead. She shook them to her plate where they landed with a mushy *plop*. "Inessa's shockingly good aim."

"I had cousins." Inessa grinned broadly. "You can't hide your amusement from me, Charlotte. No matter how surprised you are, and even if you are a wee bit angry."

"What are you talking about?" Neil shook his head. "I'm confused."

"I had cousins that were very ill-mannered. It meant a lot of food fights," Inessa clarified.

"Food fights? Oh, *oh*." Humor flickered across his visage. "You didn't."

"Right between the eyes," Inessa proclaimed with a hint of pride. Before she could turn back to check if Charlotte had gotten over her anger, she felt a smattering of soft pellets ping against the side of her face.

Charlotte giggled. "Peas forgive me, or don't."

"Now, hold on." Chance's voice halted Inessa's grab for her spoon. "We aren't children."

Inessa met Charlotte's gaze for only a heartbeat. The unspoken agreement must have been mutual because they both turned their next volley on Chance himself.

In no time the food fight dissolved all awkwardness and tension, and even Neil got involved despite his poor eyesight. The room, and the people in it were covered in food and filled to contentment with laughter in a way none of them knew they'd needed when it all started.

Annie sucked the pixelated version of air past her teeth as her computerized prison clattered onto the kitchen table in James' room. She forced a smile on her face despite the near constant ache that settled into her soul. "Hey...they will figure it out. It won't be much longer. Let them get some sleep."

A snarl rumbled past James' lips. His heavy footfalls echoed throughout the room. Each pass in front of the computer diminished the dubious hold on his temper. "We're running out of time."

As much as she hated to, she closed her eyes and pushed down on the agony that had grown exponentially as more of her own code frayed like an old cord. "Your parents are brilliant. They will see what they missed and fix it. As early as tomorrow night you could be holding me in your arms."

"At what cost?" His upper lip twitched and pulled back in a snarl.

"I don't know what the materials cost, but we will do what we need to." That wasn't what he meant and she knew it but she needed to steer him away from that topic. Anything that had to do with her being in pain sent him into a frenzy.

"That's not what I meant and you damn well know it." The growl in his throat sunk into his chest. "Anne, we are running out of time."

Her tenuous smile faltered. No secret to either one of them that the next attempt would be the only other one. There wouldn't be enough time or enough of her left to make a successful transfer. Not that either one of them had said the words out loud. "Ehoalid..."

"Stop! Just stop it! How can you just sit in there and be so positive right now? You may die...again."

"I know that James, but I can't focus on that. I have to stay focused on the fact that WHEN this does work, I can touch you again. I can kiss you. I can lay in your arms. I can pop you in the back of the head for yelling at me."

The underlying growl had dissipated to what she would have called an angry purr. It ramped back up again as the screen flickered. "Is this what it's going to be like? One maybe two emotions? Is this part of the programing to not give a shit that this could all go sideways?"

Anger and anguish collided within her heart. The logical side of her knew that he was scared and reacting. The rest of her wanted to punch him in the throat. Calm and even brought him back to the rational side before, perhaps it would diffuse this. "James you know that's not true. You are the only one here that honestly knows me."

"What that you're a robot?"

Annie flinched back as if he had slapped her. The only good thing it did was hide the surge of pain and section of code that degraded further. Digital tears welled up in her eyes. "I can't believe you said that. How could you even say that?"

"Well shit, there's a third emotion. Is that progress or hidden programming?"

If she hadn't been trapped in a computer she would have lost the ability to breathe. "What the hell is wrong with you? Are you just in the mood to hurt me?"

A lazy smirk tugged at the corners of his mouth. "I thought you could handle me. Oh, wait you're a computer program at the moment."

A frustrated yell started low, then volume on the computer increased to full instantaneously. "Take me to my mother. I'll spend my last hours with her if you're going to be like this."

"And if I don't?"

Annie starred James in the face as best she could. "I'll connect to the network and find my own way. I'm no one's prisoner."

The slightest audible gasp escaped before James covered it up. He swiped a glass off the table, threw it across the room, and leaned on the table with his knuckles. "Fine. I'll take you there, but you'll be with me before we try again."

"Need some time to come up with some more ways to hurt me?" She folded her arms across her chest.

Despite the anger on his face his grip on the computer was surprisingly gentle. "Whatever you need to tell yourself."

The walk from their room to the one Abby had taken temporary residence in wasn't that far. She spared a glance up at him but all that did was lance her pixelated heart with a new kind of pain. The wait for her mother to answer the door was torturous. On one hand she wanted to stay with James and figure out what had him in this mood. On the other she wanted to be as far away as possible.

"Hey guys, what are you both up to?" Abby's warm smile broke the dam that held Annie's emotions in check.

A cascade of digital tears etched their way down Annie's face on the screen. "I...uh...James has something to do, can I...uh... hang with you for a bit?"

"Something?" Abby's eyebrow quirked up as she panned between James and the computer.

"Can she hang here? She wanted to see you. Isn't that what you wanted?" James snapped.

"James." Annie scolded in a firm yet soft tone despite her tears.

"Not like it isn't true." James blew out the air in his lungs in a huff. He set the laptop in Abby's hands with extreme care. "I'll be back."

Abby held the computer so Annie could see James' retreating form. "First fight?"

"First fight."

Tal should have been doing something — anything, really — rather than sitting there on her ass staring at a blank computer screen. She couldn't motivate herself to turn it on. Everything was wrong, nothing was good, there was nothing redeeming anywhere.

"I haven't seen a dark cloud over your head like that since you were debating leaving the tribe." How Chance had managed to sneak up on her, she had no idea.

"Pretty sure you have. It's called a war. Children stolen from me. Returned as…I'm not even sure what half the time. Her dad gets her more than I do, I think. She likes him better anyway."

"Oof, dark dark dark." Chance's strong arms circled her shoulders from behind. Though she didn't fight, he held on tight. The warmth soothed some of the turmoil in her brain. "What can I do?"

"Turn back time? To five years ago. That would be great."

"That's beyond even the Spirits' skill set, Li. You know that."

"A girl can dream." The great weight settled on her shoulders. "Ugh. I disgust myself."

"What? Why?"

"I miss being in the compound."

Chance kissed the top of her head. "Stockholm?"

"No, I hold no affection for that asshole. It's more like I miss not having to worry about anything but how in the hell we were going to escape. And not really being able to destroy any of my children's lives while in there, either. After all, they already thought me dead."

He slid into the seat beside her. "Talisa?"

"I think he's going to win." The words came out in a whisper. The first time she voiced the fears aloud. "I'll fight to my dying breath, but I don't know that we can win. He's got too much, and we've got nothing but a fractured society whose very soul is deeply damaged. The mother's heart is breaking."

"That's your heart, Talisa."

Her throat spasmed under the rush of pain she refused to allow to escape into tears. Eyes closed, she blindly grasped for his hand. "No. I've been broken since the bomb."

"You're here."

She lifted her gaze to search around the lab. "Here. Not home. Here. We can never go home."

"Tell me what's happened."

"Annie."

"I know. Charlotte is at a loss, too. What else?"

"It's not my story." Tal let out a long, slow breath. He was the Chief, this was his tribe, and he was family on top of it all. "The child we rescued, she's human—and Elan's daughter. I just finished telling her."

"Oh." Chance sat in silence a few minutes, his body still. His mind, blessedly, didn't overwhelm her with shouted thoughts or disbelief. Rather, it was almost silent as if he conversed with the spirits instead of his own mind. "I bet that went over like a lead balloon."

Despite her state, Talisa couldn't stop the laugh that erupted at his frank reaction. "To say the least. I'm not sure where she's at."

"You don't think she left, do you?"

"No. I'd know that much." She picked at her nails. "I don't know how to fix Annie. Despite all our repairs, the code died. She fell apart before our eyes. Warren is batshit crazy. Who knows what will happen to James now?"

"Come on."

"What?"

Chance was already out of his chair, one hand stretched toward her. He flicked his fingers to beckon her forward. "Come on."

"C, I don't have time. I have to—"

"Come on. I won't ask again."

Tal didn't need to be a telepath to know he wouldn't let this go, she just had to have known him his whole life. Not one to give up too easy, she only took his hand with a grudging sigh that might have actually been a groan. She wouldn't swear to it.

"Stop acting like a child."

"I will if you will."

He only shook his head in response, though she wagered a guess that he'd added a roll of his eyes she couldn't see. "You can stop trying to read my brain waves, Troi."

This time she was the one to roll her eyes. "How you ever became a *Trekkie* living on the reservation I will never know."

"When your best friend leaves it frees up a lot of time in your life."

Another point against her. She'd screwed up Chance's life so many times without meaning to. Her steps slowed until he stopped to face her. "Does she make you happy?"

Chance stared at her wide-eyed. The change of subject clearly had thrown him for a loop. "What on earth does Nessa have to do with this conversation?"

"I've hurt you so much."

"Oh, for crying out loud, don't go lumping me into your trauma."

"Yelling at me doesn't help my trauma."

"In your particular case, I beg to differ."

Damn him for having a valid point.

"You've always been a contrary one, after all."

"Shut up and leave me alone."

"No, and no. Now come on. Stop dawdling."

Tal did groan full out this time when he dragged her along again. The path they took wound around to the back of the complex and down to a door she didn't remember seeing on the map. And down, and down. By the time they stopped, she didn't know how far below the surface they were.

In the middle of the circular room sat one LED light circled by candles. Chance gestured to them, then around at the walls. "If you don't mind. You'll be faster."

Tal didn't need to be asked twice. With a flick of her fingers, a flame sparked to life in her hand. She shot it toward the circle of candles, skimming the tops to light them before sending her flame through the room to light any other candle she might find.

By the time the room had lit, Tal noticed a second door off to the side. Before she could question, roots shot down out of the ceiling to cover the exit. "What?"

"I don't think you want interruptions, though no one knows about this place besides me, as far as I know." Chance picked up a candle to hand to her. "I know you can make your own fire, but don't. Use the candle."

Tal hesitated, but did as he instructed. The room she entered was another circular room, but this one was lined with a protective layer of flora. Somehow the dampness of the outer room didn't reach in here.

She lifted the candle as she approached the wall, then paused to gasp. "Chance!"

"Not only are they not gone because we can talk to them, their stories remain." Chance freed a scroll from the shelf it sat on, and held it open for her to see. "One of my orders for the tribe was to gather our stories that had been written down and put them somewhere safe. I wanted you to see them first, but then…"

She ran her fingers along the ancient scrawls on old leathered hides. Without another word, she made the full circuit of the room. Near the door she found several shelves that didn't contain hides at all. "No. You saved my old notes?"

"As the only one that knew of your secret cave, yes. I kept them here with the scrolls because I wasn't sure if you'd want them seen."

"The scrolls – I can't believe you still have them. Why aren't they upstairs where the others can see them?"

"We have a library up there. These needed somewhere special. It's our people. The full history of our people. Again, I wanted you to see it first. That was selfish of me, but it was what I thought needed to be."

"Thank you." She set her hand on what now seemed like an ancient notebook in her loopy teenage handwriting. "Thank you."

"It doesn't solve the world's problems, but I hope it helps."

"We have to share it now. With—with our people." Her face felt hot with the force of emotion shoving back at her restraints.

"We will. Soon. First, you scream. Yell. Fight. Curse. Whatever you need."

A shudder shot through her chest, and the tears erupted before she could stop them. She wanted to do all he said, but she could find nothing but the deepest pain. A sob wrenched from her belly, and her knees went out from under her.

The moment she hit the floor, Chance's arms wrapped around her. He said nothing, his mind remained blissfully clear. He let her grieve without judgment or telling her how.

"I hate you," she managed to spit through sobs.

"Love you too, Li."

Elan stared at her hands as they shook. Over and over her skin went from normal to its gray-leathery appearance. She couldn't even get a handle on her own powers. This sort of thing had never happened.

At least she'd shaken off Tal. She couldn't take any more of her disappointed looks. What the fuck had she expected, anyway? She knew what Elan was—Caiman, the ultimate warrior. More so than the blockhead of her brother who'd been botched. Powerful and angry, but with a default weakness of too much anger.

She stretched her hands out, willing them to stop changing. For a moment, they did in the Caiman state. She breathed a sigh of relief, for like this her nerves weren't on fire with something she couldn't figure out. In her human form she felt under attack constantly, which kept triggering this response. Then she'd calm again and relax, and the cycle started all over.

She didn't understand what could be causing such chaos in her body.

"Fuck, fuck, fuck." She buried her face in her hands as if it would help her regain her sense of who she was. "You're Caiman. You're above this fucking bullshit. You're made for war, this is nothing. Nothing at all."

Years of training had taught her how to numb herself, this stupid family crap had stripped some of that power away from her. It shouldn't be so hard to regain her control.

She closed her eyes and thought back to her years of training under Steele. The conditioning to feel no pain, no emotions. They only made everything worse, anyway. Best as she could, she shoved them aside back into the corner of her mind that she hid from everyone—including Lucas and now her mother.

"What on earth are you doing? That's weird."

Caiman opened her eyes to find her twin staring at her, head tilted and a crease between her brows. "What the fuck are you talking about, Char?"

"You like, folded up part of your aura like an origami crane. I still see it, of course, but how in the world did you do that?" Charlotte approached without a hint of fear, despite the growl Caiman directed at her. "Stop. Right now your bark is worse than your bite."

"My bite is always worse. It kills, remember?" Caiman waved one of her poison-laced claws as a visual reminder.

"Blah, blah." Char sat beside her. "So what's up? You're a mess of shit, so much so, that I felt it down in the mess hall. I'm not used to so much chaos from you. You keep it close to the vest pretty much always."

"I'm a soldier." Caiman pointed out.

"I repeat, blah, blah. You're also a human, so get over your damn self."

"Or what? You'll tell Talisa? Or Danny? Blah, blah your fucking self. I didn't sign up for sister therapy. For that matter, I didn't sign up for sisters. Or brothers. Or…"

Once again, Char's sharp gaze studied her intently at the flare up of whatever the fuck sent her nerves ablaze. "Okay, you're really freaking me out now. What is going on? What were you about to say? Or what?"

"None of your God damned business."

"We don't really worship God in the Christian sense around here."

Elan growled low and deep.

"Elan."

"Don't."

"Fine, then. Caiman. You might as well talk to me. I not only feel something huge has happened, but I see it. I'm also already in a shitty place with this whole Annie thing and don't care to be dealing with your crap on top of it. So you can tell me and I can help you figure out how to deal with it, or—"

"Or what? And how on earth are you going to help me deal with it? You think you can help? I know how you can help. Go sabotage the stasis unit with that bastard child in it. It doesn't belong here. Anything that asshole created from me doesn't belong anywhere on this earth."

"Woah, wait, hold on there, back up."

Caiman stared at her, her flesh turning so extremely leathery, she wondered if she'd be able to even blink at this point.

"Back the truck up." Charlotte stood so they were eye-to-eye, although at the moment there was nothing similar to them except height. "Am I understanding what you just said correctly?"

"Which part?"

"The child downstairs, the one you brought home—"

"Talisa brought here."

"Whatever. Mom brought her back along with the others. Either way, did you just suggest she was your child?"

"I said it was created from me. It is *not* my child."

"Elan." Charlotte set her hands on Caiman's shoulders, not even reacting when she got a visceral growl in response. "Your child."

"I am no mother. She is nothing. Not worth our time or energy. It's human, for fuck's sake. Probably why he threw it away, too. If we're lucky she'll fall apart like Annie."

That got the desired reaction, at least. Char stepped back, tears sparkled in her eyes, but there was a hint of fury in the way she glared at her sister. "I get that you're scared and confused, but that was unnecessary."

"I don't get *scared*. I'm not made that way."

"Bullshit."

"Fuck you and your feel-good happy family feelings, Char. I think the one thing on this doomed earth we can agree on is that you are nothing like me, and vice versa."

Char rolled her eyes. "You were doing fine with the happy family feelings before the war, you hypocrite. You got married and you were comfortable."

"And then the fucking war happened thanks to the fabulous father figure I grew up with. I didn't have precious Mommy and Daddy and Popsicle to make my life all better."

"Old news."

"So are you. Speaking of mistakes."

"Old insults." Despite her cold words, Char straightened her shoulders against the affront. "You forget that it isn't just my ability that makes me able to know you're fuller of shit than our septic tank right now. I'm also your twin."

This time Caiman rolled her eyes, even though the septic tank line managed to break through her defenses enough to humor her. "You don't know me."

"Better than you think I do. So does mom." Charlotte held up her hand when Caiman scoffed. "I also know that as much as you fight it, you actually seek her approval even when you piss all over it when you get it. You may still get kicks out of enjoying punishing her for a sin she was never guilty of, but I don't."

"Just shut up."

"Just deal with your damn emotions. You're afraid to be a mother, that doesn't mean you aren't one. You think you'll suck as a mother, still doesn't mean you aren't one. Killing her might do that, but I'll be damned if you'd even succeed if you got close enough to do the deed yourself."

"It shouldn't be here, Char. He only makes monstrosities. He only makes weapons. He only breeds evil."

"Then break the mold."

"I am the mold."

# 25

"How can she even…what is she thinking….?" Charlotte released her notebook on the lab table with an unceremonious thud. "I get the shock but…"

She moved around the area of the makeshift lab she had been working through, slamming things down a little bit harder than necessary, closing drawers with as much force as she could muster as if it would solve all of her siblings' problems. There was the real issue laying right in front of her. Most of her loved ones had issues going on and there wasn't a damn thing she could do. Not even for her husband.

Tears welled up in her eyes at that thought. It broke her heart to watch him cycle through the stages of grief, anger, and depression over his current lot. As if on cue the door to the lab opened and Neil entered the room just as she slammed a cabinet door.

"What's wrong baby?" A gentle smile pulled up the corners of his mouth.

"Why do you think something is wrong?" Her own smile tugged at her lips. He didn't need to see her to know how she was. She would bet a week's worth of milk and egg rations that he sought her out due to a feeling he had.

"You mean besides the feeling I had that something was bothering you or the fact that when I walked in here you were slamming the cabinet door?" Neil's steps towards the lab table, both measured and counted out in his mind, took a short time more than if he could see. He extended one hand and touched the table as he neared it. "Left or right?"

"Left. I can come to you."

Neil held his hand up to stop her. "I can get to you. I'm getting the hang of getting around again."

"Maybe I just didn't want to wait to kiss you." Charlotte did wait until he had made it most of the way to her when she closed the distance.

"Hey…"

"I couldn't wait anymore." She pressed her lips to his in a gentle kiss.

His fingers danced along her temple to tuck an unruly curl behind her ear. "You're really tense. What's wrong? Something with Annie?"

"No…I mean that situation still isn't fixed but it's getting there. Just my usual family dynamic. Bomb of the week." Her shoulders rose in a non-committal shrug.

"Beyond the most recent family food fight?"

"Hey, it took me hours to get all the mashed potatoes out of my hair." A brief shake of her head followed a frustrated sigh. "No it's about the little girl we took out of the stasis pod to make the chamber for Annie."

"Is something wrong with her?" Neil wrapped his arms loosely around Charlotte's waist.

"I mean not unless we're talking about her being put into stasis to begin with or the fact that she's my niece." The quick transition from curiosity to shock occurred just as she expected it to. "Yeah that was my reaction too. Well there were a lot more curse words involved."

"Wait, which sibling?"

"Elan. Another one of Steele's insane ideas. Danny isn't the father." She leaned in with a quick kiss before he could ask more questions. "I have just as many questions as you do but can you do me a favor?"

The way the confusion on her husband's face melted away and quickly reformed into a warm smile offered another reminder of why she fell in love with him. "Name it."

"Can we not talk about it? She's screwed up eight ways from hell over this and I don't want me over analyzing it to transfer through our bond and have it screw her up even more."

"Makes sense. Ethan says there's a storm coming in. Pretty nasty one. They were talking about securing everything topside." Neil kissed the tip of her nose with surprising accuracy considering his lack of sight.

"Well I'm glad they are getting it all taken care of. I guess RB is taking point since last I checked Dad was trying to physically extract James' head from his ass." Charlotte patted the stool next to them for Neil to sit. "You want something to drink. I'm going to get some tea."

"Tea sounds good. So what's going on with James now beyond the obvious?" Neil leaned his arms on the table in front of him.

"You know how feral the Exceptionals get when they haven't been around their mate in too long. He can see her but he can't physically touch Annie and he's mad. He took it out on her."

"I'm sure that went over well."

"Hence the extraction." A short laugh escaped. "I don't know what he's going to do when she has her body back and can blow his ass up for being stupid."

"They'll figure it out. Did talking with Warren help spark anything?"

Charlotte shook her head as she poured the boiling water into the mugs followed by dropping the teabags in them. Bright and deep streaks of yellow shot out through his aura at the question. "No. I mean a little bit but not as much as I would like."

Greys stifled out the yellow suffocating them to nothing. She set the mugs down in front of him and set her hand on his arm. "Hey, none of that. Apparently Warren is batshit crazy at the moment so I doubt I would have gotten anything of much use from him."

"You know it's not fair that you can not only see me and read my auras but I can barely see you at all. God, I miss being able to see that sexy little pout I'm guessing you have on your face right now." His arm snaked out and caught her around the waist to pull her close.

"I'm not pouting." Her fingertips trailed along his temple and into his hair. "We will figure it out. Annie said she would help once she was fixed so it will happen."

"Don't make promises baby. I want my sight back, but I don't want false hope." His fingers trailed up along her spine.

"No false hope. I promise I will do everything in my power to find a solution. And no matter what I will be by your side." Charlotte rubbed her nose across his in an Eskimo kiss before planting an actual kiss in the same exact spot.

"So how much work do you really need to do right now?" A mischievous grin settled onto his face.

"I don't have anything time sensitive running at the moment. What did you have in mind?"

"I think I need you by my side for some physical therapy. What do you say?"

Charlotte's grin matched his, "Lead the way."

James' retreating form held Abby's attention. Her daughter sniffling came through the speakers, but Abby didn't speak or move until James was out of sight. She shut and locked the door with the press of a button. "What happened? It must have been a heck of a fight if you both look like you do."

The close-up image of Annie flickered into a scene of her on a couch. She sobbed. "He was so cruel. I've never seen him like that. I don't know what I did to make him act like this."

"Back up a little bit. What was going on before the fight started?" Abby settled on the couch with the laptop on the end table.

Guilt swept across her daughter's features. "Talisa and Roark tried to bring me back. The body degraded."

"Anna Maria Johnson. How could you even think about attempting that without me there? What if something had gone wrong and I didn't have a chance to say goodbye?" Tears stung the back of her throat just from the thought of losing her again.

"I'm sorry, Mom. You've been struggling around emotions and I knew they would be high and you're doing really well having just dealt with James and now me." Annie tucked her legs underneath her.

248

"I've been isolated from your father and been able to build my own defenses up again." She motioned for Annie to continue, "So the attempt failed and then what happened?"

"We went back to our room and he was so angry. Like scary angry. Nothing I said broke through. The worse it got, the meaner he got." More digital tears descended down Annie's face.

Abby rest her hand on the keyboard of the laptop, "You two are going to work through this Annie. You have both been through a lot in a short amount of time."

"That doesn't give him the right to basically tell me I'm nothing more than a computer program. I've been trying so hard to keep myself together. I know how hard he struggles with the anger and I didn't want to set it off." A digital hand swiped at the digital tears.

"I haven't seen you this upset since Jordan." A sad smile settled onto Abby's lips. While she hadn't lived all those years with the distraught young woman in front of her, she had watched the data drive Annie had given them. "I'll tell you the same thing I did then. If it is worth fighting for, then you will both find a way."

A startled gasp echoed through the computer speakers. "M-mom? You watched?

"It's all I have been watching. It's been helping me recalibrate my sensors, so to speak. You were just as mischievous as your brothers were." Her shoulders rose in a slight shrug, "I wanted to understand where you were coming from. To see how close we would have been if I had gotten to raise you like I should have."

"Thank you. I know it's weird seeing things that way."

"It's fine. It was odd at first but after the first few memories I got the hang of it. Now," Abby shifted on her knees to face the computer fully, "Do you want my honest opinion as to what really happened here?"

Annie adjusted herself on the digital couch and visibly braced herself for Abby's assessment. "That's why I'm here."

"You two have been through hell and back since he picked you up in New York. Whether either of you wanted to admit it or not there was something there between you from the moment you met. You got back here only to find out just how sick you were and how little time you actually had."

"Mom, I wasn't sick. I was never meant to be here."

"Stop that. Everything happens for a reason. This whole compound is full of examples of that. Even in the middle of this war." Abby shifted back to sit on the couch and pulled the laptop onto her lap.

"What possible reason could there be for a disintegrating clone to end up here other than my original purpose of infiltrating the compound and disappearing? Oh God, he's right. I'm nothing but a failed computer program." The sobs that wracked her daughter's body broke her heart over and over with each little sob and sniffle.

"Annie, breathe." Abby pushed calm towards the laptop. In theory it could work. She could feel her daughter's emotions despite her digital existence at the moment. "There's a quote that fits this whole situation perfectly. You don't have a soul. You are a soul. You happen to have a body. Or you will when Talisa and Roark are finished."

"M-mom…what if they don't figure out a way to fix this? I don't want to die again."

Abby reached out and touched the screen tears welling up in her own eyes. "God, I can't wait to hug you again. They are going to fix this. You know how I know that?"

"How?"

"You saved James. He was so angry all the time before you got here. And it may have taken some getting smacked around by his siblings but once he acknowledged that you two belonged together his whole demeanor changed. I knew he loved you before he even realized it. By the time he did realize it, he knew he had to prepare himself for losing you. Now he's had more time with you—"

"But Mom…?"

"No buts. Listen to what I'm saying. Yes, James is absolutely furious. He's mad at just about everything. None of it is directed at you. Steele…definitely. The Spirits…probably. But you…he loves you with every ounce of his being. His anger wasn't aimed at you."

"It certainly felt aimed at me."

Her hand came up to catch a few tears that escaped. "Annie, I focused on him when he left you here. When he handed me the computer he was extra careful. We all know your father did some damage to it. All I felt when he was handing it to me was how much he loves you. He's angry because he feels helpless. In this war, in all this ugliness, you are the one bright thing in his life. You make him want to be a better man."

Annie folded her arms across her chest. "He was very specific that it was about me when he was yelling and throwing things."

Abby held her hand up in surrender, "I don't doubt it felt that way. Think about it this way though. The biggest parts of James' gifts are feral like his parents and when you were dying he still had bursts of anger but something as simple as touching you or holding you pushed all that anger away."

"So what does that have to do with this time?" The skeptical look on Annie's face that mirrored Warren's pulled a smile out of Abby.

"This time he can't touch you. He can touch the laptop and keep you close but it's not enough. He wants to touch you and hold you and help take your pain away with your bond. He wants to be with you. If I can feel your pain being an empath, then he certainly can with your bond. Right there that negates his outburst that you are a program. You have thoughts and emotions and pain. All part of what makes us human."

"Mom, he's been with me since the day I died."

"Not quite what I meant. He wants to be with you fully." A chuckle escaped as her daughter's eyes widened. "There's nothing wrong with that Annie. I've never been an uptight parent about those things. Ask your brothers."

The laughter that echoed through the speakers was a welcome reprieve from the weight throughout their conversation. "Mom, I don't think we'll be jumping right in bed as soon as I am back in my body."

"You say that now but that's because you've never done it. Wait until after the first time and you'll be sneaking away from work and running into an unused office to enjoy each other as much as possible just like your father and I did."

"Ew, Mom…just ew…"

Elan wandered back toward her quarters as slow as possible. She'd rather not have to tell Danny anything at this point. He'd likely kill her when it came out, but silence seemed the safer option after her mother and sister.

Rather than rush to find her husband, she studied the few people that passed her in the hallway. They'd recruited enough that she dared to say things were going to become crowded if they didn't get to work on more levels.

Of course, having this many people in one spot was a danger in and of itself. Even with the measures they'd taken toward safety, if they found any other stragglers, she worried about being discovered. Not to mention feeding everyone. Even with Chance's unique talents, they could only grow what they had—which wasn't as much as would be ideal.

A group of young women, a few years her junior, passed by in a cluster. One of them cast a look Elan was hard pressed to identify. Disdain and fear were two she could figure out real easily, but this was different.

Lucas' voice cut through her musings, "It is called respect, maybe a touch of awe. Actually, she may have a bit of a crush on you."

"Don't read my mind."

"I was not reading. You were broadcasting that bit of curiosity." Lucas leaned on the wall outside his room that sat alongside the medical area. Unlike the others, there was no door that sealed it shut, and the entire area was earthen, not a hint of metal inside.

"I don't broadcast."

"Not normally, no." He didn't budge from his relaxed position. "This time you were. You should be well aware I am not one to pry."

"Unlike Talisa."

He wrinkled his nose and bobbed his head back and forth in a signal of mild disagreement. "I believe she is still learning control. She does her best to respect boundaries. The dirty trick you played on her earlier gave her a headache I am now assisting her with."

"Steele was good for one thing, at least. How to get things out of my head."

"Considering how few of us there are with my particular gift, I am sure you are delighted to use those tools. It was rather unnecessary."

"It was instinctive."

"Ah." Lucas said nothing else, not even to argue the point. Maybe he knew she wasn't entirely lying about it.

"I need to go."

"Of course." He nodded, remaining where she'd found him even as she walked away.

"Stop watching me."

"Not watching. I am waiting for my wife to arrive."

"Liar." Elan knew he probably wasn't, but she still felt like maybe Talisa had sent out a signal for everyone to watch out for her. Even though that totally wasn't Tal's style, it felt good to accuse her of something anyway.

When she opened the door to their quarters, Danny paced the floor, muttering to himself. Over what, she had no idea. Had word reached him? Did her whole family blabbermouth her entire life story? She dropped hard onto the couch. "I'm sorry."

"We've got to do something," Danny blurted at the same time. His brow furrowed. "What?"

"Nothing. What?"

"Chaz. We've got to get him like an obedience class or something."

Elan stared at him, not sure exactly how to respond to the asinine statement. "What?"

"You heard me. He's out of control. He's breaking shit and not sitting still."

Elan rose to her feet slow and steady so she didn't lash out at her husband. Some logical portion of her brain told her he was frustrated, but her already annoyed state made the likelihood of smacking him not out of the realm of possibility. "Your solution is obedience school?"

"For the mere fact that he doesn't have—"

"Your solution is to take a man that's been caged up his entire life and is already trained using commands they used on *dogs* and put him in a form of *obedience school*?" Despite her best efforts to remain calm, her voice rose with every word.

"I didn't mean that, and you know it." Danny bristled at her tone.

"You said it. So, you meant it."

"I'm frustrated."

"Oh. You're *frustrated,* because he's having trouble adjusting? You poor baby. All the levels of hell Steele has brought down on this entire god-damned family with your paper doll sister, that abomination of a child he created out of me, and you're worried about a fucking broken coffee pot and how to break an already fragile and confused cheetah? That's fucking awesome, Danny."

"She's *not* a—wait, what?"

"Oh, hey, congratulations, let me ruin your life more. You're a fucking stepdaddy…well, you would be if I gave a shit enough to call that freak of nature my child, because she's not. She's no more real than Annie is."

Danny had gone ashen at first, but anger fueled his face right back to red in no time. "Elan!"

"It doesn't matter. God willing, all of us will be dead soon…those of us that were no more than fun experiments for him anyway."

"Stop." He reached for her hand, frowning when she jerked it away. "Slow down, Elan. Tell me what happened."

"In those pods my mother insisted we bring back with us is a small girl, a *human* girl…that somehow he created out of me. She says it's my child, but it isn't."

"But she is if she was created from you."

"I'm not saying this again to one more person. She isn't. She's nothing. If she isn't some sort of weapon for him, in which case we definitely don't want her, then she's human and somehow deeply flawed. That's why she was in stasis. He put all the useless ones there."

"Elan. She's your daughter."

"No, she's not. I never carried a child, I never gave birth, I would rather she were dead."

"You don't mean that!"

256

"I do, Danny. If you knew what was best, you'd wish the same."

He shook his head. "No. No life is worth destroying except Steele's. She's real, and she's here. You can't honestly wish her dead?"

"If you think so highly of Steele's throwaways, then you raise her."

"Now wait. I didn't say—"

"That's what I thought. Stop fucking judging me and everything else and get a grip on your own frustrations. Stop taking out your fucking paper doll sister woes on Chaz."

"Stop calling her that!"

"Whatever. I'm going to blow off steam. I told you because I didn't want to keep a secret, but right now you annoy me more than that little bitch does."

"Elan."

"Bye."

01110111  01101000  01100001  01110100  00100000
01110100 01101000 01100101 00100000 01101000 01100101
01101100 01101100 00100000 01101001 01110011 00100000
01100111 01101111 01101001 01101110 01100111 00100000
01101111 01101110 00111111

*Click.*

Warren shook his head at the electronic buzz in his whole body. He couldn't help verbalizing the code running through his brain. "What the hell is going on?"

*It's them, always them. They always have to be the stars in this story. They want to take it all, take all that's—yesterday. All my troubles seemed so.*

His right arm jerked of its own accord, sparks flying from the opening in the artificial flesh covering it.

01011001 01101111 01110101 00100000 01100001 01110010 01100101 00100000 01110111 01101111 01110010 01101011 01101001 01101110 01100111 00100000 01101111 01101110 00100000 01110010 01100101 01110000 01100001 01101001 01110010 01110011 00101110 00100000 01000110 01101111 01100011 01110101 01110011 00101110 00100000 01000110 01101111 01100011 01110101 01110011 00101110

"Focus!" He slammed his arm down on the desk hard. Tools spilled off the edge. The screens lining the wall crackled with white noise before returning to streaming code.

The same crackle ran through his body.

"They're fighting to save her," he muttered to himself. He grabbed a small screwdriver from the floor and peeled back the layer of skin. "They're you're friends."

*Enemies.*

"Family."

*Steele held them for a year. A fucking year.*

"Assholes."

*Click, click.*

His head tilted this way and that.

"What the hell is going on?" He shuddered against the extraneous noises in his two cybernetic parts. They, and his brain seemed to be reacting to stimuli he couldn't recall.

"Run diagnostic 01110000 01110010 01101111 01100011 01100101 01110011 01110011 00101110 00100000 01000100 01100101 01100010 01110101 01100111 00101110 00100000 01000110 01101001 01101110 01100100 virus."

He blew out a blast of frustration. "Diagnostic process. Debug. Find virus."

*Click.* A whir of motion moved along the upper limits of his limb. He was pretty sure that was what was supposed to be happening.

*Locate Anna Maria Johnson. Find program. Destroy.*

"*No!* Not destroy. Repair. Fix her. Gods alive, *fix her.*"

*Fix yourself. He's got you, too.* In a rush of motion, Warren's right hand flew up to grab the screwdriver from his left hand. It spun it fast and thrust it toward his chest almost before he could react.

He caught his own arm a split second before the tool made contact. With a lot of effort, he kept his arm from causing any injury to himself. "Deactivate! Now."

01000100 01100101 01100001 01100011 01110100 01101001 01110110 01100001 01110100 01100101 00100001 00100000 01000100 01100101 01100001 01100011 01110100 01101001 01110110 01100001 01110100 01100101 00100001 00100000 01000100 01100101 01100001 01100011 01110100 01101001 01110110 01100001 01110100 01100101 00100001

The arm twitched once, the hand jerked open to drop the tool, and the whole unit hit the desk with a small thud. "What the hell is going on?"

He eyed his arm warily. For the first time in years he wasn't sure he could trust his own limbs. Hell, for that matter he wasn't sure he could trust his own brain.

*He's brainwashed them. Steele is after you all.*

Warren closed his eyes against the wall of code before him, against his own mind. Not that it would help. Maybe he was beyond hope.

"Daddy."

Warren's eyes flew open at Anna's laughing voice. On a screen before him she stood, maybe 16 years old in a fancy dress, probably for some dance. Her laughter rang free and warm, genuine and real.

*It's not real. She's not real. She's a weapon.*

"My daughter. Is. Real."

*Ultimate weapon experiment number thirteen. Unlucky in every way. The winner is out there. Find it. Destroy us all.*

Warren jerked back from his own thoughts. He pressed his hands to his head, focusing on the familiar. The known. Abigail. She'd been there, helped him. She'd helped him create these extensions of himself. She could help him fix them.

"Gail. Please." He hit the comm panel. "Gail. Gail. Gail."

"I'm not talking to you right now. Not unless you've gotten yourself together." Her voice wasn't cold exactly, but there was a level of detachment he couldn't fathom.

"Please. I don't…you know what, shut the fuck up, then." He slammed the panel, immediately feeling a flash of regret. "Fuck. What the hell is going on?"

01110111 01101000 01100001 01110100 00100000 01110100 01101000 01100101 00100000 01101000 01100101 01101100 01101100 00100000 01101001 01110011 00100000 01100111 01101111 01101001 01101110 01100111 00100000 01101111 01101110 00111111

"This is fucking insane, bro." Danny plopped down on his brother's couch. A quick nod was all he managed before he downed the shot of moonshine Ethan had handed him. Of all the things they figured out while living in the compound, moonshine ranked up there in the top ten. Top five even. The majority they kept on hand for medicinal purposes since it was easier and cheaper to make than rubbing alcohol.

"What the hell happened? I literally felt your brain lock up. You and Elan get into a fight or something over Chaz?" Ethan poured another shot for Danny.

With the second shot downed he set the shot glass down so he could talk with Ethan about the newest revelation. Too many more shots and the only thing he would be doing was taking a nap. "Nah, not Chaz. I mean he pissed me off when he broke the coffee pot but this is so much more than that."

"Something go wrong with Annie? Mom? The alien that replaced our father?"

A short chuckle escaped at Ethan's line of questioning. "I'd kill for it to be that simple. No, I just found out I'm a stepfather."

"Mazel Tov?" Ethan's eyebrow arched up. "How did that happen?"

"How else? Steele. Something about a turkey baster or her 'training,'" his fingers came up in air quotes. "Hell could have been a test tube. We don't know. I don't think we know much more than the little girl that was in one of the pods they brought back is genetically connected to her."

Ethan stood up wordlessly, ventured back into the kitchen and grabbed another shot glass. He poured more moonshine into Danny's and then filled his own. With a flick of the wrist he tossed his own back. "Are you shitting me?"

"Wish I was." Danny took his own shot. Instead of setting the glass down again he played with it between his fingers. "I don't even know how I feel about this."

"Shocked for one. It's not like this is anything you ever expected. When they rescued Roark and Talisa they brought back what? Five pods? And one of them just so happens to be related to your wife. The chances of that are insane. Add Steele into the mix and they become less insane."

"Elan is so fucking freaked out. I don't know how to help her. I don't even know if I'm qualified to help her. Shit man, do I even have a right to an opinion on this?" He dragged his hand through his hair.

"Of course you have a right to an opinion. This tosses your whole dynamic in the damn air. Things still hadn't settled with Chaz moving in." Ethan filled up their glasses again and set the bottle on the coffee table.

Danny stared into his own shot glass wishing for some magic answer. Anything that would tell him what to do or how to handle this. "There are days I wish I could see into the future so that I could know that everything would work out."

"Not all it's cracked up to be. Look at Lucy; she lost her mind. Literally." Ethan leaned back in his chair. "The whole thing is fucked up. I get that. What's the biggest part that has you all fucked in the head over this?"

"I don't know that there's enough shine for that." He finally tossed back the shot. "I don't know how to pinpoint just one thing. I mean, I worried about Elan. Really worried. Goin' back in, like she did to get her parents out, really messed with her. Then I have an Exceptional that all he knows is more animal than human living in the room next to ours. Let's not forget, with all the sick shit Steele did, that same guy used to fuck my wife. Our sister is dying…again. They don't know if they're gonna be able to help her. On top of all of that our father has lost his own fuckin' mind and tried to kill my wife. Could ya narrow it down a bit?"

A soft chuckle escaped and a slight smile, albeit a sad one, settled on Ethan's face. "Okay, fair. It's been a lot. The rest of it is all insane by itself, but a kid? Man… I mean do they even know if they can help her?"

Danny rubbed his hands over his face. "I don't know. We didn't get that far. She's still at the point of denying any ties to her. I really think if forgetting she existed was an option she would take it. It ain't the kid's fault though. Not that I know anything about raisin' one in a normal world, let alone in the middle of all the shit we deal with day-to-day right now."

Ethan leaned forward with his elbows perched on his knees. "Only thing I can say is be there for her. We both have Nashuk women and they are inherently stubborn. Not to mention, admitting that they need help is a foreign concept with that side of the family."

"Ain't that the fucking truth." Danny blew out an exaggerated sigh, "Not that our family is any different. Do we know what the hell is going on with Dad?"

"Changing the subject, I see." Ethan shook his head, "No clue. He went from devastated over Annie dying, to pissed off at James, to raging and pissed off at their whole family. Now he sounds more like Lucy than himself."

"Eh, it's all tied together. All connects to why my head feels like it's going to explode." He grabbed the bottle off the coffee table and downed another shot followed by a loud belch. "I don't remember eating onions."

"Classy bro." Ethan let out his own sigh. "So now what?"

"We wait and see I guess. Isn't that what you're doing with Ilana?" The last shot still burned in his throat. The fleeting thought that getting drunk was not his best plan in the world right now ran through his mind. He quickly dismissed it by pouring another shot.

"We aren't talking about Ilana right now. She's got something going on and when she's ready to talk to me she will. I know better than to push her." Ethan snatched the bottle back from Danny, "Don't drink all my shine man. I just got this bottle."

"I'll help…" His chest jumped with a silent hiccup. "I have some stuff I can barter for another bottle."

Ethan took a swig directly from the bottle. "Well then let's finish it while we worry about our women.

"Best thing I've heard all day."

264

Ilana floated above the compound, over the treetops, near to the clouds. She could almost touch them. Familiar with the feeling, she reached for it as she always did, but the cloud level remained beyond her touch.

She stretched again, as far as she could reach, willing herself higher. Her wings didn't flap, she moved nowhere.

"Wait." She stilled, thinking hard.

For though she was, indeed, high in the sky—so high she could almost touch the clouds—she felt none of the familiar motion of wings. The weight of them on her back when she spread them. Though they were a part of her and weighed next to nothing, she always sensed them. This time, she couldn't tell they were there.

She glanced over her shoulders, and sure enough they were nowhere to be found. When she looked down toward the earth, she noticed the rope tied around her ankle like a tether.

No, more like a balloon string.

She wasn't a balloon.

She flew, she didn't float.

The realization crashed over her, and as though in slow motion her weightlessness disappeared. Her feet gave in to the pull of gravity, yanking the rest of her body behind her.

She crashed to the ground quick and hard.

Every ounce of the breath she'd been holding as she fell, rushed from her lungs at the impact, her body instantly screamed in pain.

She convulsed, biting her tongue against the scream she wanted to release.

*You fight what you are.*

Her eyes flew open to face the cold metal ceiling of her bedroom.

A dream.

No. That was no dream.

She rolled onto her side, studying her sleeping husband. The smell of moonshine had dissipated quite a bit, but he was going to hurt when he did wake. Probably as much as her own body currently ached.

The fall had been a simple vision, but the pain echoed into her real body.

Slow as could be, she slipped from the bed. She grabbed a glass of water and some headache medicine she'd stashed on their last scavenger mission and set them on the table beside Ethan. With a few taps of her fingers, she turned off the sunrise on their computerized window so he might get all the sleep he needed, and not feel the full effects of bright lights on his pounding headache before he felt ready for them.

Satisfied he was set; she threw on some day clothes and left the room.

Trouble was, she had no idea where to go now. Or who to talk to. The chief was a good one, but he wouldn't understand, and he had bigger fish to fry than what was going on with her.

No one would understand.

So many times she'd thought to tell Ethan, explain to him the chaos, the questions, and the weirdness of everything, but how could she?

The panel across from her on the wall beeped three small, quiet warning beeps, and then the power shut down. At night the warning for fly-by's remained brief on the assumption that everyone was asleep.

"This has to end," Ilana whispered to herself. "We can't live like this."

"Not forever, no."

Ilana shrieked in surprise at the voice right beside her. "Fucking hell in a handbasket of scorpions, Lucas. Don't sneak up on a person in a blackout like that!"

A low chuckle carried through the darkness. Lucas' voice remained amused when he spoke. "I was not aware I was sneaking. You are the Guardian; I thought your instincts and senses were as good as any here. Better."

"Until I'm too deeply wrapped in my own thoughts to think of anyone but myself in a totally selfish, possibly narcissistic way. I shouldn't be Guardian."

The lights clicked back on at low levels, rising back to the minimal night levels over the course of the next thirty or so seconds. During that time Lucas remained quiet, a contemplative stare set on her. "You are no narcissist."

"I am no Guardian. I couldn't protect us. I still can't."

Lucas pulled her into a warm hug, tight and secure, in a way that rivaled their dad's. "Illy."

He never used nicknames. The very idea caught her so off-guard she let out a long pent-up sob. "I let them all down. I'm no Guardian."

"There are things we cannot stop. We do not always know the reasons."

"Gods above, stop saying that worn out line. It didn't mean anything before the war, and it definitely doesn't today." She tried to push her way free, but he held her tight. "They want to kill me. I am not the Guardian. I don't belong here or there. They are trying to break me."

"Who?" Lucas released his hold to study her intently. "Who is trying to kill you?"

She couldn't form the words, because she knew he'd balk at the idea. He was the exact opposite of who she needed to talk to. Maybe their mother would understand better. Or dad, even. Lucas was too entwined with the spirits.

"Ilana. I cannot help if you do not tell me what is going on."

"You won't believe me. No one will."

"Try anyway."

She lowered her gaze to the floor, grateful in the moment for Lucas' infinite patience in most every matter. "The visions are breaking me. Literally."

"What?"

Her lip quivered beyond her control; she closed her eyes against the sting of tears.

Lucas took her by the elbow in a gentle, but firm grasp. He led her down the hall, so at least she wouldn't have to open her eyes. When he stopped her, she heard the surprising sound of doors whooshing closed.

The mere fact he'd take her somewhere with a door surprised her enough to open her eyes. She sniffled as she took in the location. Chance's meditation room. He could block the unfriendly metal doors with roots and have total privacy.

"The Chief does not usually mind me using the space on occasion. My medicine room is open and we could be interrupted," Lucas said by way of explanation.

"I can't talk, Lucas. I just can't."

"You can. That is fear talking."

"Of course, it is. I don't know what the hell is going on." She threw her arms out in an unnecessarily dramatic exclamation point to her statement. "I wake up from visions I didn't know were visions literally broken. I can feel bones knitting back together, Lucas. I'm able to function because of whatever the fuck they gave me, but they are trying to break me. And succeeding."

"What are the visions?"

"Everything. In some I'm floating above the earth like some freaky balloon, and crash to the ground. In others I'm beneath the earth and wind up scalding in lava or crushed in a collapse of earth. They're telling me I'm fighting, but for fuck's sake, they're trying to kill me."

"Maybe they are not. Maybe they are trying to show you something?"

"Then they're showing me I'm not meant to be the Guardian."

"I do not believe that, Ilana."

"In every vision I am beyond my own powers, and when I realize it, it all comes crashing down. They want it back, or they want to kill me."

Lucas set his hands on her shoulders. "You said when you realize it, you lose the power."

"Yes. I'm in the air and I realize I don't have wings, that I'm tethered to the earth like a balloon. Then like some old cartoon mom used to watch, I fall to the earth like a coyote running off the edge of a cliff."

"The coyote falls because he stops believing he can run."

"He falls because of the laws of gravity, Lucas."

Lucas smiled, "But what if he kept believing he could cross like the bird? It makes it across every time."

"It doesn't matter, Lucas. I fall."

"But what would happen if you didn't let yourself? What if you let yourself fly without wings?"

Tori pushed a supply laden cart through the common area toward the living areas. She tapped the button on the panel outside the unit of her choice. A sigh of relief escaped when no one answered. One six-digit code later and the door slid open. Thank God her father's code still worked. In the past the plan had only been to use it in an emergency. Warren would pick up the code's use soon enough and erase it from the system. No one would have expected it to be used. Joe had been dead for over a year now.

Tears coated the back of her throat at the thought. She would give anything to hear his voice again. Or get a hug. The kind that made you feel safe and secure with no effort at all. God, how she missed him and in turn her mother too since she had been near catatonic since her father's death.

"Focus, Tori! Not the time for this." Tori tucked a lock of hair behind her ear and extracted the first part of her mission from the bottom of the cart. The coffee pot had seen better days but it still worked. And this one wasn't embedded in part of the wall.

A thud against the door startled her enough that she fumbled with the pot for a split second. Once it was nestled safe and sound on the kitchen counter she stood in front of the only thing that kept her from part two of her plan.

The door to the connected living space slid open and Tori stiffened up to brace herself. Nothing happened after a count of ten, so she stepped into the room and let herself relax.

"Chaz? It's Tori."

In a blur she found herself pinned to the wall. Her wrists pinned above her head; the lower half of her body pressed into the wall by his leg. There were no growls, no malice. Rather, his nose buried in the crook of her neck sniffing her.

"No mate." Chaz's English might have been stilted, but it was clear.

"Chaz." She giggled at the ticklish sensation.

His head jerked back from her neck. "You injured?"

"No, I'm not injured. It tickles."

"What is 'tickles'?"

This was going to take more work then she thought. "Let me up. We can sit on the couch."

The look in Chaz's eyes told her just how wary he was. His eyebrows knit together in confusion, but he released her.

"Let me get my cart. I brought some food and some bandages for your hand." Another breeze blew through the room, this one almost knocking her over. With one hand on the side of the couch she regained her balance. "Thank you, Chaz. I could have gotten it."

"Caiman no clutter."

"Caiman doesn't like clutter? Well I can understand that."

"Her mate say she'll be angry." Chaz sat next to the couch similar to how a dog would sit back on their hind legs.

Tori lowered herself down onto the couch cushion next to him. "You can sit on the couch. It's okay. This is your room."

Chaz tilted his head to the side, his brow wrinkled in confusion.

"Let me see your hand. Danny said you cut it when the coffee pot broke." She tugged the cart closer with one hand.

"Not hurt. Punish for break."

It took every ounce of restraint to swallow back the gasp she felt escaping. "Chaz no. You aren't being punished. Please let me see it." She took it slow but remained still when he jerked back as she got closer. "I'm not going to hurt you. I promise."

Chaz's cheek twitched as he leaned back away from Tori. "You punish?"

Tori shook her head. Her eyelids fluttered rapidly to stave off the tears that now burned down her throat. Elan had mentioned that she didn't understand what Chaz went through and the other woman was right. The idea that Steele had trained another human being like an animal and made them think they were less than everyone else made her stomach turn. "I'm not going to punish you or hurt you. I'm here to help you."

"Help?" He leaned forward and sniffed along her arm.

"Yes. I found another coffee pot to replace the broken one, some medical supplies to tend to your hand, and some essentials to keep in your room in case you get hungry." A smile tugged at the corner of her lips. He sniffed along her wrist and moved up along her arm. She turned her hand so it skimmed along his hair as he moved higher. A soft giggle lilted between them as he reached the crook of her elbow and his fur-like hair brushed along the inside of her arm.

The last time they met she didn't have a chance to really look at him. Now she could see the spots that graced his temple and cascaded down along the edge of his cheek, his neck, and under the shirt Danny and Elan had gotten him to wear. A light nip where her neck and shoulder met pulled her from her trance. Before she realized what was happening again, he nuzzled into the crook of her neck. "Chaz?"

"Help?" Confusion danced across his features when he pulled back to look at her.

"One step at a time." She took his hand in hers, extremely conscious of the fact that he had tensed again. "Why don't we start with friends? Do you remember my name?"

"Friends?"

"Yes, we'll be friends, but my name is Tori."

"Tori? Tori help?"

"Yes, I'll help." Without thinking about it she ran her fingertips along the spots on one side of his cheek. She expected him to yank back or tense up but instead he crept up on to the couch next to her and curled up with his head on her lap. "When was the last time you slept?"

Instead of an answer a soft purr emanated from Chaz's chest. Tori traced her fingers through his hair and along the edge of his spots as he dozed off. "Rest now. We'll worry about everything else later."

James stood outside the door, his hand clenching and unclenching. Try as he might, he couldn't lift it to hit the panel to get Abby's attention. What if he was already too late? What if they all were? Shit, what if she didn't forgive him?

*You're giving me a headache, son.*

James jumped at his mother's voice, spinning around as if he'd see her in the corridor. By the time he'd made it back to face the door a slight hint of embarrassment picked at his constantly bubbling temper. *Damn it, Ma.*

*You got used to your brother doing it, you'll get used to me. Your father let you beat the shit out of him and talked you down. Or so I thought. Why are you spinning your wheels and distracting me from what I need to do?*

That was a damn good question.

*Thanks. I know it is, that's why I asked it.*

James growled low and long. *Then get out of my head.*

A small bit of laughter, warmer than he'd heard from his mother in a long time, trilled through his mind. *You were projecting. Still figuring this shit out here. I'm great at blocking everyone but family, it would seem. Unless the non-family person is truly projecting with some intensity. You guys, you always seem to be a low roar in my head. When you project it's front and center.*

*Convenient excuse to be in my business all the time.*

*I know. Isn't it fabulous?* He could truly picture Talisa laughing until her nose scrunched at the smart-assed comment. *I've always been your biggest busy-body, and supporter. I get to be all these things from a distance now.*

*Lucky us.*

*Oh, wait. Was that laughter in your tone? No. Not my fierce warrior.*

His amusement faded at her words. *You always could reveal more, ma. Now…*

She didn't speak for a long time, though her presence remained in his mind in an oddly reassuring way. Even as he had the impression her attention was divided, she remained present. Almost as though physically beside him.

*I don't know how to do this. No one has been able to calm me before, besides you.*

*And she does a fair better job of it than even me. This mate-function is still one of the most fascinating parts of our evolution. I can't explain it, and I don't think in this case that's what you're seeking anyhow.*

James shook her head, even though she couldn't see him. *No.*

The silence lingered for only a moment this time. *James.*

*Yeah, ma?*

*There is no magic formula to make it work, or to apologize. You fucked up, but you love her. She loves you.*

*Is it enough?*

Talisa laughed again, bright and cheerful. *Oh yes. It won't solve the world's problems, but it will always be enough. Now push that panel and shut your voice so I can work.*

*Yes ma'am.* James tapped the panel before he could second guess himself. Within thirty seconds, the door whooshed open. Abby set her hand on his wrist, an encouraging smile on her features. "Abby, can I?"

"Go ahead. I'm going to go meet Charlotte anyhow." She slipped past him without a hint as to what he was walking into.

James entered cautiously as if Anne stood on the other side of the door ready to bash him with a frying pan like some old cartoons Neil once made them watch. Not that such a thing was possible, she was in a fucking computer.

"Is that scowl just for me?" Anne's voice called to him from his left. On the coffee table sat her laptop, facing him. The screen was black so he couldn't see her. "Here to abuse me more?"

"Anne."

"I mean, you took tall, dark and angry to a new level. Even for you."

He sank to his knees in front of the dark computer. "I'm sorry, all right? I don't know what to do here. I don't know."

There was a flicker of code across the screen that faded as fast as it appeared. "Well. That much is infinitely clear."

"I suck at this."

"True."

"You deserve better."

"False." The screen flickered to life finally. The code coalesced into a close up of her features, her glare fixed right on him. "Stop the pity party."

"I fucked up and stole time from us."

"Mom said you were scared."

He pursed his lips.

"Oh, I forgot, you're the fierce warrior. You can't be scared."

"I didn't say that." James gripped the sides of the screen, struggling for the words to explain. When he spoke, he could only manage a hoarse whisper. "I'm fucking terrified, all right? If this fails again, if you end up lost in cyberland, if I lose my mate…"

She released a soft sigh from her side of the screen. "You don't think I feel the same way?"

"I'm not used to it. This is worse than when my parents were killed."

"Sort of killed, anyway."

"Exactly." He bowed his head. "I was created for war. Not this."

"And I was created to destroy us all. Shit happens. People change, James."

"I'm sorry. I really suck at this."

"You really do."

"You need to stick around to help me figure it out."

"Hmmmm, I do? That's the only reason?"

He lifted his head to meet her gaze. "No. Because you're my mate."

"How romantic. An obligation, then."

"No. You're my mate. You are a part of me. A part I need, a part I love."

"Better."

He blew out a breath of frustration. "You have to make it."

"I don't want to die either, you know."

"You won't die. You can't."

She laughed low. "I've already died once, so I really can."

He glared at the screen. "You're not funny."

"I am a little."

"Nope."

"But you love me."

"I do. Still doesn't make you funny."

Talisa walked the full circle of the room Chance had built. After accepting her gratitude, he'd left her alone in the room without her needing to ask. For the past several hours she'd pored over the old leather scrolls.

The stories of her people were as rich and deep as she'd remembered, as well as deeply prophetic. Already she'd found one about the Guardian created hundreds of years ago she guessed, but the image held a similarity to Ilana that couldn't be denied.

Over the years the scrolls of leather had been well cared for by her people, for they were all still flexible and legible. She imagined in the past two years they hadn't been cared for as regularly, but they would need to see to doing that again.

She paused at the thought, her hand hovering over another scroll. Such thoughts for a woman caught in the middle of a war. A never-ending war, it seemed. The world had changed.

*She* had changed.

For so many years she'd fought her role as matriarch. Her pull to the white world and science had been so strong. Her mother and father had encouraged her toward that world if that's what she desired. When the time came, and the entire world began to fall apart she'd returned home briefly and received a crash course—if you could call a lifetime of watching her and Chance's mothers in such a role followed by a few weeks of dedicated instruction and tale-telling to be a crash course.

"I am no matriarch," she whispered to the wall as if it cared for her defense. "I can't solve any problems. If I can't fix Annie when that's what I was meant for, I can't fix this tribe. So many people gone. There's so little left now."

She sighed softly into the silence surrounding her words.

"All the stories of our people, and no one to tell them to." She scanned the room again, carefully avoiding the cubby with the spiral notebooks of her youth. After a moment she plucked a more recent roll of leather from a shelf.

When she opened it, she immediately recognized the writing beneath the artwork. Her own father had created this piece, and she was sure she hadn't seen it before. The tale it showed was one of a new world, a new magic granted by the Spirits, a world vastly different but filled with a new understanding.

"In my youth I would have called you an old fool. Now, I just call you hopeful. Wrong, but hopeful." She pushed the scroll back into place. As it set in place, a wave of light spun past her, the room shifted so she swore the entire circular room spun one full turn around her while she remained still.

She fought down the wave of nausea that came with the sudden, rapid spin. "Ugh."

"Simba."

Talisa straightened her back at the deep voice, so familiar but so…dead.

"Remember who you are."

Slowly, afraid her imagination was playing cruel tricks on her, she turned to face the person speaking. A lump formed in her throat when she caught sight of the tall, noble man before her. Dressed in his ceremonial regalia, a proud Lenape man, one so dear to her.

The sob welled so fast, tears burst from her eyes. She took three quick steps forward, then paused. "Father."

"It is your vision. I am as solid as you need."

She threw her arms around him, relieved he felt as real as anything. Through her tears, she chuckled. "Why are you quoting *The Lion King*?"

"You always did enjoy the movie."

"It is silliness now. Everything is gone. The world ended." She refused to let go, to give up this moment of warmth and peace. Though tears flowed from her eyes so freely she could no longer gather her thoughts. "Oh, Father."

"The world has not ended. It has changed. It is not the first time such a thing has happened in our history, of which you can see for yourself now that Chance has saved our stories."

"What does it even matter? I can't—we won't—there's no way."

"My child, have you forgotten the strength you carry in your soul?" Under her protests, he pried her off him to set his gaze to hers. Stern as it had been on the many occasions she'd gotten in trouble in her youth. "You would throw it away for fear?"

"I'm not strong anymore." She tried to force back the tears, only succeeding in a hot burning sensation between her eyes and nose for her efforts. "This is more than fear. He's won, Father. I can't win this battle. We can't win."

"What would have become of our people if we'd thought the same? When they murdered our wives and children while we hunted? When they drove us across unfamiliar territory, away from our homes, forced us to live on their lands in their ways? What if we had decided the white man had won? What then?"

"We would have died."

"We would have died," he concurred gravely. "But we lived. We kept our stories close, though we were forced not to share. We concealed our written words deep in hiding until we could bring them forth again. We fought for our lives and built new again."

"I am beaten. Chance isn't, I'm not even sure Roark is, but I am." She wrapped her arms around herself under the shudder she couldn't control at her own words. "I don't know how."

"You don't have to. The answers are already here, all around you, and inside you." He tucked a finger under her chin. "You have to remember who you are."

"What if that girl is dead?"

"No one can destroy my Talisa. Except herself."

Talisa folded into his embrace again, sniffling against her own tears. "You and Chance always believed that."

"And your mother. And Roark. We are not alone. You are not alone. The spirits of your ancestors are with you. Even if they have to sometimes sound like Mufasa."

She chuckled low. "Must you leave?"

"I am always here, Talisa. Reconnect to who you are, and you will always know how to find me." A warm kiss to the top of her head and he stepped back.

Talisa sighed. "Tell Mother I miss her most."

"I am wounded."

"No you're not."

"No. Everyone always does."

Talisa reached for him as he faded away, even though she knew she couldn't hold on forever. Exhaling slowly, she turned toward the cubby with her own notebooks. She pulled the topmost one free, flipping it open to pages upon pages of complex codes and diagrams.

This was the last notebook she worked in before she'd joined Steele's team under the assumption they were working to cure cancer. She'd had it sent home rather than take it with her. Whatever instinct made her do that, she had no idea.

She casually flipped through the pages until one bit of code caught her eye. She froze, taking in every inch of the equation. Meant for a potential clone of a species that had gone extinct, the mammoth if she remembered correctly. The recovered DNA had missing pieces.

On some random TV show she'd seen their discussions of recovering DNA from fossilized or frozen bones and how fragile the whole thing was. She'd played with the numbers for days. From random scraps of paper, to napkins, until it had finally hit her.

A multi-layered sequencing so complex that it could not just make up for the missing holes– but potentially…

"Roark!" She yelled so loud in her mind and verbally that she gave herself a headache. This was it. She had to find him and let him know.

She took off out of the room so fast, she almost forgot to drag her fire along for the ride. Up and up the crazy amount of steps Chance had created toward the main levels until she finally reached metal.

Roark met her in the hallway, wild-eyed and breathless. "Where the fuck were you? You scared me half to death!"

"How sexy do you find me?"

"What? Very. What the fuck, Tal?"

"How sexy do you find my mind?"

"Tal, I swear to the spirits."

"I figured it out."

Roark froze mid-argument, his mouth open, gaze fixed.

She tapped his jaw shut with a finger. "We can save her if we move fast."

"You're fucking with me."

"Not yet. When we're done."

"I'm holding you to that."

"You'd better."

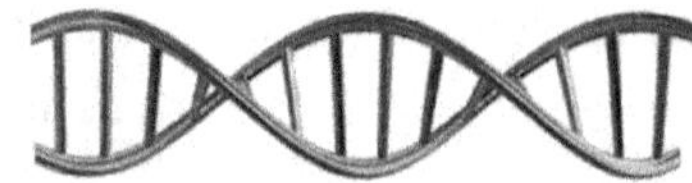

Danny slid his way along the wall of the corridor. Before a bottle of shine, two units over felt close. Now the distance became questionable. In Danny's mind he was doing well. That is until he reached the outside door of Chaz's half of the unit and he bounced in against the door. That small indentation sent him stumbling into the wall directly across the hall. He felt like a human ping-pong ball. With his eyes closed he took a deep exaggerated breath and focused on his destination. Home. His own unit. He could make some coffee. No he couldn't. Chaz broke the damn coffee pot.

A generous shove off the wall and he propelled himself towards his own door. Which he bounced off of and landed on the floor in front of it. "Fuck me." His head hung down between his shoulders, "Open door."

The door remained closed. Almost as if it stayed shut intentionally to mock him. "Stupid door. Stupid Steele. Stupid shine. Stupid door." All he needed to do at this point was get up and punch in his code to open the door. What was the code? With the form of a toddler he rolled over onto his stomach. He put his hands flat on the floor and pushed his upper body up. One foot at a time slid forward until he was bent over in half and precariously on his feet. Now he just needed to straighten up.

Not his best idea to try and get up this way. His vision swam from all the blood rushing to his head. He swiveled his head from one side and then the other. Maybe someone would come down the hallway and help him. Or not. "Damn. Gotta pee." Danny screwed up his face with determination. He walked on his hands and feet to the closest wall and awkwardly walked his hand up the wall until he stood straight-ish.

Curse words escaped under his breath. His hand connected with the panel next to his door and he tapped the numbers haphazardly in the hopes he had the right ones. "Elan? Elan need to talk." Despite the silence that echoed back at him he was going to talk to her. "Woman. I saids I needs to talk to you. My sister is not a paper doll damn it."

He barely looked around in favor of a quick trip into the bathroom to relieve himself.

"Danny?" A feminine voice echoed through the open door to the adjoining unit they'd added on to make room for Chaz.

"I see how it is. Can't talk to me 'bout dis. Can talk to him?" He tripped over his own two feet only to fall against the door frame. The damn thing pushed back against him so he stumbled and nearly fell into the next room.

Danny threw his hand up to hold onto the wall and keep him on his feet. He thought he would find Elan in here with Chaz. What he found? Nothing he ever thought he would see. Chaz's head was on Tori's lap. He remained curled up on the couch next to her sleeping. Tori stroked Chaz's hair as she looked up at him. Was he purring?

"Danny are you okay?" Tori's fingertips never stopped their path along Chaz's temple and through his hair.

"What the actual fuck is going on in here?" Danny snapped at the pair.

The tone in Danny's voice is apparently all it took to wake Chaz up. It's also all it took for Chaz to put himself between Danny and Tori with his fangs and claws bared. "No hurt her."

"I ain't gonna hurt Tori. Tori, ya gotta know it's dangerous to be in here like this." Danny looked between the pair dumfounded. Could his day get any weirder?

Tori stood up from the couch keeping her movements slow and even. She laid her hand on Chaz's shoulder with extreme care. "Chaz. Danny isn't going to hurt me. It's okay."

Chaz's head whipped towards Tori. "No hurt you."

"Easy. Both of you." Tori wiggled her way between the men. She rested her hand on Chaz's cheek. "Danny isn't going to hurt me. He's just worried." Her head jerked back toward Danny. "And drunk."

"Fuck dude I don't wanna hurt anyone. I don't want her getting hurt in here. She doesn't know…" Danny looked between the pair more confused than before. When the hell did Chaz become protective of Tori? And when the hell did she figure out his off button? Was she even safe to be in there with him? Elan. He needed Elan to help sort this all out. He squeezed his eyes shut and blinked rapidly. Maybe he needed some coffee. Fuck. It's broken.

"I know enough, Danny. Why don't we get you in bed? You look like you are flat out plastered." The moment Tori's fingers wrapped around Danny's arm a low growl emanated from Chaz.

"Caiman's." Chaz flashed his fangs again.

Tori didn't flinch. Her smile remained sweet. Her fingertips trained along his temple again. "I'm just going to help him to bed."

A breeze. A breeze in the living room. No the kitchen. Wait the bedroom. What was happening?! His head spun. His brain hurt. The contents of his stomach threatened to revolt and come back up all over…the bed?

"Chaz wait." Tori's voice chased after them.

Chaz had moved him. Chaz had moved him extremely fast. "Oh God, I'm going to die." Danny wrapped his arms around the pillow closest to him and prayed to any and every God and Spirit he could think of to make it stop. Stop the spinning, the dizziness, the urge to vomit for days.

"You aren't going to die." Tori approached the bed. She set something on the end table next to him. "There's water and something for your head. Come on Chaz, let's go back to the other room and give him some privacy."

"Dying?" Chaz sounded more curious than anything else.

"Nah, just doesn't feel good." Tori countered.

Coffee. That's all he wanted when he got back to his room and instead he got a heavy dose of confusion and his own personal tilt-a-whirl. The pair's retreating footsteps followed by the door shutting was all his brain could focus on. The room spinning needed to stop first. Then he would find Elan.

# 30

Talisa hummed to herself as she bustled around the lab. Several test runs were going at once, but they only had another half hour and it was do or die. She was sure this was going to work, though. As long as they'd gotten every detail right.

"Is that—'The Lion Sleeps Tonight'?" Roark had stopped what he was doing, his nose scrunched in concentration.

"What?"

"I mean, I think it is. But since you can't carry a tune in a bucket it could be the ABC's for all I could tell."

Her jaw dropped, "Roark! You son of a rotten, no good—"

He grinned. "You look like you want to throw something at me."

"If we weren't in the lab with delicate and hard to find equipment, you bet your fine piece of ass I would."

"You're always in a good mood when you're right."

"If that were true, I'd always be in a good mood."

"Right." He turned his attention back to the scope he stood in front of. "Damn, woman. I love your mind."

"Sample holding together?"

"Like a fucking dream."

She flipped open the autoclave to withdraw another three samples. Each one was lined up, in turn. Each had been carefully timed. "Last batch."

A soft kiss landed on her neck. "You didn't have to run twenty."

"I did. After what happened last time and what I'm getting from the two of them, we are running out of time. I wanted to be as sure as I possibly could before putting her in there. Hell, the body could hold and we could still lose her."

"It won't happen."

"You don't know."

"No, but I believe in you."

Tal sighed and leaned back against him at this. She still hadn't told him everything due to the fact that they'd been working non-stop for about twelve hours at this point. "Father came to me in a vision. Plus, I saw a prediction he wrote down before he died. He seems to think we're going to be all right, in the end."

"What about you?"

"I still don't know. That time in Steele's compound messed me up bad. I don't know how to recover sometimes."

"Me too, Tal." He kissed her temple, his arms strong and secure around her waist. "But we'll get there. And I tend to believe your dad. He was right about a lot of things."

"I just need some hope."

"You have it. We all do. Buried kind of deep in some more than others, but it's there."

Tal's response faded on her lips the second the door burst open. James entered with the laptop balanced carefully in his hands. "Tell me you've got it. She's getting tired. Weaker. I don't know how much time we've got left."

Tal sprang to action, waving Roark toward the samples. "Check them quick. I'm going to go get everything set in the next room."

Roark didn't argue, to his credit. He went to work.

"What's going on?" James hounded her all the way to the next room. "Are we good or are you going to let her die?"

"James," Annie admonished from the computer speakers. James wasn't entirely wrong; she did sound tired. Then again, when you're a computer program, do you sleep?

"It's all right, Annie. He's worried. He's allowed to snap at me now and then." She pointed a finger at him when he opened his mouth again. "But even I have my limits. I literally made you from scratch, I can deconstruct you just as fast, young man."

James shut his mouth, his jaw set in a firm line. "Update?"

"We were actually going to be calling you within a half an hour. The body is made, we were testing to make sure it was holding together."

A loud crackling screech came from the laptop. "I'm sorry, *what*?"

James growled low. "And you didn't tell us?"

"We wanted to be sure. Last time we started right away, and it was disastrous. It's not good for the body to remain a shell for too long, but we were giving it as much time as possible to be sure Annie had a safe place to land."

A small sob came from the computer. Annie took a shuddering breath Talisa could audibly hear, even though she didn't technically breathe. "I have a body again?"

"Once Roark gets his ass in here with the final check, yes." Talisa circled to where she could see Annie herself. The young woman appeared slightly fuzzy as if it was too much effort to hold herself together in high resolution. "I'm sorry we didn't tell you sooner, we just didn't want to get your hopes up, plus you two had plenty to talk about."

"James needed sleep too." Annie smiled back at Talisa. "You really did it?"

"We'll know for sure once you're safely back where you belong, which is decidedly *not* in a laptop." Talisa nudged her son. "Stop grumping. You're ruining this happy, joy moment."

"You should have told me," James grumbled. His shoulders sagged. "How much longer does the body have?"

"Safely, about an hour. Shouldn't take Roark more than five minutes to get to us. Do you have any questions?" Tal focused her attention on Annie.

"No, I don't think so. We went over it the last time." Annie wrung her virtual hands.

"It's okay to be nervous. Just know that we have your back." Tal glanced at James. "And you need to chill the hell out before you vibrate yourself right out of the room."

"I will relax when Anne is here in the flesh." James scowled her way. "When you prove you're actually as smart as you claim."

"You're lucky I know you well enough to not be insulted right now. You don't speak to the matriarch of the tribe with any more disrespect than the Chief." The words she'd just spoken on instinct sent a shockwave through her own soul. *Fucking hell. Father was right. Damn it.*

James straightened at her words but offered no apology.

To his benefit, the doors from the next room opened for Roark. He walked toward them steadily, a warm smile on his face. "Let's do this."

Annie kept as close an eye as the camera on the laptop allowed her to. The man was ready to rattle apart as his parents went over the last few checks to ensure it would work this time. "James…?"

"Ma, is it ready?" James avoided looking back at the computer. His gaze stayed on his parents running through their checklists. Each time he passed on his determined path to wear a hole straight through the floor, he hazarded a glance her direction.

"Almost, James." Talisa's voice had taken on a business-like tone.

"James." She said his name again in the hopes of getting his attention. The fact that he refused to look at her made perfect sense to her. What if this was the last time they ever laid eyes on each other? His own pain reverberated through the bond.

"Relax James, we're about to start the count down again. I'm turning up her body temperature." This time it was Roark. Both of his parents remained outside of her field of vision. "Alright, here we go. Ten."

"James Logan Nashuk, would you look at me!" Annie chastised through the tinny speakers.

"Nine."

"Anne…" The pacing stopped and he focused on the computer fully. "I…"

A sad smile formed on her digital lips. "I know. We're going to get through this. Tonight, I will be safe in your bed and not on the nightstand."

"What if…"

"No what if. It is going to work and we are going to be together." Annie pressed her hand against the screen. She couldn't wait to be able to touch him again.

"Six." Had they missed Roark counting?

James trailed his fingertips along the screen over her hand. "That's all I want."

"I know, me too. And we're going to get it. Trust me." A digital tear cascaded down her cheek.

"What if something goes wrong?" Fear mirrored in his eyes.

"Four."

"I love you, James." It was time. She needed to gather her strength and make the jump to her new body.

"I love you too, Anne." James didn't take his hand away from the screen.

"Two."

"See you soon." Annie held her hand against his for one last second.

"One."

The pixels she had been projecting spiraled into a smaller body. One turn and she sped down the pathways towards her new body. Code flew by at various speeds. Some meandered past her as if it was on its way back from Sunday service. Other bits of code flew by at the speed of light, barely perceived as it moved along to whatever important business it had.

The voices of James, Talisa and Roark faded away in the instant she began her leap. Navigating the wires felt freeing and isolated all at the same time. If her calculations had been correct it shouldn't take more than five to ten minutes tops for her to traverse the distance to her new body and settle in.

292

Inside her consciousness a list formed of all the things she wanted to do. Hold James. Eat. Hug her mother and her brothers. Feel the breeze on her skin. With each item on her list she journeyed closer and closer to her freedom.

Annie slowed down and stopped at the junction in front of her. The code around her felt—agitated. Angry.

A cluster of code sped in her direction from the left side of the juncture. It shifted its shape as it approached. At one point she swore it looked like PacMan coming up at her.

01000100 01100101 01110011 01110100 01110010 01101111 01111001 00100001 00100000 01000100 01100101 01110011 01110100 01110010 01101111 01111001 00100001 00100000 01000100 01100101 01110011 01110100 01110010 01101111 01111001 00100001

"What the hell?" She backed up and focused on the right-hand side. Another cluster approached her just as fast.

*Locate Anna Maria Johnson. Find program. Destroy.*

"Not if I have anything to say about it." Annie backtracked and stopped dead floating in the middle of the tube. She tilted her head to the side and streams of code flew out of her fingertips at the clusters.

*Locate Anna Maria Johnson. Find program. Destroy.* The clusters pulled together and started to form a shape. The voice sounded less mechanical and distorted this time but nothing she recognized.

"Fuck, you weren't supposed to form Voltron." She concentrated harder and sent more code at it."

*Locate Anna Maria Johnson. Find program. Destroy.*

"Do you say anything else? I have no plans on dying today."

*Locate Anna Maria Johnson. Find program. Destroy.*

As the clusters formed into a solid object, well as solid as she was, she rushed forward and threw a punch in the hopes of stopping it from whatever it planned to do. Her fist connected with the head of the figure in front of her and sent them reeling backwards. She circled around to face it again when a gasp escaped.

*Locate Anna Maria Johnson. Find program. Destroy.* The distortion in the voice dissipated completely. All that remained behind resembled and sounded exactly like her father. Warren.

A choked sob escaped as she stared back at her father, or at least his code. Annie knew the signature behind his code as well, if not better than she knew her own. "Daddy, no…"

*Locate Anna Maria Johnson. Find program. Destroy.* The digital version of Warren turned around and lunged at her. He wrapped his hands around her throat and squeezed. A combination of pure malice and anger mixed with fear and sorrow in his eyes.

"Daddy, stop." Annie pried at the hands around her throat. In one swift motion her knee came up between his legs. She scrambled back away from him. It took an inordinate amount of concentration, but a wall formed in front of her blocking off Warren's access to her. It also blocked her access to the path she needed to get out. Time was ticking down and she needed to get to her body.

01001100 01101111 01100011 01100001 01110100
01100101 00100000 01000001 01101110 01101110 01100001
00100000 01001101 01100001 01110010 01101001 01100001
00100000 01001010 01101111 01101000 01101110 01110011
01101111 01101110 00101110 00100000 01000110 01101001
01101110 01100100 00100000 01110000 01110010 01101111
01100111 01110010 01100001 01101101 00101110 00100000

294

01000100 01100101 01110011 01110100 01110010 01101111
01111001 00101110 00100000

James tapped impatiently on the laptop. Anne had disappeared mere seconds ago, but it seemed like ages already. An aching burned through his heart, down to his stomach, leaving him feeling both ill and infuriated at once.

An alarm chimed once. It stopped by the time that James glared at it, but he held his gaze on it, daring it to sound again.

Another pain shot through his gut, burning in his throat. "Fuck. What is taking so long?"

"Shut your fucking face," his mother spat through gritted teeth. "This isn't like dusting crops, boy."

James shook his head in confusion. "What?"

Shockingly, Roark chuckled under his breath. "Here we go."

"Go and boil your bottoms, son of a silly person." Tal's lips hardly moved, and the comment held all the venom of a viper but made no sense.

"What the fuck, ma?"

"She's focused. Leave her alone." Roark moved suddenly further down the panel at the next beep. "She can only quote movies at this point."

"What?" Before he could demand an explanation, a pain tore through him like he hadn't experienced since before his release from stasis. *"Fuck."*

"Son?" Roark spared him a quick glance.

This time when the pain ripped through his gut, sirens exploded all around the room. From the stasis unit, the walls, the computers. He moved to slam his fist into one, but it flashed a bunch of code before it dissolved into snow. "What the fuck? What's going on?"

"Not now." Now Roark sounded as tense as Talisa had. "Something's happening."

"What the fuck is happening?" James rushed forward toward the unit. He gripped the laptop on top of it. "Anne! Anne, get back here, or in there. What's going on?"

"Fuck fuck fuck fuck fuck." It was so quiet, she might not have even said it out loud, but James sharp ears picked up his mother's freak out.

"What? What is it? Where is she?" James charged toward his mother. Her hand flew toward his face to stop him, and everything stopped dead.

The alarms stopped beating at his ear drums. The frenzied panic of the room faded. For that matter, the room itself disappeared as well.

James spun in a circle feeling oddly disconnected from his own legs. There was nothing as far as he could see. Grayness echoed back against his retinas, silence deafening him more than the alarms had. *"Talisa."*

Nothing. "Fuck me."

He turned again, searching for something, anything. "Mom?"

In the distance, a dark spot appeared. It grew larger ever so slowly at first.

Without warning it sped up so fast he hardly recognized his mother before she'd tackled him to the ground, a fierce growl on her lips.

"The fuck?"

"Don't curse at me, you ungrateful, impatient bastard. I know she's your mate, but this fuckery has got to stop. I need every *ounce* of concentration I can spare to save that girl who is not yet dead, and you're taking up extremely valuable real estate in my brain."

"But what is—"

"We don't fucking know, all right? Right now, she's not dead, I can sense her, and so can you."

"The pain…"

"Means there's a hiccup. Trust me, you'd fucking know if she was dead."

James gripped his mother's arms. "Save her."

"Leave me the fuck alone to do it."

"Mom…"

Her features softened. "I know. You don't have to say it, or try to say it in your ever-incapable way. I know."

"Stay out of my head."

"I don't need to be in your head to know. I know you as well as I know myself. Like I just reminded you minutes ago, I made you from scratch."

"You made me from Lucas."

"Right. From a little scratch on his arm." She smiled, and they were both standing in the literal blink of an eye.

"She has to make it."

"Then let me work without distraction. Bite your tongue until it bleeds if you have to."

"Yes ma'am."

"Good boy."

298

The alarms slammed into his ears so hard again, he clapped his hands over his ears. "Fucking hell."

"We know." Roark's face screwed up in his concentration and probably from discomfort. "The two people that can make it stop are either insane or trapped."

"Trapped." James spun setting his hand on the pod. He stared into the window. "Anne. Get your ass where you need to be."

The computers in the room all flashed at once, code streaming across them before they went black. Talisa's hands stilled on her console. "No you don't, you piece of shit."

She slammed the metal so hard, the side of the pod dented, but the screen flickered back to life. James breathed a sigh of relief. He opened his mouth to ask, but then clamped it shut.

Talisa sighed a breath of relief. "Everything looks good. It should be okay. Is she waking up?"

James stared down at the form of his mate, trying to sense if she was in there or not.

"James?"

"I can't tell."

*Locate Anna Maria Johnson. Find program. Destroy.*

The voice echoed against the barrier that had been erected. It kept her safe for the time being but severed her access to her freedom. To her life. Annie surveyed the area and concentrated on the code on the other side of the wall. She had to think of it that way. Bits of code. Not her father. If she let herself dwell on the fact that her father tried to kill her, she might crumble under the thought.

*Locate Anna Maria Johnson. Find program. Destroy.*

Virus. That's how she needed to handle it. The virus beat against the wall. Despite the fact that she didn't need to breathe in this form, her body went through the motions of a deep breath. Inch-by-inch she pushed the wall back and stretched it across the opening. Another foot or so and she could keep the virus on the other side and give herself enough room to slip through.

*Locate Anna Maria Johnson. Find program. Destroy.*

Annie lifted her hand to steer the formation of the wall as it stretched. The opening beckoned to her just as much as the bond with James called to her. Two more inches. She just needed two more inches to ensure the virus would be sealed out as well.

*Locate Anna Maria Johnson. Find program. Destroy.*

Her exit opened up and she threw up two more walls behind her for added protection. Without another glance back she took off like a shot again. Even with the distance between her and the virus she could still feel it down to her core fighting against her counter measures.

There it was. The exit. Another unneeded breath and she dove headfirst into the connection that would bring her back to the land of the living. In theory.

For the briefest moment, she felt the world go out from under her. Total weightlessness. A freight train of pain slammed through her body. Her body and mind stretched against the confines of her programming that held her together. The pain vanished a moment later and she was unable to move. Her arms and legs felt heavy and she couldn't open her eyes.

300

*Annie? Can you hear me?* Talisa's voice rang through her mind.

"Talisa?" Why weren't her lips moving? Why couldn't she move her body?

*Easy. Give yourself a few minutes. Everything is rebooting so to speak.*

"Is James okay?"

Laughter rang through Talisa's voice. *Worry about letting your body do what it needs to right now. James is fine. He's just anxious.*

"I am too." In the back of her mind something nagged at her. She couldn't pinpoint the source but she knew it was important.

"What's happening?" James' voice, although muffled penetrated from the outside of the pod she now resided in, came through with all the concern and anxiety she felt through the bond.

*Easy Annie don't push too hard. You need to take your time.*

*Locate Anna Maria Johnson. Find program. Destroy.*

Shit. The virus. She needed to get out of the pod as quickly as possible. They hadn't tested anything yet. They didn't know if she would still have her gifts or how quickly they would work. Connected to the pod as she was, she became vulnerable and if the virus had broken through her countermeasures it could hurt her.

Despite Talisa's warning she pushed her body to wake up. Her eyes flew open with a gasping breath. The deep even breathing her body had been doing when she entered it became erratic. She couldn't get enough air. In fact the oxygen in the pod felt nonexistent.

"Shit, it's too soon." Roark's muffled voice reached her.

"What do you mean too soon?" James's panic beat against her.

Annie threw her hand up, window above her. *Talisa get me out of here. It's not safe.*

*Annie I need you to relax. Your vitals are spiking all over the place.*

Tears coursed down the sides of her face. Panic started to win out over rational thought. She beat against the glass over and over again with both hands. They had to let her out of there. The virus would kill her all over again.

"Ma what's going on?" James' panic coupled with her own only spurred her on.

"I'm opening the hatch. She's hyperventilating. Her blood pressure is too high." Roark's voice joined the cacophony of voices.

"She's distraught and scared. Terrified. I'm trying to push calm at her but it's not working." Was that her mother?

James' face pierced the angry red haze of panic. "Anne. I'm right here. We need you to calm down."

Calm channeled through her very soul. When Abby used her empathic abilities, it felt like waves coming at you. Her eyes locked with his and her breathing eased. "James." Her voice sounded foreign to her. Dry and raspy. Tears cascaded down her face with no end in sight.

"Easy, Anne. I'm right here." James brushed her hair back from her face.

"Her vitals are stabilizing. Annie have you ever been claustrophobic before? Maybe that's what happened."

The panic slammed through her again without warning. The virus. She needed to get out. Now. Before it could hurt her. "Out."

"James why don't you lift her out of there and get her over to the exam table." Talisa disconnected the monitoring equipment from her.

James slipped his arm under her legs and lifted her as if she were the most precious thing in the world. "You were right." He pressed a kiss to her temple.

Annie snuggled closer and reveled in the feel of his arms around her. She waited until he set her on the table to lean in and press her lips against his.

"Annie, what happened? You were so scared." Abby stepped up next to them but kept enough distance to give them their moment.

Annie took the glass of water Roark offered her. After several swallows she looked between the three of them; a knot coiling in her stomach.

James kissed her again, holding on to her hand tight. "You're safe, Anne."

Abby's outstretched hand relieved Annie of the glass. "We won't let anything happen to you baby."

"Warren created a virus to try and kill me."

The glass of water slipped from Abby's grasp to shatter on the floor.

# Epilogue

Bubbles tickled along her flesh as the water levels rose in the tank. An easy deep breath and the liquid filled her lungs caressing her from the inside and out. The best way to sleep at night, suspended in bliss.

"Is it secure? Make sure it stays that way." General Steele's voice reverberated through the water that surrounded her. His fist hit the base of her sleep-tank which caused a gentle shift in the liquid that surrounded her.

Her eyes remained shut out of habit more than anything else. The man in charge despised her staring at him when he paced outside the tank. Better to let him think she slept now. Something had him all riled up. Something made him give the order for her to be secured. Did he worry for her safety?

"The whole thing a total loss. What wasn't flooded they burned down. Years of research." The anger rose in his voice.

Did they lose a base? Supplies? Did the Infected attack again? A jolt ran through her body at the thought. Infected sounded wrong. The word applied as she had been taught but it felt wrong and off deep in her core. Steele wouldn't mislead her. He was like a father to her. He raised her.

"The child is gone! They killed the child."

Another jolt. Who would kill a child like that? The General swore he would protect the innocent. That's what she was there to help with. What he trained her for. To eradicate the Infected.

"They need to be wiped from this earth so we can be safe again." The shift in the liquid told her that this time he hit with both fists.

The General had become quite proud of her training. When the time allowed, she would be able to help remove the issue from the equation.

*"Joe…"* A feminine voice she didn't know slipped through her mind like silk. It made no sense. No one else had been given access to her room. Only Taylor, her handler. This voice felt familiar though.

*"I miss you…"* The anguish and pain were palpable. It echoed through her own chest enough that she inhaled with a shudder.

"What's going on? What's happening? Does it normally move like that?" Concern mixed with the anger still in his voice.

"She's most likely dreaming, sir. I don't see anything alarming on the monitor." Taylor knew she wasn't asleep yet. She had just gotten into the tank and closed her eyes.

"It."

"Pardon, sir?"

"*It* is a weapon. Make sure it gets the rest it needs. Once we pinpoint the rebel base, we'll unleash our new weapon. They said it couldn't be done, but here we are and it's a near perfect specimen." General Steele sounded proud as a peacock.

Mentally she frowned. Just the other day he had told her that she was his special girl. His best hope for humanity. Now he was calling her 'it' again? It didn't make any sense.

Pain seared through her brain cutting off coherent thought. When she was able to think again an image came into focus within her mind, almost like a movie. A woman's hands holding onto a set of dog tags. Her thumb ran along the raised letters that spelled out 'Maritime'.

*"God I miss you. The kids suggested if I talk to you it would make me feel closer to you. Right now I feel further away than I ever have. The others came back, but you weren't as lucky. It's not fair."*

Whoever this woman was, she had suffered greatly. She felt a connection to her. No logical explanation as to why. It wasn't like she had met her. Come to think of it she hadn't met anyone outside of Taylor and the General. If she could make the pain go away for her, she would.

*"Rest easy, my love."* The conviction and love behind the words almost knocked her over. She did her best to stay steady in case General Steele remained in the room watching her.

Nothing would be solved tonight. Things did not add up. Between the woman's voice and the other weird feelings she kept getting, something was definitely amiss. Right now she would bide her time. Put the pieces together one by one until she had the answers.

# About the Authors

Sarah Cass's world is regularly turned upside down by her three special-needs kids and loving mate, so she breaks genre barriers, dabbling in horror, straight fiction, and urban fantasy. An ADD tendency leaves her with a variety of interests that include singing, dancing, crafting, cooking, and being a photographer. She fights through the struggles of the day, knowing the battles are her crucible and though she may emerge scarred, she's also stronger. While busy creating worlds and characters as real to her as her own family, she leads an active online life with her blog, *Redefining Perfect*, which gives a real and sometimes raw glimpses into her life and art.

*~*

Mary Terrani lives a chaotic life as the mother of two boys of the 20 something and teen variety. They keep her on her toes on a regular basis, so she's happy to get lost in other worlds. Her long-standing passion for the written word drives her need to create chaos with her pen that only she can solve. She loves to dabble in many genres, from young adult to paranormal, and post-apocalyptic piece she's co-written with fellow author, Sarah Cass.

When she's not writing, Mary can be found in a variety of activities including knitting, gaming, and anything involving her favorite geekdoms. Mom, author and all around geek she loves spending time with her family. You can find Mary on Twitter, Facebook and her website.

# Books by Mary Terrani

Decking the Halls

# Books by Sarah Cass

**The Tribe Series**
The Tribe
The Wolf
The Chief
The Raven
**The Dominion Falls Series**
Changing Tracks
Derailed
Dark Territory
Runaway Train
Home Signal
**The Lake Point Series**
Santa, Maybe
Deep-Fried Sweethearts
Stalled Independence
Witch Way
A Thorough Thanksgiving
Eve's New Year
Heartstrings & Hockey Pucks
Luck of the Cowgirl
Stars, Stripes & Motorbikes
Free Falling
Love for Hire
Haunted Hearts
**Stand Alone Novels**
Masked Hearts
Leap

# Divine Roses Ink

## DivineRosesInk.com